W9-DBL-697

YEARS
of the
LOCUST

A Novel

YEARS
of the
LOCUST

A Novel

Thomas L. Seltzer

TATE PUBLISHING & Enterprises

MAIN LIBRARY
Champaign Public Library
200 West Green Street
Champaign, Illinois 61820-5193

Years of the Locust
Copyright © 2011 by Thomas L. Seltzer. All rights reserved.

No part of this publication may be reproduced, stored in a retrieval system or transmitted in any way by any means, electronic, mechanical, photocopy, recording or otherwise without the prior permission of the author except as provided by USA copyright law.

This novel is a work of fiction. Names, descriptions, entities, and incidents included in the story are products of the author's imagination. Any resemblance to actual persons, events, and entities is entirely coincidental.

The opinions expressed by the author are not necessarily those of Tate Publishing, LLC.

Published by Tate Publishing & Enterprises, LLC
127 E. Trade Center Terrace | Mustang, Oklahoma 73064 USA
1.888.361.9473 | www.tatepublishing.com

Tate Publishing is committed to excellence in the publishing industry. The company reflects the philosophy established by the founders, based on Psalm 68:11,
"The Lord gave the word and great was the company of those who published it."

Book design copyright © 2011 by Tate Publishing, LLC. All rights reserved.
Cover design by April Marciszewski
Interior design by Stephanie Woloszyn

Published in the United States of America

ISBN: 978-1-61777-659-5
1. Fiction / Mystery & Detective / General   2. Fiction / Christian / Suspense
11.07.22

ACKNOWLEDGEMENTS

If it takes a village to raise a child, it takes another sort of small community to raise a novel after the author gives birth. Therefore, there are many people to thank for bringing *Years of the Locust* to life. I will name just a few here, but the rest of you know who you are. I'm convinced no one accomplishes anything truly worthwhile without the help of many others.

My wife, Jennifer, tops the acknowledgement list. She is an amazing woman with so many talents and skills that I can only say that I am blessed to have her. After listening to me talk about this story, she lived through the writing and then spent hours helping me edit it. Thanks, Jennie. You are the love of my life, and you've made me a better man.

My editor, Kalyn McAlister, goaded me on through two rewrites. She kept challenging me to make the novel better, and I'm convinced that her suggestions resulted in a far better final product than the manuscript I sent to Tate Publishing a year ago. I also want to thank my friend, the late Bill Call, for his help in developing the character of bounty hunter Ezra Goldstein.

Lastly, I want to thank scores of friends and well-wishers for your encouraging words before, during, and after the writing of *Years of the Locust*. I hope you're not disappointed in the final product that you now hold in your hands.

PROLOGUE
April 1968

"Are you sleeping, Corporal Tanner?"

"I'm praying, sir," the handsome youth said with a smile.

"Why bother?" Sgt. George Murphy said, shaking his head. "God can't hear you."

"No disrespect, sir, but I think he can."

"Not from Hill 881S."

Tanner knew Sgt. Murphy well enough to know that the large grizzly bear of a man was no atheist. He was only making the point that this isolated hill in war-torn South Vietnam *appeared* to be God forsaken. Two months earlier, Hill 881S was a scenic spot. Tanner had snapped a picture looking north from 881S in January to send to his wife back in San Antonio, Texas. The view looked like something you'd see from a rustic cabin in the Blue Ridge Mountains.

What a difference six weeks could make. The same view now looked like the surface of the moon following all of the Arrotta air strikes and Supergaggle prep fire that had peppered the hill. The Battle of Khe Sanh had begun in northwestern Quang Tri Province, Republic of Vietnam, on January 21, 1968. For the past fifty-three days, the isolated marine base and hilltop outposts had been under constant North Vietnamese ground and artillery attacks.

Casualties were high, and the only thing keeping the 2nd Battalion 9th Marines from being overrun was Operation Niagara.

The massive aerial bombardment campaign, launched by the U.S. Air Force, utilized the latest technology to target enemy forces on the ground and keep the marines supplied. It was their only lifeline.

Tanner had arrived at the village of Khe Sanh on January 7. He had left his teenage wife behind to go and fight a war in a land he knew little about. While many of Tanner's friends had been drafted, he had enlisted. His father had served in the same marine battalion during World War II, fighting alongside his brave comrades in the Battles of Guam and Iowa Jima. Tanner was proud to follow in his father's footsteps but longed for the war to end so that he could return home to Rachel.

How he missed his wife. He kept a picture of her in his Bible. The first thing he did each morning was open the Bible to the page where he had been reading the previous day. The picture would fall out, and he would hold it in his hand and gaze longingly at Rachel, with her slightly protruding tummy. Inside her belly was something more precious than Tanner could describe—*his* child.

Tanner didn't know if he would soon be the father of a boy or a girl. It didn't matter to him. The only thing that mattered was that the baby was healthy and that he, or she, grew up to love Jesus. Tanner had accepted Christ as his personal savior at a young age. His father, a pastor of a small Hill Country church near San Antonio, had introduced him to the Lord. He looked forward to doing the same for his child.

Each morning, he would pray for Rachel and the baby and then ask God for the privilege of returning to them. The death toll had been rising since the beginning of the Tet Offensive, and Tanner had already lost several friends. While some went home in body bags, others went home without limbs to face lives irreparably altered by the war. Some left the battlefield with emotional scars that would change their lives forever. Tanner prayed that he might return alive and whole, in body, mind, and spirit.

Before he returned home, Tanner had a job to do. There was a formidable enemy surrounding them on all sides, but there was a higher purpose for him being on Hill 881S right now. God had him here for a reason that went beyond this war. Perhaps, it was to share God's Word and encourage his comrades. Perhaps, it was to disciple Private Eric Adams, who had given his life to Christ six weeks ago. Tanner had rejoiced when Adams had put his faith in Christ after weeks of Bible study together.

Tanner had been studying the book of Second Timothy, and he had just been reading the fourth chapter during his quiet time.

> But you, be sober in all things, endure hardship, do the work of an evangelist, fulfill your ministry. For I am already being poured out as a drink offering, and the time of my departure has come. I have fought the good fight, I have finished the course, I have kept the faith; in the future there is laid up for me the crown of righteousness, which the Lord, the righteous Judge, will award to me on that day; and not only to me, but also to all who have loved His appearing.

The first rays of dawn signaled a new day dawning. It was time to go to work. As assistant team leader, he shared the responsibility of patrolling the area around the marine encampment to ensure that the enemy didn't break through their lines before the overland relief expedition reached the isolated marine base. Too many of Tanner's friends had already died, and the young man was eager to do his part to protect the others.

Picking up his M-16, Tanner started walking toward the light.

CHAPTER 1
April 2010

Debris blew past the truck as Wes Tanner guided the vehicle slowly down the dilapidated street in the seamy west-side neighborhood. Iron security grates protruded from shabby storefronts in between boarded up buildings, and trash littered the sidewalk. Wes saw two men huddled together on the corner, and another man was lurking in the doorway of a nearby building about ten feet away. It looked to him as though a drug deal was going down. Wes saw money change hands before the two men separated. The man in the doorway looked suspiciously at him as he passed. Wes didn't belong on this side of town, and the thought crossed his mind that he might be well-advised to turn back before it was too late.

The west side of San Antonio had in recent years become a no-man's land. It had the reputation of a place where a person could catch a stray bullet just as easily as a cold. Rival gangs roamed freely, and the sound of gunfire was an all too familiar sound to the law-abiding citizens that huddled inside their small frame homes at night. Even the police were reluctant to patrol there. A man alone on the west side had reason to be fearful—especially if he was an Anglo. A police reporter might be sent over here to cover a shooting, but a columnist? The assignment editor at the newspaper had made it sound so interesting, but she failed to mention that the subject lived in the heart of the west side.

If Wes survived the outing, he figured on having a good column. The man he was going to interview was a private investigator and bounty hunter named Ezra Goldstein. The former rabbi had a colorful history dating back almost forty years. He had served in the Israeli army as a scout and sniper during the 1973 Yom Kippur War and during the campaign against the Palestine Liberation Organization in Lebanon in the early 1980s.

In more recent years, he had gained a reputation for being able to track down escaped fugitives. Most of his work came from bail bondsmen facing financial losses from bail jumpers. However, he also handled high-profile private investigations.

Directly ahead, Wes saw a Hispanic woman leading a small child by the hand into the middle of the street. Wes had to slam on the brakes to avoid hitting her. Their eyes met for a brief moment as she passed in front of the truck. Empty eyes, the writer in him noted, with the light long ago snuffed out by the adversity and disappointments of life. To Wes she looked almost as though she might welcome a vehicle striking her down.

The more affluent San Antonio northsiders like Wes could only imagine what life was like for people on the west side. The two sides of the sprawling city were only twenty miles apart. But, for all they shared in common, it could as easily have been two thousand miles. Wes frequently saw people on the news speaking through tears of loved ones lost to senseless violence on the mean streets of the west side. Young people no older than his fifteen-year-old daughter or thirteen-year-old son were caught in the whirlwinds of a culture threatening to suck them into an abyss.

When Wes saw the bounty hunter's west-side address, he was surprised. Why would a man who was well paid for his work choose to live here? But after further consideration, it seemed fitting that a tough man like Ezra Goldstein would live where he could keep his ear close to the ground. Wes thought of the old law of nature. It was the survival of the fittest, and Goldstein could survive anywhere he chose to live. He would have plenty of experience on mean streets like these, flushing the rats out of the dark corners of society and returning them to their cages.

As he drove, Wes continued to keep one eye on the narrow, winding streets and one eye in the rearview mirror for possible trouble coming up from behind. He peered at addresses on storefronts until he finally found the address he sought. He pulled into a parking place in front of what looked like an old country store. There was a sign hanging over the door reading: "EZRA GOLDSTEIN. CONFIDENTIAL INVESTIGATIONS." Under that was a Bible verse: "Behold, he shall come up like a lion from the swelling of Jordan against the habitation of the strong." (Jeremiah 49:19).

When Wes entered the building, he stepped into what appeared to be an Old West museum with a wooden floor and cracked walls. There were numerous pictures of Goldstein, dressed like a cowboy, a biker, a rabbi, and a businessman lining the wall. In one picture, he was dressed in a long, black kaftan and broad-rimmed hat. The common denominator in all of the pictures was Goldstein's stone-cold eyes; unruly, curly, brown hair; thick beard; and weathered skin. In several pictures, Goldstein was handcuffed to men that he had apprehended. In all cases his quarry looked hopelessly defeated.

Wes noted that the other wall space was taken up with antique guns and wanted posters. There were even memorabilia for sale on the U-shaped counter running along the walls. As his eyes panned the room, Wes saw a light on in a side office.

"Hello?

"Shalom," said a voice from the office. A moment later, Goldstein stepped out into the front room. He was wearing a sleeveless black T-shirt, silver-capped boots, bicycle gloves, and a yarmulke. "Can I help you" he said with a thick Brooklyn accent.

"Ezra Goldstein?"

"In the flesh. Your name, sir?"

"Wes Tanner with the *San Antonio Express-News*."

"Good day, sir," Goldstein said, stepping forward and extending his hand. When Wes shook his hand, Goldstein bowed and twisted his head slightly.

"Quite a place you have here, Mr. Goldstein."

"Thank you, sir. I've always been an admirer of the Old West. Often told my maker that he made a mistake when he plopped me down here in the late twentieth century. If I'd been born a century or two earlier, I would have been right at home. And I think I'd might have known a better breed of men. What do you think?"

"They don't pay me to think," Wes said with a grin on his boyish face. "Just report."

Goldstein looked at him slyly and laughed.

"A journalist with a sense of humor. I like you, already, Wes Tanner. And I'm flattered that you find me worthy of a story. You were even willing to take a bit of a risk to get your story, weren't you?"

"I wouldn't have wanted to come down here and see you at night," Wes admitted. "You probably don't spend too many nights down here, either."

"On the contrary, Wes, I spend many nights down here. I live in the back," Goldstein said, pointing to a hallway leading to another part of his building. "I always thought it was a waste of hard-earned money to maintain an office and a residence at separate locations. Would you like to see my inner sanctum?"

Wes rose to his feet and followed his host to the front of the store. Goldstein turned his front door sign around to read "CLOSED." He then locked the outside door, which Wes noted was made of heavy oak wood with a large glass pane in the middle. It was covered by a black wrought iron security grate. Against the doorframe was mounted a solid steel plate into which two extra-long deadbolts could be secured.

After locking the front door, he led Wes down the hallway to the back of the long warehouse-type building and into an area that was blocked from view from the front. The back door, which led out to the back alley, was made of solid steel. This door also closed onto a solid steel doorframe and was secured by two heavy deadbolts.

"I'll bet you don't get broken into much." Wes nodded to the door.

"If the deadbolts don't keep 'em out, my Walther P38 will do the trick."

"Do you live here alone?"

"All alone," Goldstein said as he unlocked a door off the hallway and led them into his home. The living quarters consisted of a bedroom, full bath, long, narrow kitchen, and a spacious den. All of the comforts of home were here at his disposal.

"So, you're not married?"

"Not anymore. I've been a widower for thirty years."

"Your wife must have died young," Wes said, fishing for more information.

"She was twenty-seven. Killed at a market in the Western Galilee region of northern Israel by a PLO rocket attack."

"And you never got remarried?"

"Never felt like settling for something less than what I had," Goldstein said as he moved into the kitchen. "So, are you a happily married man, Wes?"

"I'm a married man."

"Only a writer could edit my sentence in such succinct fashion. So how long have you been just a married man?"

"Eighteen years, but we're here to talk about you, not me."

Goldstein picked up a half pint of cognac and a large crystal tumbler and led Wes into his den. It was dark with no overhead lights. The room was paneled with knotty pine, which was varnished to a glossy finish. Oil-burning lamps shone from small antique tables in all four corners of the room, bringing forth the natural glow of the wood and casting a soft golden ambience.

A large stone fireplace occupied almost one entire wall. On the mantle was a menorah. On one side of it was a dated, oval-framed picture of a couple that Wes guessed was Goldstein's parents. On the other side was a square-framed picture of a beautiful, dark-skinned woman that was probably his late wife. On the wall adjacent to the fireplace was an antique Motorola stereo cabinet.

Goldstein walked over to the stereo, put on an old record, and sat down in a black leather recliner in the center of the room. He motioned for Wes to sit down on the couch across from him. "Will you have a drink with me?"

Wes held up his hand. "I'd better keep my wits about me."

Goldstein swished a generous shot of cognac around in the bottom of his glass and let his head fall back into the plush foam-padded headrest. The room filled with strains of Frank Sinatra's "Strangers in the Night." As Wes prepared to begin his interview in earnest, he was confident this would be one of his better columns.

CHAPTER 2
April 2010

Nicole Tanner breathed a sigh of frustration. She glanced at her wristwatch again as she stood on the driveway next to a real estate sign in the front yard of the affluent north San Antonio home. It was a quarter past six, and the wind was blowing her hair into a tangled mess. Her feet hurt after being wedged into high-heeled shoes for almost ten hours. Who ever came up with the idea that these kinds of shoes were fashionable? It had to be a man. Nicole would wait five more minutes and then she'd head home.

There were plenty of no-shows circled in red on her desk calendar at work. It was not uncommon in the residential real estate business for a prospective buyer to call, schedule an appointment, and then not show up. Often, there was not even a follow-up phone call to apologize. Since Realtors like Nicole worked on commission, it was easy to blow them off. It didn't cost the no-show a penny to stand her up.

Nicole had become accustomed to it, but the home she was prepared to show would sell for more than $400,000, and the commission she stood to make on the sale would fix a lot of mistakes. Mistakes? Nicole checked them off one at a time in her mind. Mistakes like a maxed-out credit card that she used to purchase her expensive wardrobe. Her husband hit the roof when he saw the bill, but Wes didn't understand much about her business. You had to dress like you were successful—even if you weren't. She had started in real estate after her kids were all in school , and her income had grown steadily until the recession had set in two years ago. Now, she was struggling to make sales, and the Tanners were struggling to pay their bills. Wes told her they needed to tighten up until things got better. He blew up every time she busted the budget with her credit card, even threatening to cut it up if she didn't stop using it.

It was easy for Wes to criticize her for spending too much money instead of getting off his duff to earn more himself. Her husband had been in the newspaper business for almost twenty years, and he earned less than $50,000 per year. This left Nicole to assume the role of primary breadwinner.

Nicole's musing was interrupted as a silver Lexus swerved quickly into the driveway and came to a stop about one foot from her knees. Startled, Nicole quickly composed herself before the man exited the vehicle. She brushed her bangs out of her eyes and smiled. "Mr. Gonzalez?"

"Sorry I'm late, Nicole," Raul Gonzalez said with a thick Spanish accent as he grasped her extended hand. He was athletic looking, heavily muscled, and in the Mexican tradition, wore a striped polo shirt that fit very tightly around his biceps. Gonzalez was looking not at her face but directly at her breasts.

It wasn't as though Nicole had never been undressed by a man before. In spite of her hard-knock adult life, which included some late-night, hard-drinking bouts with numerous clients and coworkers, Nicole was still very attractive for a woman in her late thirties. But most men were more subtle than Raul Gonzalez.

Nicole had been taught early in her real estate sales career not to "qualify" her buyers. She had learned it was easy to qualify yourself right out of a sale. Just the same, Nicole had a critical eye for detail when meeting a client for the first time. This man was well groomed to the last detail and wore clothes and jewelry in a manner that indicated they weren't worn just to impress. It was obvious that this man was wealthy.

"Where's your wife, Mr. Gonzalez?" Nicole asked casually, recalling that he had told her on the phone that both of them would be coming.

"She couldn't make it. Had to feed the kids."

"How many children do you have?"

"Two."

"How old?"

"Six and four."

"Well, I think this house would be perfect for you." When Nicole reached the front door of the house, she paused to check her pocket for her iPhone. Somehow she didn't feel right about this one and thought she should call a friend at the office to join them. Grabbing her empty pocket, she realized she had left the phone in her car. An odd feeling tickled the hairs at the base of Nicole's neck. Her intuition told her she should go back to the car and get her phone, but this would mean leaving her buyer standing at the front door. That would be rude, and Nicole didn't want to offend the man. There were too many other Realtors that would love to work with this kind of buyer. She decided to press on with the showing.

Nicole fumbled to get the lockbox key, glancing quickly behind her at the man, who had pressed up very close to her. Once inside, she waved casually with a sweeping motion of her arm. "There's a study off to the right and formal dining to your left."

There was no comment. Nicole turned to look at the man's face, trying to gauge his first impression of the house. He didn't even glance at the elegant dining room, with the table perfectly set. "Is the master bedroom downstairs?" he asked in a husky voice.

"Yes. One down. Four up."

"I'd like to see the master bedroom."

Nicole nodded, instantly regretting that she had been so quick to agree to show the master bedroom first. She started walking toward the back of the house, sensing that Gonzalez was watching her as she walked ahead of him.

Be calm, she told herself. *Be calm, and be in charge.* Overcoming the urge to run out the back door, Nicole led Gonzalez to the master bedroom. When she reached the door, Nicole stepped aside so the buyer could see. An ornate king-sized bed and other attractive furniture adorned the bedroom. Gonzalez stared at the bed. Slowly, his gaze moved back and rested on her chest again. Nicole wished now that she hadn't worn her low-cut dress.

"Tell me about your husband, Nicole."

"He's a newspaperman," she said slowly, uncertain about the question.

"What's he like?"

"What do you mean?"

"What is he like? What kind of a man is he? Is he an hombre like me?" Gonzalez was standing between Nicole and the door. She shifted her weight back and forth nervously. Nicole had told Gonzalez over the phone that the owner of the house was out of town. He knew they weren't going to be interrupted.

"Did you want to see the upstairs?" As Nicole tried to squeeze past Gonzalez, he put his arm up to block her. She brushed his arm and then backed away.

"He doesn't satisfy you, does he?" Gonzalez said with his dark eyes dancing.

Nicole didn't answer. She avoided his glance until he took a step toward her. Startled, she backed up another step.

"Mr. Gonzalez—"

"It's Raul. And I always satisfy a woman."

"Always?" Nicole asked. Fearing the worst was just ahead of her, she had made a split-second decision on a way to get out of this predicament. Gonzalez smiled, took another step toward her, and lowered his head. He kissed her squarely on the lips. Nicole gradually responded to the kiss. Then she pulled away and looked at him.

"Let me prove it," Gonzalez said hungrily, nodding to the bed.

"Okay, but it can't take too long."

"It won't take long." Gonzalez reached to unbutton her blouse, but Nicole put her hand on his to stop him.

"I want to clean up first."

"Why?"

"It's very hot outside. I've been perspiring."

"I don't care."

"I'm going to take a shower," Nicole said firmly.

"I'll take one with you."

"No."

"Why not?" Gonzalez looked at her now with a hint of skepticism in his eyes.

Nicole smiled seductively. "That's a real turnoff. Do you want me to be turned off or turned on?"

"I want you to be turned on."

"Okay." Nicole touched his face. "I'll take my shower. You get ready for me. I'll be just a few minutes."

Ducking inside the bathroom, Nicole closed the door behind her and locked it. She turned on the shower and then glanced at the window. As she opened it, Nicole wondered if the alarm system would signal her imminent departure. After a nervous glance at the door, she removed the screen. Nicole was relieved when no alarm sounded.

She heard footsteps in the bedroom and the doorknob turning from the other side.

"Nicole?"

She climbed out of the window, ran through the backyard and around the house.

Nicole's heart felt like it was coming out of her chest as she ran. Not inclined to pray often, she found herself uttering a silent prayer. *Please, God. Let me get out of here.*

She glanced at the front door as she unlocked the car. There was no sign of Gonzalez yet.

If he had undressed when she went into the bathroom, it would take him a few minutes to dress again before he could pursue her.

As she was backing out of the driveway, she saw Gonzalez step onto the front porch. He was still standing there, looking at her, as she drove down the street and passed out of sight.

CHAPTER 3
April 2010

When six-year-old Summer wandered into the kitchen , Natalie was just starting dinner for the Tanner family. Summer was pouting over something.

"Hi, Summer."

"Hi," Summer replied, with a sullen tone that begged attention.

"What's wrong?"

"Nothing."

"Are you sure?"

"Yes."

Natalie had all of the ingredients out for her sesame ginger grilled chicken—sweet-sour sauce, hoisin sauce, sesame seed, clove garlic, fresh ginger, oriental chili sauce, and six small, skinned, boneless chicken breasts—set on the counter. Allowing twelve minutes to grill, there was still plenty of time to get to the bottom of Summer's problem and get dinner on the table by six. "Did something happen at school?"

"Suzy doesn't want to be my friend anymore."

"I thought Suzy was your best friend."

"I thought so, too."

"So, why not now?"

"'Cause I'm friends with Cindy."

"What's wrong with that?"

"Suzy doesn't *like* Cindy."

"Hmm. Do you want to know what I would do?"

"Sure."

"I'd stay friends with Cindy. Suzy will come around. If she doesn't, then maybe she wasn't much of a friend after all."

Summer seemed resigned. "Yeah, that's kind of what I was thinking, too," she said, as she turned her attention to her aunt's meal preparation. "What are you making, Aunt Natalie?"

"Sesame-ginger grilled chicken."

"Can I help?"

"Sure."

"Mom never lets me help," Summer said as she poked at a chicken breast with the tip of her index finger. Natalie playfully acted like she was going to slap Summer's hand, and the child quickly pulled it away with a smile. The revelation that Nicole didn't cook with her daughter came as no surprise to Natalie. She knew how impatient her sister could be with her children. Nicole generally was too busy with her own problems to listen to Summer's rambling stories. From Natalie's perspective, her sister viewed her own children as an impediment to realizing her full potential in life.

Summer was tugging at her skirt, and Natalie quickly turned her attention back to her niece. "We start by combining all of these ingredients," Natalie said as she put them in a saucepan.

"What about the chicken?"

"We have to grill it first." On cue, Duncan, the family dog, trotted over to see if any food scraps might fall his way. Natalie glanced down at the little terrier mix, and smiled. "Just waiting for me to make a mistake, aren't you, boy?"

"Maybe Duncan should sample some chicken," Summer said.

"Duncan can eat his own food."

Summer began to set the table as Natalie put the finishing touches on dinner. Soon, the aroma from the chicken drew Monty, Summer's thirteen-year-old brother, into the kitchen. Monty was at that awkward age when the boy was becoming a man. He walked across the kitchen and stared into the oven. "Aunt Natalie, I'm *really* hungry."

"Dinner is almost ready."

"When's Mom going to be home?"

"She had a showing. She said you could go ahead and eat without her."

Satisfied that he would soon be able to fill his stomach, Monty sat down at the table.

"Summer, call your sister," Natalie said.

After Summer ran upstairs, Natalie walked into the study. A middle-aged man with thinning hair sat in front of his computer, staring at the screen. Here was Wes, pouring himself into another novel. Nicole's husband had been writing for as long as Natalie had known him, but he had never published anything. Yet.

"How's it going, Hemmingway?"

Wes looked up and smiled weakly at his sister-in-law, "Slow."

"What chapter are you on?"

"Seven."

"When can I read it?"

"When it's done."

"When will that be?"

"Six months."

"You're asking me to wait six months to read the next great American novel?" Natalie teased. "That's way too much to ask."

"You said the last one was the great American novel before every publisher in the country turned it down."

"Wes, I thought *The Silent Place* was fantastic. I can't believe your agent couldn't find a publisher for it."

"Thanks, but you seem to be alone with that opinion." Wes shook his head. "I'm wasting my time. I'm really not that good of a writer."

Wes continued to stare at the computer screen for another moment before stealing a glance at Natalie. When he got down on himself, she would humor him and allow him to sit on his pity pot for a while. Eventually, he'd climb down and continue his endeavor.

"I still can't believe none of your novels have been published."

"A publishing house gets thousands of submissions each year. The chances of an unpublished fiction writer getting a first novel published are about the same as hitting the lotto."

"You're a good writer, Wes. You've just got to keep plugging," Natalie said with spirit as she sat down on the couch facing the desk. Wes started to say something but stopped when Jordan appeared in the doorway of the study.

"Are you coming?"

"Coming?"

"To dinner?" Jordan gave her father the look. Natalie knew it was the look only teenage girls can give their dad. It said, simultaneously, "I love you so much," and "Dad, you're such a dork." Natalie wondered what happened to the little girl that used to sit in her lap while she read her stories. It seemed like yesterday. Now, just a month short of sixteen, Jordan had come of age. She was almost as tall as her mother, and just as beautiful, with a woman's figure and silky hair. Natalie shuddered at the thought of how many over-sexed boys had already taken note of these features. How would she ever remain pure until marriage?

"Well?" Jordan asked Wes again. "I'm hungry."

"Coming," Wes said.

As Natalie followed Wes and Jordan out of the room, she couldn't help but wonder what their life would have been like if she was his wife, instead of Nicole. She was suddenly flooded with guilt. Feeling ashamed, she looked down at her feet and asked the Lord for forgiveness. These were the kind of thoughts she must crowd from her mind forever.

CHAPTER 4
April 2010

Nicole Tanner entered her home wanting only to be alone. A hot bath and a glass of wine sounded good to her, but her sister was walking toward her from the living room with an inquisitive look on her face. "I was worried about you. Did you get my message?"

"Bad day at the office," Nicole snapped as she walked past her and headed into the kitchen. She set her purse on the counter by the microwave and began fishing around in it until she found her phone. She hadn't checked her messages, so she dialed into her voice mail and listened to a message from a prospective buyer who was interested in meeting her tomorrow. Nicole was startled when Natalie walked into the kitchen and turned on the overhead light.

"Turn off the light, please."

Natalie turned off the light and waited for her to make eye contact. Instead, Nicole pretended she wasn't there as she busied herself looking through the day's mail. Why couldn't Natalie just go away? She wanted to be alone, and she certainly didn't want to talk with her sister about what had happened. Natalie would probably tell her it was all her fault for dressing too provocatively.

The house was stone silent, and Nicole suddenly was aware of the loud ticking hand of the clock above the stove behind her. "Turn on the TV, the stereo, *something*, Natalie. It's like a tomb in here."

"Are you hungry? I can heat you up something."

"I already ate." Nicole walked into the living room and sat down on the couch. She flipped on the television and turned to CNN. Natalie, following her at a safe distance, stopped at the easy chair next to the couch and waited. She was looking intently at her with that judgmental look Nicole hated. Natalie had always acted more like a mother than a big sister, and Nicole had no patience for that kind of an attitude tonight.

"Where's Wes?" Nicole finally asked.

"He went to the bookstore."

"Where are the kids?"

"Jordan and Monty are spending the night with friends."

"On a school night?"

"There's no school tomorrow."

"Oh, I forgot."

"Nicole, I want to talk with you about Jordan."

"What about her?"

"I overheard her talking with a friend on her cell phone. I think they were going to meet some boys this evening. That's why I was trying to call you."

"How could they do that? Jordan can't drive."

"But her friend, Amy, can," Natalie said. "You may want to call her and check in."

"I just want to unwind. I'm going to watch some TV if that's okay with you."

"She's your daughter."

"That's right," Nicole shot back. "So mind your own business."

"I'm sorry you had a bad day."

The front door slammed, signaling Wes's return. Nicole turned her attention back to the television, hoping Wes would go into the study and leave her alone. But he walked back to the family room instead. "Hi, Nicole." She didn't answer, knowing that if she conversed with him, he would certainly ask her about her day.

"What's wrong with her?" Wes asked Natalie.

"I'm sitting right here, Wes. Don't talk about me like I'm not in the room."

"I'm going to take off," Natalie said, turning to leave.

"Thanks for dinner," Wes said, as she passed him.

"Thanks for dinner," Nicole repeated, mockingly.

Wes took the remote, turned off the television set and glared at her.

"I'm sorry." Nicole closed her eyes. "I had a rough day. Okay?" She stood up. "I'm going to take a bath. Can you pour me a glass of wine and bring it back to me?"

Wes nodded and started for the kitchen as Nicole headed for the bathroom. Closing the bathroom doors behind her, Nicole opened the medicine cabinet. She reached for a bottle of pills, opened it, and popped a couple of Xanex in her moth. Nicole had convinced her physician to write a prescription for the drugs after describing the bouts of anxiety she had been experiencing.

After downing the Xanex, Nicole slipped out of her clothes and started drawing the water for the bath. When the water reached the appropriate level in the tub, she flipped on the jets and climbed in. The heated air bubbles immediately began to soothe her body. She leaned her head back, closing her eyes.

"Here you go," Wes said as he entered the bathroom with two glasses of red wine in his hands. He walked over to the tub and handed one to her.

"Thank you."

"You're welcome," Wes said, staring down at her in the water as the bubbles rose around her. Nicole realized she had made a mistake by asking him to bring her a glass of wine. He was surely thinking amorous thoughts. There was no chance of that happening tonight. She looked away but still felt his eyes on her.

"So, how was your day?" Nicole asked.

"It was good. I interviewed a real character over on the west side. Ezra Goldstein. Bounty hunter. Former Israeli sniper. It's going to make a great column."

"That's nice."

"You want some company in there?" Wes asked hopefully.

"Wes, how many hints can I drop to tell you I'm not in the mood?"

"You're never in the mood."

"Just go away and leave me alone."

"What's your problem?" Wes asked her angrily.

Nicole crossed her arms over her chest. "A man tried to rape me, Wes, " she whispered, blinking back the sudden rush of tears.

"What?" His mouth was open, but there was no sound. "You said *tried*?"

"No," she snapped, "he didn't rape me. I got away."

"How?"

"I escaped out the bathroom window."

"Who was he?"

"Sshhh," Nicole said, putting her finger to her mouth. She couldn't stand it to hear him raising his voice to her.

"There's nobody here. Tell me!"

Nicole looked at Wes incredulously and started to cry. She couldn't believe her husband's lack of sensitivity. "Wes!"

"What?"

"Look at yourself. All you care about is this man. What about me?"

"Did you call the police?"

"No."

"Why not?"

"The same thing happened to Marty last year," Nicole said, trying to rein in her sobs. "She reported it to police and they did n-nothing."

"They did nothing?"

"They said it was just her word against his."

"Do you have this guy's address?"

"Why?"

"I'm going to pay him a visit."

"And do what? Beat him up?"

"Maybe."

"This guy would take you apart."

Nicole could see immediately that her words had the desired effect. Like a skilled surgeon, she made the cut and saw her victim bleed out. The anger slowly faded from Wes's eyes, and his body assumed a deflated posture. Sometimes, anger simply removed the social barriers of civility, and this was one such occasion. Nicole meant to hurt Wes with the truth because he needed to stop being angry and feel her pain. Since he lacked empathy, this was the only way to bring him to that point. Shaking his head, Wes turned and walked out of the bathroom.

Wes went out on the back porch and lit a cigarette. He soon found himself staring blankly at the glow of the gas lamp on his neighbor's patio as he sipped his glass of wine. Wes knew how Nicole felt about him, so the cutting words she spoke came as no surprise. Nicole would always see him as something less than a man. Wes wanted to go back into the bedroom and give Nicole a piece of his mind, but he resisted the urge because it wouldn't accomplish anything. After eighteen years of marriage, Nicole wasn't going to change her mind about him. Miracles just didn't happen.

Miracles. That was a subject for church and churchgoers. He had heard a lot about miracles from his grandfather, the pastor of a small Hill Country church in Kerrville, who had preached for years about miracles. Wes recalled the time when Pastor Roger Tanner had stood up in front of the church with a family that claimed their son had been healed by God of a brain tumor. Everyone was praising God and offering up prayers of thanksgiving. It was funny how people were quick to praise God for anything good that happened but never blamed him for the bad things. If God was so wonderful, then why was the world in such a mess?

Wes could see that Nicole had turned the light off in the bedroom. He put out his cigarette and walked back into house. Setting the half-finished glass of wine in the sink, Wes went into the bedroom, undressed quietly in the dark, and slipped into bed beside his wife. Her back was toward him, but he knew from the cadence of her breathing that she wasn't yet asleep. He started to say something but stopped, turning his back to her as he slipped the pillow under his head. In a short time, the rigors of his day caught up with him, and he was asleep.

CHAPTER 5
April 2010

It was almost eleven before Nicole made it to her desk the next day. Wes insisted they go to the police station and file a report on the incident involving Raul Gonzalez. A police officer had taken down the information and promised nothing except to turn the report over to a detective. When Nicole sat down at her desk, she called up her Yahoo account on the computer and began typing an e-mail. Noticing someone in the doorway, she quickly cleared the personal e-mail from her screen and turned to face her friend, Marty Chavez.

"There you are." The attractive Hispanic woman smiled.

"Wes made me go to the police station."

"You reported the incident?"

"Yeah."

"It's a waste of time, Nicole. You know that, don't you?"

"What?"

"Going to the police. They won't do a thing to the creep."

"That's what I told Wes, but he made me go down there."

"They should castrate him."

"Wes?"

"No." Marty laughed. "The creep. All men, for all I care."

"You might regret that some day."

"I doubt it. Start with my ex. Hey, congratulations."

"For what?"

"I heard that you closed on that house in the new development on Tuesday."

"That's my only sale in two months. You've already closed two this month."

"Sure. Two poor Mexicans. You doubled me on the one. How do you do it?"

"Total needs selling."

"Your client *needed* to buy that house?"

"No," Nicole shook her head. "*I* totally needed the sale. I've got my car payment to make. We owe Visa, MasterCard, and Talbot's. And Jordan starts college in two years. Do you know how much college costs these days?"

"It's brutal." Marty nodded empathetically.

"Wes brings home his little paycheck from the newspaper and looks to me to do the rest. And the economy isn't getting any better."

The phone rang at Nicole's desk.

"I'll let you go," Marty said. "Can you have lunch today?"

"Sure. I'll be ready to go in an hour."

"This is Nicole Tanner," Nicole said, disappointed when she learned it was only a police detective. It was unlikely that he was in the market for a house. The detective asked her if she could come back down to the police station. "Okay." Nicole sighed. "I've got two showings after lunch. Can we come at five?" She hung up the phone and dialed her husband's number. "Wes... The police want to talk with us again."

Wes stood in front of the San Antonio Police Department building, tensing his muscles as the anger welled up inside him. He had seen Nicole's Mercedes drive past him and turn into the parking lot across the street. But she was talking on her phone, and it was five more minutes before she finally got out of the car and started walking toward him. Wes had been waiting out in front of the police station for thirty minutes. Taking a drag from his cigarette, he tossed it on the ground.

"Glad you could make it," Wes quipped as she walked up.

"Sorry to keep you waiting, dear. I wouldn't want you to be late for one of your earthshaking interviews with the director of the animal shelter."

"I know my job's not anywhere near as important as yours," Wes said as they walked up the steps and into the building, "but it does help pay the bills."

"Barely."

Wes didn't take the bait. He could tell that Nicole was spoiling for a fight, and his job had been a sore subject for years. Nicole seemed to relish every chance to put him down and belittle his chosen profession. Her friends' husbands all made six-figure incomes, and Wes made less than half of their salaries. Seldom did a day go by that he wasn't reminded of that fact.

Inside the police station, they turned down a hall and found seats on a wooden bench in front of a sign that read: *Homicide, Robbery, Sex Crimes, Night CID.* Nicole crossed her legs and looked down at the floor. Wes started to say something but stopped. These days, she seemed like a stranger to him.

"Do you have any closings coming up?" Wes finally asked her.

"No. We're in a recession and no one is buying anything in case you hadn't noticed."

Wes looked up to see a big biker-type walking by them. The man glared at Wes as if to ask, "What are you two doing here?" before sitting down on the bench next to them. A moment later, a loud pop signaled the unlocking of an electronically controlled door off to their left. Wes looked up and was surprised to see a familiar face.

"Wes." The handsome Hispanic extended his hand. "What are you doing here?"

Wes rose to his feet, taking the man's hand firmly in his own. "Unfortunately, it's not a social visit." He looked down at Nicole, who looked disinterested at the idea of meeting someone new. "Frank Salas. This is my wife, Nicole Tanner."

"Nice to meet you, Mrs. Tanner," Salas said, and Wes noticed him giving Nicole the once over with an approving nod.

"Frank and I went to high school together," Wes explained to Nicole as she shook his hand. She hadn't even bothered to get up for the introduction.

"So you're from Kerrville?" Nicole asked politely.

"Yeah. My father was a ranch hand back in the day. I couldn't wait to get out of there."

"You've done pretty well for yourself," Wes said. "You're a detective now?"

"That's right. And I'd better get back to work before they demote me," Salas said. "Good to see you, Wes. Let's grab a beer soon."

Before Wes could sit down on the bench, he heard the electronically controlled door again and turned his head to see a large man dressed in a white, short-sleeve shirt and tie approach them. The detective had the weathered look of a man who worked his fair share of hours outdoors in the sunshine. He was lean and looked fit, with no sign of a paunch. His graying hair was cut high and tight, military style.

"I'm Detective Tommy Niebring," the man said, extending his hand.

Wes shook his hand. "Wes Tanner."

"Pardon me, Mr. Tanner, but are you the Wes Tanner that writes the column for the *Express-News*?"

"Yes, sir."

"I read your column. You're a funny guy, and you make sense— most of the time."

"Thanks, I think."

"Let's go back to my office," Niebring said. With a wave of his hand, he led the couple through the door and down the hallway to a small, sparsely furnished office, whose only window was largely obscured by freely growing ivy. There were no commendations, plaques, or photographs on the wall, as Wes had expected to see. But there was a photograph. A younger Niebring stood holding the reins of a paint-colored horse. In the background was a barn and behind that, sagebrush.

Niebring motioned for the couple to sit down in two chairs that were arranged on the other side of his desk. Directly in front of him, Wes noticed a single file open, with only a one-sheet police report in it. On either side of Niebring, however, Wes also noticed that there were many files arranged haphazardly on his desk. "Looks like you stay busy," Wes said with a nod toward all the files on his desk.

"You don't know the half of it, Mr. Tanner." Niebring shook his head. "We stay pretty well covered up." Niebring wiped his forehead with the back of his hand, looked sincerely at Nicole, then at Wes, and continued. "Mr. and Mrs. Tanner, we have more than a hundred full-time detectives working as regular officers for the San Antonio Police Department. Last year alone, we had 2,600 felony cases filed within this jurisdiction." He made a casual sweeping motion with his forearm in the direction of the case files on his desk. "Most of these we will never clear, unless we get a tip or unless somebody that we already have in custody cops to one of these crimes. We call those 'gimmes,'" Niebring said.

Niebring leaned forward and focused his gaze on Nicole. "We have questioned Mr. Gonzalez in reference to the incident—"

"Let me guess," Wes cut him short. "He denies it?"

"He didn't deny it," Niebring continued patiently. "His version was different than the one your wife gave us." Niebring held his hand up in a sort of preemptive stop sign signal, and Wes assumed what he was about to say was expected to arouse an angry response from the couple.

"Gonzalez said he believed his interest in you was reciprocal," Niebring said, turning his gaze to Nicole.

"Why would he believe that?" Wes asked.

"He said your wife kissed him and told him she would have sex with him if it didn't take too long." Niebring now turned and looked at Nicole while he spoke, gently tapping on his desk with the tip of his ballpoint pen. "Is that true, Mrs. Tanner?"

Wes looked at Nicole. He was waiting for her to jump up, hopping mad, and tell the detective that Gonzalez's account was absurd. How could the detective believe something like that? Instead, Nicole squirmed nervously in her chair. Niebring glanced quickly at Wes, then back to Nicole.

"Is there any way he could have been led to believe that you were interested in him, Mrs. Tanner?" Niebring rephrased the question.

"I don't think so."

"You don't think so?" Niebring slumped into the back of his chair and laced his fingers behind his head.

Nicole was shaking her head, clearly uncomfortable with the direction the detective was taking her. When she didn't respond, Wes jumped in. His honor seemed to be at stake here, too.

"What are you doing, Detective? She's the victim. Remember?"

"Mr. Tanner, you weren't there, were you?" Niebring asked firmly.

Wes went silent and looked over at his wife. The detective had a point. Wes was *not* there.

"Mrs. Tanner? Can you answer the question?"

Nicole looked away.

"Did you kiss him?"

"I didn't kiss him *back*."

"But you didn't pull away?"

"No."

Wes felt like someone had punched him in the gut. Nicole hadn't told him the whole story. He was now left to wonder how much of what she had told was fabricated. It took this wily cop to bring the truth to light. Nicole was staring at the floor, her hands in her lap, rolling her thumbs one over the other in a paddlewheel motion.

"Mrs. Tanner, we don't like to put anybody on the spot. But we have to know *exactly* what happened, or we can't proceed. Why didn't you pull away from him?"

"I was scared. He blocked the door. I thought he was going to rape me."

"Mr. Gonzalez said you told him to wait in bed while you got cleaned up."

"He was blocking the door. I went into the bathroom and locked the door so that I could get away from him."

"Out the bathroom window?"

Nicole nodded.

"Did it ever occur to you that this was the only way she could escape from being raped?" Wes was glaring at Niebring now, trying to get his attention away from the wilting woman sitting next to him.

"Sure, it did. And I have no doubt that that's the way it probably did happen. But, as long as there was no verbal rejection, and in the absence of any real physical coercion on the part of Mr. Gonzalez, we just don't have an awful lot to work with here," Niebring said, softening his tone as he continued. "Mr. Tanner, I have seen defense lawyers go on the attack against complainants in courtrooms for twenty years. If she can't make her case here in this office with me, she will be very hard pressed to make her case in court."

"What are you saying?" Wes asked.

"What I am saying is that, according to the strict letter of the law, what you are looking at here is possibly an assault by contact. In Texas, that's a Class C misdemeanor. You can go to municipal court with that if you want, but based on what I have here, this is not a felony matter," Niebring said, standing up to signal an end to the interview.

CHAPTER 6
April 2010

Nicole's emotions were in tumult as she walked out of the police station. Her initial feelings of shock and humiliation had turned to anger when she felt her husband pull away from her after the revelation in the detective's office. Nicole had little doubt that Wes was dealing with his own array of emotions, but she didn't care about his feelings at this point. She was the one being held up for ridicule, and he had turned against her. He didn't even try to understand her predicament alone in that house with a man threatening to take advantage of her.

"Did you have *anything* you wanted to say to me?" Nicole finally asked as Wes lit a cigarette. They were waiting to cross the busy street.

"I have a lot that I'd like to say to you, but my grandfather told me to not use that kind of language in front of a lady. But then I'm not really sure *you* qualify."

"You're scum."

"And you're a tramp."

Nicole slapped him.

"Truth hurts, doesn't it?"

"I hate you, Wes."

"Do you think you're telling me something that I don't know?"

"I'm not a tramp," Nicole said, starting to sob.

"You kissed a man and agreed to have sex with him."

"It was a ploy to escape from him."

"But why didn't you tell me everything that happened? Why did I have to find out that kind of information from someone else?"

"Because I knew you wouldn't understand."

"You're right, I don't understand."

"What don't you understand?"

"Why didn't you just run?" Wes said, his anger evident. She knew he was near the boiling point, but that didn't bother her. In fact, she welcomed his anger. If he blew his lid, she would be justified in launching a devastating retaliatory strike.

"What do you think, Wes?" Nicole said through clenched teeth. "Do you think I wanted to have sex with him? If I wanted to have sex with him, I would have."

"I've got to go," Wes said, turning to leave.

"You're just going to walk away?"

Wes didn't turn his head or acknowledge her question as he crossed the street, heading for the parking lot. Nicole couldn't believe he would just leave her standing there. Recovering from her surprise, she started after him but had to wait until traffic passed. By the time she reached the parking lot, Wes had already climbed into his truck. She reached the vehicle as he started the engine. Surely, he would roll down his window. She tried to open his door, but it was locked. Furious, she pounded on the window, but he just smiled at her. It was that smug smile she loathed. Nicole was forced to release her grip on the door when he started to back out of the parking place. There was nothing she could do but watch as he sped out into the street, barely missing a car in his lane.

At that moment, Nicole hated Wes more than anyone in the world. He was a worthless man that had brought her nothing but misery. There were so many other men in the world that she could have married. More attractive men. Smarter men. But she had settled for *this* man. Nicole was convinced that she had wasted the past eighteen years of her life in this loveless marriage. She had thought about divorcing him more times than she could count, but she dismissed the idea for the sake of the children. Nicole's father had divorced her mother, and she didn't want to subject her own offspring to that fate. They would have to choose which parent to spend holidays with, and Nicole feared they would choose Wes over her every time.

Nicole turned slowly toward the street. Nueva, which ran in front of the San Antonio Police Department, was still buzzing with traffic. She glanced at her watch. It was almost 6:30. The afternoon heat had not abated much, although the sun was nearly spent in the western sky, signaling a merciful end to a long, frustrating afternoon. She walked over to her car, anxious to get home, get cool, and divert her mind from the events of the day. But she was going nowhere quickly with this traffic. Nicole took a deep breath and exhaled, turning her attention to the scene in front of her.

A Hispanic teenage boy, about seventeen, was walking quickly down the sidewalk. A girl about the same age was walking ahead, in an obvious attempt to distance herself from him. Finally, the boy was able to catch up to her. But instead of grabbing her, he simply ran past her far enough to cut off her walking path, then turned toward her and began to plead his case. The girl listened for a moment and then laughed. In moments the two were arm in arm, walking north down the sidewalk against the stream of oncoming traffic. *Kid stuff*, she thought to herself. Even when they thought they had it bad, they had it so good. She had a fleeting memory of a life that easy, but it was so long gone.

Wes was still angry an hour after he left Nicole. He was back at his desk at the newspaper, trying to write his column on Ezra Goldstein. But he couldn't concentrate. Perhaps, he should have felt guilty for leaving Nicole standing alone in the parking lot, but he had no regrets. Nicole had treated him far worse than he had treated her, and she deserved no respect. When she wasn't cutting him down with her words, she was ignoring him.

Worse than the neglect was the act of deception in recounting the Raul Gonzalez encounter. Wes couldn't begin to count the number of half-truths and white lies his wife had told him over the years. For every one he knew about, how many more went undetected? Nicole wanted them to believe she had been frightened at the house yesterday. She was playing the part of the helpless woman, doing whatever she could to escape an aggressive man. Wes knew Nicole too well to be taken in by the little drama in the detective's office. There were many words that could be used to describe his wife, but helpless was not one of them. A beautiful woman gets plenty of attention from men looking to satisfy one of their basic animal appetites. Wes was sure Nicole had plenty of practice handling men like Raul Gonzalez. She had never complained before about being frightened or feeling helpless.

Wes's cell phone rang. He looked at the caller ID and noticed the call had originated from home. If it was Nicole, he didn't want to talk with her. But it could be one of his children. He answered the phone.

"Wes? It's me."

"What do you want?" he asked coldly.

"That Raul Gonzalez guy called me while I was gone. He left a voice mail message. He threatened me, Wes."

"Threatened you?"

"Listen," she said. Wes could hear her dialing into her voice mail before she pressed the cell phone up to the receiver. Wes could barely hear the ominous voice of a Hispanic man speaking with a heavy accent.

"Ms. Tanner. This is Raul Gonzalez. I was eating lunch with my wife, brother, and sister-in-law today when the police stopped by to tell me to come to the police station for questioning. My four-year-old son was there, too. You got me good, Ms. Tanner. You got me real good. There is an expression in your country, 'What goes around, comes around.' We have unfinished business. I'll be seeing you soon, sweetheart."

"My God," Wes said when Nicole came back on the line. "This guy is crazy."

"What should I do?"

"We need to call the police again."

"The detective told us we didn't have a case."

"He'll feel differently now. Do you have the detective's card?"

"Yes."

"Text me the number. I'll call him."

"Wes, I'm scared," Nicole said, and Wes could hear the fear in her voice. "Could you please come home? I really don't want to be here by myself tonight."

CHAPTER 7

April 2010

Storm clouds gathered overhead, and a wind shift hinted at a change in the weather. Wes had hardly noticed that the sun had disappeared an hour ago. He was focused on the drama being played out on the field in front of him. Sitting next to him in the stands at McAllister Park, Natalie glanced at him and smiled.

"You're so intense."

"This is a big game."

"I liked your column this morning. Good insights and funny as can be."

"Thanks." Wes turned his attention back to the diamond, where his son was laboring on the mound. Their team led by one run, but this game was not over. There were runners on first and third, and the boy on first had a big lead. Working from the stretch, Monty took a peek over his shoulder before delivering the pitch. "Ball one," the umpire yelled as the runner took off for second base. The catcher came up from the crouch, ready to throw.

"No throw! No throw!" Wes screamed frantically from the stands as the shortstop raced over to cover second.

"I think he heard you." Natalie laughed as the catcher returned the ball to Monty.

"It's a good thing. If he threw down, the runner would have broken for home."

"They might have gotten him at the plate."

"Not worth the risk."

"Now they have the winning run in scoring position."

"I'm glad he stole the base," Wes said. "Now, Monty can focus on the batter. He pitches better from the windup anyway." After two quick strikes, Natalie and Wes were screaming words of encouragement. Then, two balls followed.

"Full count," Wes moaned.

"We've got a base open."

"Their cleanup hitter is up next. Monty needs to get this guy."

"He will."

"I hope you're right," Wes said, turning his attention back to the game. He watched anxiously as Monty kicked and fired. The batter swung, but the ball was already in the catcher's glove.

"Yeah!" Wes leaped out of the stands like a gazelle, pumping his fist in the air.

"I told you," Natalie said as Wes hugged her happily.

"Let's go get Monty and celebrate with some ice cream."

"I can't."

"Why not?"

"There's just twelve days left until the tax-filing deadline."

"Thanks for coming, Nat." Wes hugged her.

"Hey, I wouldn't have missed this game for the world."

"I wish his mother felt the same way."

"I know she would have been here if she could."

"She never comes to his games. She didn't even come to the play at school to see Jordan. But you're always there. You're more of a mother to her children than she is."

"You know she has to meet her clients when they're available to meet."

"Why are you always sticking up for her?"

"I'm not sticking up for her," Natalie said defensively.

"I've never heard you say a bad thing about anyone."

"I try to see the best in everyone."

Wes and Monty were still in high spirits when they arrived home from the game. It was almost six, and Nicole was in the study. The desk was covered with papers, and she was peering at a multiple-listing directory on the computer screen.

"You missed a good game," Wes said.

"Somebody has to work," Nicole said sullenly without looking up at her husband or son.

Leave it to Nicole to pour ice water on even her son's baseball game victory, Wes thought to himself as he tossed a clutch bag full of baseball gear into the corner of the study.

Nicole looked up when the bag hit the floor. "Don't leave that in here."

Jordan had sneaked up behind him. She playfully ran past her dad and brother, then turned to face them. She was wearing a halter top and tight, faded jeans. Her attire was far too suggestive for Wes's taste, but he decided not to say anything about it.

"Hi, Dad. Did you guys win?"

"Yes, ma'am. Three to two. Your brother closed out the game with a stellar performance on the mound. What are you up to?"

"I'm going to Starbucks."

"Need a ride?"

"Nope. Amy's picking me up."

"Amy's driving?"

"She got her license last week."

"Great," Wes said sarcastically. "It's comforting to know you'll be riding with an experienced driver."

"You're *not* riding with Amy," Nicole interjected.

"Why not?" Jordan shot back angrily.

Nicole looked up for the first time. Her eyes were cold, and it was clear that she wasn't in the mood to offer an explanation to her defiant daughter.

"Why not, Mom?"

"Because I said so."

"Dad." Jordan turned to Wes, her eyes pleading for help.

"Nicole, I'm sure it will be okay. I'll talk to Amy before they leave and—"

"It's not okay," Nicole said condescendingly as if she were speaking to two ignorant children. "It's against the law for her to ride with a new driver for six months."

"I'll take you," Wes said, interceding in hopes of ending the conflict before it escalated. But Nicole wasn't finished yet. She was staring at Jordan's halter top.

"You're not going anywhere dressed like that."

"Mom!"

"Where did you get that skimpy top?"

"Amy gave it to me."

"Go to your room and find another top."

"What, do you think a bunch of boys are going to attack me?"

"Is that what you want?" Nicole asked pointedly.

"Mom, you're so *not* cool. I wish you could be cool like Dad." Jordan glared at her mother before she rushed out of the study.

"Why do you let her talk to me like that?" Nicole asked after Jordan had disappeared from the room. Wes looked at Monty, who was looking at the floor, clearly embarrassed. Wes also felt embarrassed, not wanting his son around to hear his parents arguing again.

"Monty, can you take Duncan for a walk?"

"Is that the best excuse you could find for getting rid of me?"

"Yeah." Wes nodded, waiting until his son left the room before he closed the door and turned back to face Nicole. "Do you think you might practice enough self-control to wait until we're alone before you start berating me?"

"Why don't you ever stick up for me with the children?"

"You don't need anyone to stick up for you."

Wes saw a look of surprise that hinted of hurt feelings, but Nicole's expression quickly faded back into a sour look as her eyes returned to the computer screen.

"What's for dinner?" Wes finally asked.

"Whatever you want to fix. I need to go down to the office."

"On a Saturday night?"

"I have two closings on Monday morning."

It was almost ten o'clock when Wes got home. He had been gone almost two hours, and Summer was standing in the foyer when he entered the house. She was in her pajamas. "What are you doing out of bed?" Wes asked her.

"I want Mommy to say goodnight to me."

"Your mother's not home yet?"

"She promised to tuck me in when she came home."

"I'll call her," Wes said. In the study, he dialed Nicole's office number and got her voice mail. Wes dialed her cell phone and also got voice mail. "Paging Nicole Tanner. You have a daughter that wants you to tuck her in. Please come home."

"Is she coming?"

"She's coming. Now get back in bed."

As soon as Summer disappeared around the corner, Wes booted up his computer and started working on his novel again. He had tried to write earlier in the day, but Nicole kept interrupting him with jobs around the house. By the time he had completed all of them, it was time to head to the ballpark.

"Hi, Dad," Jordan said, standing in the doorway. "Where've you been?"

"The bookstore."

"What are you doing?"

"Writing."

"Your column, or your novel?"

"My novel."

"Hey, when's Mom coming home? I want to talk to her."

"I don't know."

"Is she still at the office?"

"I guess."

"Kind of late, isn't it?"

"Yeah. I called when I got home, but she hasn't called me back yet."

"Aren't you worried about her?"

"Why should I be worried about her?"

"Because of the threat that man made?"

"How did you know about that?" Wes looked surprised. "Did she tell you?"

"No. Summer did."

"Summer? Eavesdropping again, I guess."

"Aren't you *worried* about Mom?" Jordan repeated her question.

"Not really. She probably just lost herself reading some boring real estate contract. I'm sure she'll be home when she finishes up."

"Do you still love Mom?"

"Of course I do."

"It doesn't sound like it."

Wes noticed the concern in his daughter's face.

"I guess I could drive down to her office and remind her what time it is."

"Can I go with you?"

"Sure. Monty can hold down the fort."

CHAPTER 8
April 2010

When Wes turned the key in the ignition to start his truck, an oldies station was tuned in on the radio. The song being played was "Sweet Child O' Mine."

"I remember that song from my college days," Wes told his daughter with a smile.

"Guns n' Roses?"

"Yeah. Do you listen to them?"

"I've heard this song."

"Sweet child o'mine," Wes said, singing along. "She's got eyes of the bluest skies. As if they thought of rain." Wes continued to sing, pretending to sing the song to Jordan. "Sweet child o' mine. Sweet love of mine."

"Dad, you're killing me," Jordan said around giggles, trying to catch her breath as Wes drove out of their subdivision. "Did you sing that to your girlfriend back then?"

Wes smiled. "As a matter of fact, I did."

"What was her name?"

"It was your aunt Natalie."

Jordan's mouth dropped open. "You dated Aunt Natalie?"

"Yep."

"I didn't know that. How long did y'all date?"

"Three years."

"Oh, my gosh. *Then* you started dating Mom?"

"That's right."

"Why did you stop dating Aunt Natalie and start dating Mom?"

"I met Aunt Natalie in college. Your mom is two years younger. I would see her when I would stop by and see Natalie at her house. She was always just Natalie's little sister until one day when I saw her in a different light."

"Wow." Jordan shook her head. "I can't believe I never knew that. What other secrets do you have, Dad?"

"That's about it. Do you mind if I smoke?"

"Go ahead. It's your funeral." Wes rolled down the window a few inches and lit a cigarette. They rode in silence for a minute, but Wes could tell Jordan was still thinking about it. She finally looked at him again. "Did you love Aunt Natalie?"

"I thought I did at one time. But looking back, I probably didn't even know what love was back then."

"I feel like I might be falling in love," Jordan said wistfully as she leaned her head back in the seat.

"Let me guess? Your heart is all aflutter. You swoon every time he walks into the room. You think about him all the time—"

"That's it. Exactly."

"That's not love. That's infatuation."

"What's infatuation?"

"It comes from the root word *folly*. It's a foolish attraction without basis."

"What do you mean?"

"People are attracted to each other based on feelings," Wes tried to explain. "There may be no good reason for the attraction except some chemistry between them."

"What's wrong with chemistry?"

"Nothing, except that it doesn't last. Chemistry propels them to the altar, and then the chemistry wears off. Like another old song goes, 'You've lost that loving feeling.'"

"So they get divorced?"

"Sometimes."

"Have you and Mom ever talked about getting a divorce?"

"Why would you think that?" Wes asked, turning to a strategy of evasion that he employed whenever he didn't want to tell the truth, or state an outright lie.

"I don't know. I just wondered. Y'all fight a lot."

"No more than any married couple."

Wes was relieved to see his daughter grow silent. He was uncomfortable talking about his marital relationship with Jordan. A light rain had begun to fall, and Wes felt a need to focus on the road ahead of him as he began to ease over to the right-hand lane in anticipation of his exit from the highway. Traffic was heavy as they passed the Quarry Market, where throngs of late-night moviegoers were leaving the theater.

"Still a lot of people out," Wes said to break the silence as they drove down the tree-lined thoroughfare that led into Alamo Heights. Wes had no great love for this part of the city that was home to trendy businesses, posh restaurants, and spacious, old ranch-style homes. He had asked Nicole repeatedly to move her office closer to home, but she stubbornly refused. She told Wes she wanted to be more centrally located in the city, and she didn't want to miss opportunities to sell homes in the wealthy Alamo Heights and Terrell Hills area. That was typical of Nicole, Wes thought, to put her job ahead of her family if it meant more opportunity for business and the almighty buck.

When Wes pulled into the real estate office parking lot, he saw Nicole's Mercedes parked next to the building. There were no other cars in the parking lot. Wes noticed a light on in the front of the office, but the rest of the building was dark. He parked the truck and they walked briskly up to the office.

"Nicole?" Wes pushed the door open and entered the lobby. "Nicole?"

"Maybe she's back in her office," Jordan said from behind him.

"I didn't see a light on back there."

"I'll go check." Jordan ran down the hallway. Wes followed slowly behind her. When Jordan reached the door to Nicole's office, she flipped on the light. "She's not here," Jordan said, staring at her mother's desk until Wes stood next to her. There were papers scattered about, and it looked like she had been there recently.

"Mom?" Jordan yelled at the top of her lungs.

"Let's look around," Wes said as he turned and started back down the hallway. Father and daughter walked through the entire building, searching each room. There were no other lights on, and there was no sign of Nicole.

"Where is she, Dad?" Jordan asked with a trace of fear in her voice.

"I don't know."

"Could she have walked to a convenience store?"

"It's possible. Your mom likes to walk, although I would think she'd know better than to walk alone at night."

"Is there a convenience store close to here?"

"Not too far. Let's drive down there."

Wes and Jordan got back in the truck and drove the half-mile to the well-lit store. They checked inside and out, even visiting with the attendant about whether he had seen anyone fitting Nicole's description. He hadn't. Wes called Nicole's cell phone again. There was still no answer.

"Dad, what happened to her?"

"I don't know, sweetheart."

"That man," Jordan said, her eyes wide. "Oh, my God. He killed her!" Jordan screamed hysterically. "He killed my mother!"

"No," Wes said, holding her shoulders. "I'm sure she's okay."

"She's not okay," Jordan cried. "He killed her."

After Jordan had wept in his arms for several minutes, the sounds of her muffled cries ebbed and were silenced as she pressed her face into his shoulder. Wes looked up and was surprised to see a light shining through the windshield. Howling winds aloft had sheared away the clouds and swept clean the face of the moon. It hung like an eerie portrait etched in golden watercolors against the night sky.

"Jordan, let's go home," he said softly.

CHAPTER 9
April 2010

It was after midnight as an exhausted Wes Tanner sat on the couch answering questions from two San Antonio police officers. Jordan and Monty sat on either side of him, and neither looked the least bit tired. Both children were quiet, and Wes knew they were frightened.

"Mr. Tanner, would your wife have left the office for any reason that you know of?" Officer Dave Griffith asked. Wes guessed Griffith was in his mid-twenties and probably fairly new to the police force.

"Not that I know of." Wes hesitated as he tried to think. "Not without her car."

"Could a friend have picked her up?" Steve Saenz, Griffith's partner, asked.

"Not at that time of night."

"What about Miss Marty?" Jordan asked, looking first at her father, then at the police officers. "She could have picked Mom up." Marty Chavez, Nicole's coworker, was also her closest friend.

Wes shrugged. "I could call her."

"It's late," Griffith said. "You can call her tomorrow, if—"

"Maybe she walked down to the store to get something?" Saenz suggested.

"She wouldn't have stayed long, even if she went. Besides, my daughter and I drove to the store. She wasn't there, and no one there had seen her."

"When was the last time you saw her?" Griffith asked.

"Shortly after six."

"Daddy? Where's Mommy?" Summer asked as she came down the stairs, rubbing sleep from her eyes. Wes got up and walked over to her, picking her up in his arms as she reached him. Summer rested her head on Wes's shoulder. "You promised you'd send her up to tuck me in."

"We're not sure where Mommy is, honey."

Summer saw the police officers, and Wes could tell she was becoming anxious.

"Did something happen to her?"

"I'm sure she's okay."

"Why are they here?" Summer asked, pointing at the two officers.

"They're going to help us find your mother." Summer did not look reassured. "You need to go back to bed." Wes started up the stairs, still carrying his daughter.

"I don't want to go to bed until we find Mommy."

"I'll wake you up when she comes home."

"Will she come up and tuck me in?"

"Yes."

"Promise?"

"Promise," Wes said, reaching the top of the stairs. He looked down at Jordan, Monty, and the two policemen. "I'll be right back."

After spending several minutes with Summer in her room, Wes was finally able to return to the living room. He answered more questions, and then the two officers rose to leave. Griffith turned to him. "Mr. Tanner, did you need a ride back to your wife's office to pick up her car?"

"Yes, I do."

"Will your children be okay?"

"Are you okay, honey?" Wes asked Jordan.

"Sure. I can put Monty to bed."

"Not if you know what's good for you, Sis," Monty warned her. The two officers chuckled as Wes followed them out the front door.

"Mr. Tanner?" Griffith's expression was now serious as Wes locked the front door behind them, away from the children for the first time since the officers had arrived.

"Yes?"

"We saw a report that Mrs. Tanner filed Friday against a man who allegedly made advances on her inside a house. That's why we're here."

"You know about that?"

"Frankly, Mr. Tanner, we wouldn't be here otherwise," Griffith explained. "The police don't generally respond to a missing person report in the first twenty-four hours."

"People take off for all kinds of reasons," Saenz added. "Many of them show up the next morning with a logical, or even illogical explanation."

"Do you know that the same man threatened her?"

Griffith raised his eyebrows. "Threatened her?"

"That's right," Wes said, lighting a cigarette. "He called Friday night and left a threatening voice mail message. I saved it."

"What did he say?"

"Something about being humiliated in front of his family when the police came to pick him up for questioning. He told Nicole they had unfinished business and he would be seeing her soon."

"Did you report this?" Saenz asked.

"I left a message for Detective Niebring this morning."

Griffith looked up. "Detective Niebring?"

"It's Saturday. He probably didn't get it," Saenz said. "I'll call him on his cell."

Wes noticed a change in the officers' demeanor when Niebring's name was mentioned. Up until that time, they had been only courteous and professional. Now, it was as if a member of their own family had become involved. The mention of the detective by name seemed to give the whole affair a new aura of credibility. Griffith and Saenz had been walking toward their patrol unit parked in the driveway. Saenz now returned to the front porch to re-engage their complainant.

"Tell us more about this incident," Saenz said, reaching for a notepad and pen.

"The man's name was Raul Gonzalez," Wes said, putting out his cigarette. "My wife was showing him a house when he cornered her in the master bedroom and became very aggressive with her. She was able to get away from him."

"And Niebring was assigned to the case?" Griffith asked.

"What did Detective Niebring say about your complaint?" Saenz asked.

"He said the police really couldn't do much at that point."

"That's true." Saenz nodded. "That's the frustrating thing about our job. We can't arrest someone based on a threat. Unless it's the president or someone like that. We have to wait until he actually *does* something."

"When someone *does* something, it's too late."

"That's the frustrating part."

While the two men were conversing, Griffith had walked back to the squad car. He was sitting in the driver's side with the door open and his legs swung out on the pavement. Griffith was talking on the radio, probably checking out his story, Wes surmised. Now he rejoined them on the porch.

"We left a message for Detective Niebring on his cell phone," Griffith said. "I'm sure you'll be hearing from him early tomorrow if she hasn't turned up. I suspect he'll want you to come to the station again."

"Tomorrow is Easter," Wes pointed out.

"It doesn't matter. If your wife is still missing, he'll want to get right on it."

"I'll be glad to go down to the station," Wes said.

"You said you saved that voice mail message?" Saenz asked.

"Yes."

"Leave that message intact. Detective Niebring will want to hear that and make his own copy of that recording." Wes nodded in agreement. "We'll be sure that he gets a copy of our report in the morning," Saenz said. "We'll take you to get your car now."

CHAPTER 10
April 2010

Wes, Jordan, Monty, and Summer sat on the wooden bench outside the secured area at the police station, waiting to talk with the police. Wes glanced at his watch impatiently, desperately wanting to step outside and have a smoke, but resisted the urge to avoid missing the detective. For the most part, the children appeared to be doing well just hours after Nicole's disappearance. Jordan was reading a book, while Monty was listening to his iPod. Summer was writing a letter to her great-grandfather that she would hand deliver later that morning.

Wes had called his grandfather at six o'clock that morning to tell him what happened. Roger Tanner recovered quickly from his shock and insisted that Wes drive to Kerrville after he met with police. As was his custom, Roger spoke in a reassuring tone, quick to comfort and encourage him.

"Your children need to be with family," Roger said. "Meet me at church."

Wes's grandfather had been the pastor of Shepherd of the Hills Baptist Church for more than fifty years. Roger was still going strong at eighty-six. The deacon board had hired a younger pastor ten years ago to handle many of the daily responsibilities of running the church. But no one wanted Roger to retire, and he still preached on alternate Sundays.

Wes, who had moved to Kerrville when he was thirteen to live with his grandfather, had counted the days until the time came that he could leave that little Hill Country town. Now, he actually looked forward to returning to a place where life was simpler and more peaceful. Wes loved to sit on Roger's porch at night and talk with his grandfather until both men gave up from exhaustion. After Wes married Nicole, his trips back home had become more and more infrequent. Nicole said she hated to make the fifty-mile drive, but she was always eager to drive to Houston or Dallas for a taste of big-city life. The fact was that she *hated* small towns and always made fun of "those small-town hicks" that frequented Kerrville. The only reason they went at all was because the children insisted on it. Roger was an adoring and adored great-grandfather, so the trips to see him were always viewed with eager anticipation by all of the children.

After Wes had told Roger the news about Nicole, he immediately called Natalie. He could tell that the call had awakened her, and he apologized. Natalie gasped when he gave her the bad news and immediately uttered a prayer for Nicole. Wes was forced to cut the conversation short when Summer came into the room. Wes had promised to call her later when he could find a private place away from his children.

"Dad, how long is it going to be before we talk to the detectives?" Jordan asked, looking up from her book. Before Wes could answer, they heard a loud pop and saw the door open. A well-built Hispanic man came out with an older man following close behind. The younger man avoided making eye contact with Wes, turning back to shake hands with the other man.

"Thank you for coming, and we'll be in touch, sir," the older man said as the other man turned and walked quickly past the Tanner family. Wes wondered if the younger man could be Raul Gonzalez. If it was, then why hadn't he been arrested? Wes's attention was diverted from the younger man when the older man addressed him.

"I'm Detective Mendoza," he said with hand extended. "I'm Sergeant Niebring's partner. Sorry for the wait. We're ready to talk with you now."

"Let's go, kids," Wes said after standing up and shaking Mendoza's hand.

"Mr. Tanner, Sergeant Niebring would like to talk alone with the children first."

"Don't you want to talk with us together?"

"No. We'd prefer one at a time." Caught off balance, Wes mulled the request while Mendoza turned his attention to Summer. "How about you, young lady? Do you want to come back and see where the detectives work?" Summer was unsure and looked at her father for direction. "I'll get you a soft drink if it's okay with your dad."

"Is it okay, Dad?"

"It's okay." Wes nodded to Summer, who stood up to follow Mendoza into the detectives' offices. Wes settled back on the bench. One-by-one, the children were led back to meet with the detectives as Wes became increasingly agitated. When the time came for Wes to go back, he was fuming.

When Mendoza led Wes into the small, fluorescent-lighted room, Niebring looked up from behind his metal desk. He appeared to be sizing him up. When the detective rose to his feet, he offered his hand with a smile. "Good morning, Mr. Tanner."

"Good morning, Sergeant Niebring."

"Have a seat."

"Are you going to interrogate me?"

"What makes you think that?" Niebring said with a poker face as Wes sat down in a chair across the desk from him. Mendoza retreated to a chair in the corner of the room.

"I guess because I'm in an interrogation room with two detectives."

"We're just going to ask you some questions about your wife's disappearance."

"Am I a suspect?"

"We don't even know if a crime has been committed," Mendoza interjected.

"*Has* a crime been committed?" Niebring asked pointedly.

"You know what I know," Wes said as he shifted uneasily in a chair.

"Let's go over yesterday's events."

"Okay."

"When was the last time you saw your wife?"

"Around six p.m."

"Around six p.m.?"

"That's when she left the house. She was going to her office."

"And that was the last time you saw her?"

"Yes."

"Did you speak with her after she left the house?"

"No."

"Did you call her?"

"Yes."

"What time was that?"

"Around ten."

"Were you worried about her?"

"I started to get worried when I left her a message and she didn't call back."

"So you went down to check on her?"

"Yes."

"Were you worried that something had happened to her?"

"The thought crossed my mind after the threat from Gonzalez."

"If you were worried that something had happened to her, why did you take your daughter with you?"

"Why shouldn't I have taken her?"

"What if you got down there and found her shot to death? Blood all over the place. Is that the kind of scene that you'd want your daughter to walk in on?"

"That's not really what I expected to find." Wes was becoming increasingly agitated by this line of questioning, and now he felt accused by Niebring of being an irresponsible parent, or worse. Wes didn't like the detective's attitude or his tone.

Niebring studied the police report on his desk and then looked up at Wes. "You reported your wife missing shortly before midnight?"

"That sounds right."

"When did you go down to her office?"

"We left the house around ten thirty."

"When did you get to her office?

"Around eleven."

"Why did it take you almost an hour to report her missing?"

"My daughter and I drove to a convenience store near her office to see if anyone there had seen her."

"Did you really believe she would go out for a walk in the rain?"

"No. But it was worth checking."

"So you were conducting your own investigation?" Niebring said, starting to twirl his pencil. "Checking out every possible lead instead of calling police."

"I didn't want to bother the police if there wasn't a good reason."

"You didn't think finding an empty office with the light on a good reason?"

Wes started to say something and stopped.

"It doesn't sound like you were really that worried about your wife," Niebring said, furrowing his brow. "Were you worried about her, Mr. Tanner?"

"Not initially."

"Even though she had been threatened and was by herself?"

"I was worried more than you were, Detective. You didn't even return my call."

"I didn't get your message until this morning."

"I guess you don't check your messages on the weekends?"

"Generally not."

"If you had, this whole thing might have been prevented," Wes said pointedly.

Mendoza leaned forward in his chair and softened the atmosphere. "Mr. Tanner, you're on edge as a result of the disappearance of your wife. We're trying to help."

"You could have helped if you had arrested the man who tried to rape my wife. That only seems reasonable to me."

"Mr. Tanner, we've already established the fact that Mr. Gonzalez *didn't* try to rape your wife," Niebring said. "He thought they were going to have consensual sex."

"That's his story, not hers."

"Did you have a fight with your wife yesterday?" Niebring asked as he stopped twirling his pencil and looked intently at Wes.

"No," Wes snapped back. "I barely saw her all day."

"Did you notice anything unusual about her behavior yesterday?"

"She seemed a little preoccupied."

"What do you mean preoccupied?"

"Preoccupied. It's in the dictionary. It means she had other things on her mind."

A flash of rage lit up Niebring's face before he leapt to his feet and kicked a trash can across the room. Wes was startled and lurched sideways in his chair. "Who do you think you're talking to?" the detective demanded.

Wes swallowed hard as he sat very still and stared back at Niebring. He wasn't expecting such an angry outburst from the man who had been so polite to him two days earlier.

"I'm trying to figure out what happened to your wife, and you're acting like this? I won't come to your house and treat you like that, so don't come to my house and treat me like this. If you killed your wife, just shut up. Don't say another word. Otherwise, I want you to answer my questions respectfully. Am I clear?"

"Yeah, you're clear."

"Let's proceed. Did you kill your wife, Mr. Tanner?

Wes chuckled softly. "You're a piece of work."

"What did you do with the body?"

"Are you going to charge *me* with murder?"

"Answer my question."

"I'm not answering any more questions," Wes said. "You can talk to my lawyer."

CHAPTER 11
April 2010

Natalie Guerra attended mass on Easter Sunday at San Fernando Cathedral seeking some measure of comfort just hours after hearing of her sister's disappearance. San Fernando Cathedral, a historic landmark in San Antonio, was founded in 1731 and had stood stately and picturesque for almost three centuries in the same downtown location. The church, established by the first settlers arriving from the Canary Islands at the Presidio of San Antonio, has a commanding presence, with its twin white steeples and austere white stone exterior. There is a rose window over the front door. The restored interior is in traditional French gothic form, with stained glass windows placed high in the walls.

As she entered the cathedral on this Easter morning, Natalie recalled the first time she had worshipped there. Her ex-husband had taken her to mass at San Fernando while they were still dating. She had been awed by the splendor of the cathedral. Inside, immediately to the left, a white stone container held the remains of the defenders of the Battle of the Alamo, including Jim Bowie and Davy Crockett. Although Natalie lived far from downtown, she had continued to attend San Fernando Cathedral with her husband until he left her.

Natalie, badly shaken by the news of her sister's disappearance, sought peace and anonymity today within the walls of the

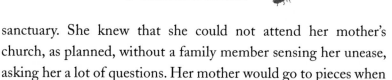
sanctuary. She knew that she could not attend her mother's church, as planned, without a family member sensing her unease, asking her a lot of questions. Her mother would go to pieces when she heard about Nicole's disappearance, and Natalie was not ready to deal with that yet.

As it turned out, the quiet splendor of the old church seemed to her the perfect place for a retreat. In the past, God had given her peace during the darkest moments of her life. She prayed, hoping to experience His peace again. While she prayed for Nicole's safe return, she knew her faith was weak. Natalie feared the worst. The worst thing imaginable was that her sister had been murdered the previous night. Wes hadn't been able to tell her much that morning except that Nicole had gone to her office and had not returned. Natalie recalled her sister doing some foolish things in her life—especially in her younger days. But Nicole wouldn't walk off into the night, leaving her car behind and her office open. Wes told her there were no signs of a struggle, so everything pointed to an abduction.

Natalie felt sick to her stomach as she sat alone in the church. Scenes from every horrible movie she had seen flashed through her mind. Had someone forced her sister into a vehicle at the point of a gun or knife? Might her sister have begged for her life, only to later lose it at the hands of a man with no conscience? She shuddered and tried to push the horrible thoughts out of her mind as she watched a procession of choirboys, clad in white vesture and carrying candles, walking slowly across plush crimson carpet toward the altar. Behind the altar stood the monsignor, his head bowed in solemn prayer as he prepared holy communion in side-by-side silver chalices. His Latin utterances were barely audible above the prayerful murmurings of the faithful. As Natalie knelt on the prayer bench in front of her, she let her forehead fall gently onto the back of her clasped hands, and she poured out her heart to God.

After church, Natalie drove to her mother's house, where the family was assembling for Easter lunch. She knew that the news she was bringing would be a crushing blow to her family as they celebrated the holiest day of the year. All they could do now was join her in praying that things were not as they seemed.

"Natalie! I missed you at church this morning."

"I'm sorry, Mother."

Natalie's mother had seen her daughter's troubled expression an instant after she opened the front door of her home. Natalie could hear her younger sister and husband laughing inside, and the voices of her niece and nephew echoed from the second story of the house. "Natalie, what's wrong?"

Stepping inside the house, Natalie closed her eyes briefly before speaking words that would shatter the day. "Nicole is missing."

"Missing? What do you mean?"

"She disappeared from her office last night. Wes went to check on her when she didn't answer her phone. She was gone."

Natalie looked into her mother's eyes, waiting for the words to sink in. "I don't understand," Nancy Hobbs said. "Where would she have gone?"

"I don't know. Her car was still parked out front. There was a light on in the office, and the door was unlocked."

"Oh, my God." Nancy staggered backward, looking like she might faint. Natalie put her arm around her mother to steady her. When the older woman looked at her again, her eyes were full of fear, begging for some reasonable explanation. Before Natalie could continue, her sister approached.

"Happy Easter," Nina said with big a smile. Noticing the expression on their faces, her smile vanished. "What is it?"

"Nicole is missing. She disappeared last night from her office," Natalie said.

"That man!" Nina gasped.

"What man?" Nancy looked at her daughters.

It occurred to Natalie that Nicole must have told Nina about Raul Gonzalez, but her mother didn't know. Nancy was a chronic worrier, and Nicole would have spared her the details of that day. Natalie quickly told her about the incident at the house and the threat.

"Oh, sweet Jesus," Nancy said, breaking into sobs. "He murdered my daughter."

"We don't know that," Natalie tried to reassure her. Nina wrapped her arms around her mother and held her until her weeping subsided.

"What *do* we know?" Nina demanded.

Nina's husband, Russ, had come in from the living room and joined them. Without speaking, his eyes sought an explanation. "Nicole is missing," Nina said.

"All I know is that Wes went down to the police station this morning to talk to the detectives. They've already been over to Nicole's office to investigate," Natalie said.

"Did they arrest the man that threatened her?" Nina asked.

"I don't know."

Dinner plates were virtually untouched that afternoon as the family drew together to offer one another encouragement. It was the middle of the afternoon when Natalie's cell phone rang. It was Wes, and she stepped outside to talk in privacy. Wes told her about what happened at the police station and how the detectives had questioned him like a suspect instead of trying to help. They hadn't even arrested the man that had threatened Nicole one day earlier.

When Natalie hung up the phone, she decided to leave the family gathering. She could tell by the sound of Wes's voice that he needed her by his side. Jordan, Monty, and Summer needed her, too. She left the house over the objections of her mother and other family members.

"**A**unt Natalie, can you spend the night?"

Summer posed the innocent question at eight o'clock after her father had told her it was time to get ready for bed. Natalie's youngest niece had been clinging to her since she arrived at the Tanner home four hours earlier. It was as though she now drew her security from having her aunt by her side.

"I can't spend the night, honey."

"Why not?"

Natalie could tell from Wes's expression that he wasn't going to be much help.

"Because a woman doesn't spend the night in the same house with a man she's not married to," Natalie said, hoping that might end the discussion.

"Suzy's mom has a boyfriend that spends the night with her."

"You don't know that," Wes interjected.

"Yes, I do."

"How?"

"Because he was there the last time I spent the night with Suzy."

Natalie and Wes exchanged startled looks, and Monty laughed out loud. Natalie thought he had been watching television in the great room, but he had obviously been listening to their conversation.

"That's not the right thing to do."

"I know that," Summer said with a nod. "They slept in the same bed. You don't have to sleep in the same bed with Daddy. You could sleep on the couch."

"It's still not the right thing to do," Natalie tried to explain.

"Why not?"

"Because people that didn't know us might think that your father and I *were* sleeping together."

"How would they know you were here?"

"One of our neighbors might see Aunt Natalie leave in the morning," Wes said.

"I don't care what our neighbors say. I want Aunt Natalie to spend the night."

"No," Wes said firmly.

Natalie wasn't sure whether it was the finality of her father's answer, or the tone, but Summer burst into tears. Natalie walked over to Wes, speaking softly so she wouldn't be overheard. "Wes, can she spend the night at my house?"

"What about school?"

"I can take her."

"Okay."

"Summer?" Natalie said over the sobs. "You can spend the night with me."

"Okay." Summer suddenly brightened through the tears.

CHAPTER 12

It was one of those South Texas summer days when the sun seemed like it would never go down. The four young people on the red and white fiberglass ski boat were streaking across Lake Travis without a care in the world. It was 1989, and the challenges and difficulties of adult life were still ahead of them, but this particular afternoon was full of laughter and fun. Their bodies were strong, their minds were clear, and their souls were full of optimism. It was good to be young and so alive.

Wes glanced over at his girlfriend in the seat next to him. Natalie smiled back. It was a comfortable if not passionate relationship. Wes and Natalie had met during their freshman year at the University of Texas. They had been going steady since then, and Wes figured they would be married sometime after they graduated next May.

In the front of the boat, Wes could see Nicole's long legs stretched out in front of her. Wes had asked Natalie if Nicole could accompany them on the outing. It was his idea to set up his college roommate with Natalie's little sister. Johnny Jenkins' mouth had dropped open when he first saw the young woman, and he mouthed the word "thank you" to Wes as he stared at the slender, well-endowed teenager with the long, silky hair.

Although the sisters looked like siblings, they had little in common. Natalie was quiet, studious, and responsible, while Nicole was boisterous and fun-loving. Nicole was also a flirt, and she had been flirting with Wes for months. Truth be told, Wes liked the attention and the boost to his male ego. Unlike Natalie, Nicole laughed at his jokes and told him how clever he was. Wes found Nicole to be exciting and unpredictable.

At first the four of them took turns water skiing. When they grew tired, they hauled in the skis and rope and set the throttle for a cruise. The sun was searing them, and they applied suntan lotion on one another and took turns pushing each other out of the boat. But mostly they just sped around the lake as if they owned the place.

Wes, Johnny, and Nicole drank beer and did a lot of laughing and cutting up. At one point, with the boat running at full speed, Johnny left the steering wheel unattended, jumped over the front bench seat and into the back of the boat. The boat swerved wildly to the left. Nicole, who was still on the front bench seat, screamed and quickly grabbed the wheel to right the boat.

"Johnny!" Natalie said. "Are you crazy?"

"No. I'm hungry," he said.

"He's crazy, too," Wes said.

"Who made these?" Johnny asked as he reached into the cooler, grabbed a sandwich, and pulled it apart.

"I did," Natalie said somewhat defensively.

Johnny held out the two thin slices of white bread and offered it to Wes for a look, as if he were presenting evidence. There was nothing between the slices of bread except for a single slice of Velveeta American cheese. That was it. Wes, Johnny, and Nicole started laughing hysterically. Johnny proceeded to eat seven of the sandwiches, and Wes an equal number. The girls ate three apiece. Nicole was still laughing as Wes and Johnny dug around in the pool of melting ice in the bottom of the cooler, looking for more of the sandwiches to eat.

Johnny jumped back in the front seat and took back control of the steering wheel from Nicole, who loaded a tape into his duly named "redneck" boat stereo. The stereo was nothing more than an old automobile eight-track tape player that was mounted under the dashboard of the boat. A pair of four-inch automobile speakers were mounted under the dashboard on the left and right hand sides of the boat, giving the system a stereo effect. The speakers were no longer even in their cases, with only gray cloth covering their inner workings. Johnny had somehow jerry-rigged it all to the boat battery using red and black wires, with a little black electrical tape wrapped here and there.

Wes donned his shades, poured a scoop of lake water over his head, and lit a cigarette as Nicole walked to the back of the boat. She reached over and grabbed a beer from the cooler. The cooler was next to Wes, and her warm skin brushed up against him. "Hey, can I see some ID?" Wes asked with a smile.

"ID?" Nicole looked at him curiously. Wes was looking at Nicole's skimpy bikini, revealing more than should be seen.

"Yeah. I don't think you're old enough to drink a beer."

"Are you going to bust me?"

"Maybe."

Nicole's eyes were dancing flirtatiously. She seemed to be asking him if he liked what he saw. Out of the corner of his eye, Wes could see Natalie watching them with a hurt expression. He refused to look at Natalie, so she got up and walked to the front of the boat. At that moment, the sounds of James and Bobby Purify's "I'm Your Puppet" wafted from Johnny's tinny speakers and filled the air around the little fiberglass cruiser. "Just pull my little string, and I'll do anything. I'm your puppet... I'm your puppet."

Nicole sat down next to Wes on the rear bench seat and shot a glance at her sister as if to say she had staked a claim. Nicole had also slipped on her sunglasses, and she stretched out her long, sun-toned legs, allowing them to rest on the top of the cooler in the middle of the boat deck. As the music played through the stereo, Wes and Nicole exchanged a long, lingering gaze. She threw her hair back to catch the wind as Johnny steered the craft directly down a sunlit strip of water that seemed to lead on endlessly into the setting summer sun.

Wes snapped out of his daydream. It was the day after Easter, more than twenty years after that fateful day on the lake. Wes thought about his decision and how it had changed his life. He had broken up with Natalie a few days later and started dating Nicole. They had dated for more than a year before they married. Wes had allowed his hormones to rule his head. In his mind, he knew that Natalie was the kind of woman a man should want to marry. Natalie was a woman of character and depth. Nicole was selfish and shallow. Wes had married the wrong sister, and he had lived to regret it.

Wes was on the back porch smoking a cigarette when Natalie stopped by to pick up Summer's Snoopy lunchbox. Wes was surprised and pleased to see her. Summer gave her father a big hug and appeared happy, but Natalie's face was drawn.

"Any word at all?"

"No." Wes shook his head. "You look tired, Nat."

"I didn't sleep very well."

"Did you keep your aunt awake?" Wes asked Summer. She shook her head.

"She didn't keep me awake," Natalie replied, and Wes understood. Of course, she had been lying awake all night worrying about Nicole.

"Jordan! Monty!" Wes called. He put a couple of boxes of cereal on the table and reached into the cabinet for bowls. "Has Summer had breakfast?"

"I fed her."

"Aunt Natalie makes the best eggs," Summer said enthusiastically.

"Better than mine?"

Summer nodded and Wes pretended to pout.

"I'm sorry, Daddy. You told me to always be honest."

"Truth hurts, doesn't it?" Natalie quipped.

"Sure does. Hey, how about lunch? I can meet you somewhere near your office."

"I can't, Wes. I'm covered up at work."

"A girl's got to eat," Wes pointed out.

"I'll eat something at my desk."

Summer was quiet on the way to school, and Natalie debated about whether to question her or leave her alone with her thoughts. Natalie knew she was thinking about Nicole, and she decided it would be best to get her niece to talk.

"What are you thinking about, Summer?"

"Nothing much."

"It looked like you're thinking about something." Summer was silent, and Natalie knew she would have to draw her out. "Are you thinking about your mommy?" Summer nodded. "Tell me what you're thinking. Please?"

"Do you think Mommy is dead?"

"I don't know," Natalie said, wondering if it would be better to lie. Lying was something that people did all of the time. Sometimes, it was even done for good reasons. Natalie could have told Summer that she thought her mother was just fine and would return home soon with a logical explanation for why she had disappeared. But lying wasn't in Natalie's DNA, and she couldn't bring herself to lie—even when it might spare the feelings of a child for a short time.

"She might have gotten amnesia," Summer said, struggling to form the last word. "I saw a movie once where someone got hurt and forgot who they were. It was a long time before they remembered. That could have happened to Mommy."

"I guess that's possible."

"I'm sure that's what happened. As soon as she remembers who she is, she'll come back home. I'll be really happy then."

"I'll be really happy too."

Summer rode on in silence for another moment, but Natalie knew she was still struggling with thoughts a six-year-old couldn't possibly process.

"Now what are you thinking?"

"I was just wondering if God knows where Mommy is."

"Oh, yes." Natalie nodded. "God knows where she is."

"I hope he takes good care of her."

CHAPTER 13
April 2010

After Jordan and Monty left on the school bus, Wes called the managing editor at the *Express-News* to explain why he wasn't at his desk. It was less than thirty-six hours after Nicole had been reported missing, but the editor already knew. The weekend police reporter had picked up the story at the police station. Worse yet, it had already been aired on the radio and television news that morning. Wes's boss told him that he should stay home. In fact, he could have as much time off as he needed. Wes thanked him but promised that he would continue to write his daily column.

A moment after he hung up the phone, it rang again. A reporter from one of the television stations wanted to know if he would consent to an on-camera interview. Wes declined the offer, but the reporter wouldn't take no for an answer. While he was still talking to the newsman, someone else was clicking in on the line. Wes checked caller ID and saw that it was Nicole's friend, Marty Chavez. This provided a good excuse to end the conversation with the reporter. Wes told Nicole's friend that he didn't know anything more than he knew Saturday night.

Wes was still on the phone with Marty when the doorbell rang. Several people had called during their conversation, but Wes hadn't picked up any of the calls. Most of them had caller IDs that were blocked, and Wes guessed it was more reporters trying to get his story. When he opened the door, Nancy Hobbs was standing on the doorstep. "Wes? Have you heard anything?"

"No." Wes shook his head, and Nicole's mother brushed past him and into the house like she was there to take charge. "How are the children doing?"

"Okay, considering."

"I've been praying all night. That's all we can do. Right? Are you hungry? Can I fix you something to eat?"

Wes told her he wasn't hungry, hoping she might leave. Instead, Nancy went into the kitchen and started cleaning up. Wes could understand why she had been married four times. A little of Nancy went a long way. Still an attractive woman as she neared Social Security age, Nancy had recently retired from her job as an office manager at a doctor's office. With plenty of time on her hands, she would often pop in unexpectedly. Nicole's mother had always driven her crazy, but now it was worse. Growing up, Nancy seldom made time for her three daughters. She was into her men, or herself, and the girls were left to fend for themselves. Now, making up for lost time, Nancy was always calling them or dropping in. She invited them to go shopping or to lunch or to get their nails done. Nicole told Wes the three sisters agreed Nancy needed to find a new husband.

An hour later, the doorbell rang again. Wes was outside smoking, but Nancy took it upon herself to open the door. A moment later, she came out on the back porch to tell Wes that there was a reporter waiting to talk with him.

"You're kidding me." Wes shook his head. "How do they know where I live?"

Nancy shrugged her shoulders. Wes put out his cigarette and followed her inside. He immediately recognized the young man dressed in a suit on his doorstep. Brad Mills was the police reporter at the *Express-News*.

"Wes, I'm sorry," Mills said. "Any word?"

"Nothing, Brad."

"Can I come in?"

"Sure." Wes stepped back from the doorway to allow him entry.

A few minutes later, the two men were sitting at the breakfast room table drinking coffee. Mills continued to offer sympathetic remarks, but Wes knew where it was going.

"I want to do a big story on Nicole, with your comments."

"I don't want to blow this out of proportion."

"We're not blowing it out of proportion. A woman disappeared from her Alamo Heights office. Vanished into thin air. People don't just vanish from Alamo Heights. Her husband and children are left to wonder what happened. This is a story our readers want to know about. It's a big story."

"Brad, I report on the news. I'm not comfortable with *being* in the news. Go ahead and write your story, but please keep me and my children out of it."

"Wes, you're a newsman."

"I'm a columnist," Wes corrected him.

"You know what makes a good human interest story. It's people. This time, it just happens to be you. But the story still needs to be told."

"But it's *my* life. It's my children's life—"

"Wes." Mills held up his hand to stop him. "Let me help you. Please."

"How can you help me?"

"I know you want to find your wife. Let me interview you. After we run the story, I'm sure the AP will pick it up. Millions of people are going to read it. With that much exposure, there's a chance that someone out there has seen or heard something."

As Wes studied him, thinking it over, Nancy walked up behind him.

"Hi," she said, extending her hand. "I'm Nancy Hobbs. Nicole is my daughter."

"Very nice to meet you, Mrs. Hobbs. I was trying to convince your son-in-law to let me do a story on Nicole. I think a front-page story will help us find her."

"I think that's a great idea."

"Nancy," Wes said with a flash of anger. "This isn't your decision."

"Wes, we need all of the help we can get."

Wes reluctantly agreed, and Mills called a photographer, who arrived at the Tanner home ten minutes later. Wes led them to his study. While the photographer snapped a couple of photos, Mills turned on his tape recorder. Wes provided some background on Nicole and then described the events of Saturday night in detail.

"Your wife's car was parked out front?"

"Right."

"Locked?"

"Yeah."

"No signs of a struggle inside the building?"

"No."

"Do you know of anyone who might have wanted to harm your wife? Had anyone ever threatened her?" Mills asked.

Wes hesitated. "I'm not sure I should say."

"Wes, I'm trying to help," Mills insisted.

"A man made sexual advances toward my wife. She was showing him a house, and he came on to her. We filed charges, but so far the police have done nothing."

"Nothing?"

"They questioned him, but they said we didn't have a case. You know. His word against her word."

"You mentioned a threat?"

"No, I didn't," Wes shook his head. "You did."

"Did this man threaten your wife?"

"Yes," Wes offered reluctantly.

"At the house?"

"No. He left a message on her voice mail after he was arrested and released."

"What did he say?"

"He said something about having unfinished business with Nicole, and 'I'll be seeing you soon, sweetheart.'"

"Did you save the message?" Wes nodded. "Can I hear it?" Wes let Mills listen to the message. The reporter seemed shocked. "The police haven't arrested this guy?"

"No, they haven't."

"Do you think he abducted her?"

"I, uh…" Wes hesitated, wondering how far he could really go with these kinds of particulars. "That wouldn't be for me to say," Wes said finally.

"Wow." Mills shook his head. "Who was this man, anyway?" The reporter said the last part casually, without looking at Wes.

"I'd better not say any more, Brad."

"I understand. Hey, can I get a picture of you and your mother-in-law together?"

Wes agreed. Mills asked a few more questions while the photographer snapped pictures of Wes and Nancy. After that, Mills turned and gave a nod to his photographer, signaling that he was wrapping up the interview. "We should have the story written and posted on the website by noon."

CHAPTER 14
April 2010

Although he could have stayed home, Wes decided to go into the office on Tuesday morning. It would take his mind off of everything that had happened for a while. Wes dropped the children off at school, but an hour later the nurse at Summer's school called. His daughter was in the clinic, telling the nurse she felt sick, although her temperature was normal. Wes knew what Summer needed was some attention and the security of her own home. When he told the sports editor about Summer, he was shooed out of the newsroom. Wes drove back to the school to pick up Summer, who clung to him for dear life until they got into the car. When they pulled into the driveway, Wes was surprised to see a Cadillac parked in front of his house. Detectives Niebring and Mendoza climbed out of the car and walked toward him.

"Summer, you go on inside, honey," Wes said, handing her the key. "I need to talk with the detectives. I'll be along in just a minute."

"Maybe they found Mommy," Summer said.

"Maybe they have good news, Sunshine. Go on inside. I'll be there in a minute."

Niebring smiled at Summer as she walked past him. He waited for the little girl to go inside the house. Then he turned on Wes. "What are you trying to pull, Tanner?"

"What do you mean?"

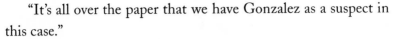

"It's all over the paper that we have Gonzalez as a suspect in this case."

"I didn't tell them that."

"What did you tell them?"

"I told them a man had made sexual advances on my wife and left a threatening message on her voice mail. I also told them that police hadn't arrested the man. I didn't give them Raul Gonzalez's name. They got that on their own."

"Well, you did enough."

"What do you mean?"

"Gonzalez and his family are gone."

"Gone?"

"They left town. If I don't miss my guess, they've left the country."

"How do you know they left?"

"I went by his brother's house after I read the story in the paper. As I suspected, they'd already packed up and left."

"You mean you weren't watching him?" Wes asked incredulously.

"Watching him? We don't have the manpower to sit on every suspect in every case we're working on."

"I guess you'd better go after them."

Niebring took two steps toward Wes until their noses were only inches apart. "Tanner, don't you ever again suggest how I should do my job."

As Wes backed up a step, Mendoza stepped forward and gave his partner a soft, cautionary tap on the shoulder. Niebring acknowledged his partner. He took a moment to simmer down then stepped closer to Wes. Their faces were only inches apart again. "If you had kept your sorry mouth shut with that newspaper reporter, Gonzalez would still be in San Antonio."

Wes was beginning to form a healthy fear of Niebring and his tough, bullying manner, but his frustration over the way the whole affair had been handled to date caused him to momentarily set caution aside.

"I thought for sure that you would have arrested Gonzalez after my wife disappeared," Wes said, looking directly at the detective. "But since you didn't do that, it seems that you could have at least kept the prime suspect from fleeing to Mexico."

Niebring's right eyebrow was arching up and down in anger as he glared at Wes. His voice was menacing but barely a whisper as he spoke. "I'm looking at my prime suspect right now." Wes stared at him, speechless. "I talked to your insurance agent yesterday, Tanner. Do you want to tell me why you took out a five hundred thousand-dollar life insurance policy on your wife three months ago?"

"Because she didn't have any life insurance."

"But you didn't get any life insurance for yourself."

"I have some at work."

"How much?"

"Fifty thousand."

"You have fifty thousand. She has five hundred thousand dollars. Is she worth ten times as much as you?"

"I couldn't afford more."

"But you could afford it on her?"

"Not that it's any of your business, but she's a nonsmoker. Her rates were a lot cheaper than mine. I was planning on getting more when I got a raise."

"I'm sure you were," Niebring said with a smirk.

Shaking his head, Wes turned his back on them and walked up the driveway to the front door of his house. As he reached the front door, Wes saw the curtain fall at the bottom corner of the big picture window that looked out onto the driveway. He had just enough time to see Summer's face disappear behind the curtain. Wes's youngest daughter had witnessed the entire episode with the police.

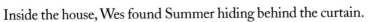

Inside the house, Wes found Summer hiding behind the curtain.

"Summer?"

"Yes?"

"What are you doing?"

"Nothing."

"Summer, you were watching me talking with those men, weren't you?"

Summer nodded.

"Why was that man yelling at you, Daddy?"

"He wasn't yelling."

"Tell the truth, Daddy."

"You got me." Wes smiled. "He *was* yelling at me. He was angry.""

"You were, too."

"I was, too."

"Why were you angry?"

"I'm frustrated, Summer. We're all frustrated because your mommy's missing."

"Daddy?"

"Yes?"

"Do you think Mommy was murdered?"

"Murdered? Where did you get that from?" Wes asked, artfully dodging the direct question from his daughter. He wasn't about to share his true feelings with her.

"I overhead Jordan and Monty talking last night."

"You were eavesdropping?"

Summer dropped her head.

"What did you hear?"

"Monty asked Jordan if she thought Mommy had been murdered." Summer's eyes filled with tears and her voice broke as she continued. "And Jordan said yes." Wes knelt down and took his daughter into his arms and comforted her as she continued to cry.

When she finally pulled her head back from his chest, her eyes were red and puffy.

"Was she murdered, Daddy?"

"I don't know what happened to your mother, Summer. I just don't know."

CHAPTER 15
April 2010

Wes sat at a small table near the door and watched the locals as they began to fill the bar after work. There was no happy hour here. The bar was small and drab, and Wes could smell stale beer and the perspiration of the blue collar crowd that frequented the downtown watering hole. The men that drank here drank to forget their long hours of labor with so little to show for it.

"Can I get you something?" the waitress interrupted his musings.

"I'm waiting for someone. He should be here soon," Wes said, looking up to see a cute woman in her early twenties staring back at him. She was just a few years older than Jordan. The waitress wore a loose white cotton T-shirt and shorts, which attracted looks from men at the next table. One of them, old enough to be her father and then some, was eying her long legs in a way that made Wes want to get up and punch him.

"Perfect timing, if I might say so myself," Detective Frank Salas said as he ducked in the door and sat down at the table across from Wes. "My friend here is buying, so keep 'em coming."

"Keep what coming?" the waitress asked him.

"A draft and a shot."

The waitress turned to Wes. "A draft and a shot for you, too?"

"Bud Light."

"That's the difference between me and him," Salas told the waitress. "I don't need anything light because I work out every day."

"You can see, he's quite a specimen," Wes said, pointing to the detective's bicep.

"I don't have a soft desk job like my friend, here. Did you know my friend is a famous columnist?" Salas asked the waitress, who was beginning to look bored. "I'll bet you read his column every day in the *San Antonio Express News?*"

"You bet wrong." The waitress moved over to the next table. "So how about those Spurs? Is there another championship in our future?" Salas asked.

"Probably not in our lifetime."

"You're such a skeptic."

"I'm a realist," Wes corrected him. "Duncan and Ginobili are on their last legs, and Parker will probably be gone at the end of this season."

"They may surprise you."

The waitress reappeared at their table with two mugs and a shot glass. She gave one beer to Wes and set the other two drinks in front of Salas. Wes watched the shot disappear down Salas's throat as he reached for his wallet. By the time Wes had paid the tab, Salas's beer glass was empty. "Round two, please," Salas blurted out.

Wes raised his eyebrows. "Tough day at the office?"

"They're all tough. Too many bad guys and not enough of us good guys."

"You guys would do better if you spent your time chasing bad guys and not picking on us good guys."

The smile disappeared from Salas's face, and he eyed Wes coolly. The pair had been friends, but not close friends, during their teenage days in Kerrville. They had met for beers only a

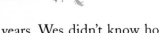
handful of times in the past twenty years. Wes didn't know how sympathetic the detective would be, but he needed to find out.

"What do you mean?" Salas asked with a poker face.

"I'm sure you know about my wife's disappearance?"

"I know."

"I showed up at the police station on Sunday morning, thinking I was going to be answering some routine questions. Instead, Sergeant Niebring and his partner started interrogating me like a murder suspect."

"They're just doing their job."

"Doing their job?" Wes looked at him incredulously. "If they were doing their job, they would have arrested the man that threatened my wife two days before she disappeared. They would have kept him from escaping to Mexico."

"Raul Gonzalez? We had nothing to hold him on."

"Nothing? He left a threatening message on my wife's voice mail. He—"

"Ssssh," Salas placed his index finger over his lips to quiet Wes before the entire bar was listening to their conversation. "Gonzalez had an alibi. He was with his wife, brother and brother's family the night of your wife's disappearance."

"That's not—" Wes stopped when the waitress reappeared with a beer for Salas. He waited until she left before he continued in quieter voice. "That's not an alibi. Didn't you guys ever consider that the man's family would lie to protect him?"

Salas didn't answer the question until he had inhaled the second shot and downed the second beer. He appeared to be loosening up.

"Of course we considered that. He is still a suspect."

"So, you'll pursue him in Mexico and extradite him?"

"I doubt it. He's in the wind, now. Gonzalez is a Mexican national, and he probably knows how *not* to be found. If the

Mexican authorities could find him, I wouldn't bet on them extraditing him either."

"So, now what?" Wes asked pointedly.

"Wes, I've already told you more than I should have. You know we're not supposed to comment on an ongoing investigation."

"Then, tell me this much. Is Gonzalez the only suspect?"

"What do you mean?"

"Am I a suspect?"

"Like I said, I shouldn't comment on an ongoing investigation. But suffice it to say that you didn't help your cause on Sunday morning by playing the lawyer card."

"Sergeant Niebring told you about that?"

"I was watching," Salas said quietly. "I saw them interrogate Gonzalez, and I saw them interrogate you. I have to tell you, Wes. You came off a lot worse than Gonzalez. He was eager to cooperate. DNA. The truth box. The whole nine yards. You're asked a few questions and then want to lawyer up. Frankly, it left Sergeant Niebring wondering what you had to hide."

"I have nothing to hide."

"I'm not saying that you do. What I *am* saying is that it doesn't look good."

"So I *am* a suspect?"

"When something happens to a woman, her husband is always considered."

"But Gonzalez threatened her," Wes insisted. "Then she disappeared. Then he disappears. It seems pretty obvious, doesn't it?"

"Fifteen years of police work has convinced me of one thing."

"What's that?"

"Things aren't always as they seem."

"Maybe not. But what about this time, Frank?"

"What about it?"

"Do you think Gonzalez killed my wife?"

"I don't know."

"I know you don't *know*. But you saw him being interrogated. What do you *think?*"

"There's plenty of circumstantial evidence against him."

"But he can't be investigated because he's not here."

"Clearly."

"So, what would you do if you were in my shoes?"

Salas gazed at him, appearing to have a difficult time focusing.

"If I were you, and I believed this man was responsible for my wife's murder?"

Wes nodded.

"I'd consider hiring a bounty hunter to go after him?"

"Hmm." Wes nodded thoughtfully. "I know just the man."

"Ezra Goldstein?"

"That's the man."

"How do you know Goldstein?"

"I interviewed him for a column, which you obviously didn't read."

"Sorry," Salas said as the waitress reappeared to inquire about another round of drinks.

"Not me," Wes said, raising his hand to indicate he was through for the evening.

The waitress turned her attention to Salas. "How are you doing?"

"I guess I'm done, too. It wouldn't look too good for a detective to pick up a DUI."

It was a few minutes after seven when Wes entered the house. He was surprised to see Natalie in the living room. She was working on homework with Jordan. Monty was still at the kitchen table finishing his desert.

"Look who the cat dragged in," Jordan quipped.

94

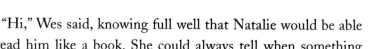

"Hi," Wes said, knowing full well that Natalie would be able to read him like a book. She could always tell when something was bothering him.

"Wes? Is something wrong?"

"I didn't know you were coming over." Wes avoided the question.

"Jordan called me and said you were going to be late. She said Monty and Summer were rebelling at the idea of frozen pizza again."

Wes smiled at Jordan. "So you rescued her."

"Have you eaten?" Natalie asked. "There's plenty of casserole left."

"I *am* kind of hungry."

"I'll warm it up for you."

"Where were you, Dad?" Jordan asked Wes as he started to follow Natalie into the kitchen. Wes had been at home all week and to suddenly disappear around dinnertime aroused her curiosity. She had asked him where he was going earlier, and he had only told her that he was going to meet someone.

"What is this? The Spanish Inquisition?" Wes tried to sound casual.

Jordan's cell phone rang, and she answered it. "Hi, Amy...I got your text...My aunt was helping me with my homework. No! He didn't!" She ran upstairs and disappeared into her room.

"Come into the study," Wes said to Natalie to be private. Natalie followed him through the French doors, and Wes closed them. He turned to face her.

"I met a police detective downtown for a beer."

"Sergeant Niebring?"

"No." Wes smiled. "I don't think Sergeant Niebring would meet me for a beer. It was an old friend. I thought he might know something about our case, and he did."

"What is it?"

"My friend confirmed that police are *not* going to pursue Gonzalez in Mexico."

"Why not?"

"I don't know. They don't think they can find him or get him back into the U.S."

"So they're dropping the investigation?"

"No. My friend told me that Sergeant Niebring considers *me* a suspect."

"What?" Natalie was incredulous. "How could he come to that conclusion?"

"Because he needs to pin this on someone."

"Don't be so cynical, Wes."

"Don't be naïve, Natalie. A police detective's job is to build a file of information that he can turn over to the DA so they can charge someone with the crime. It doesn't really matter to them whether the person they charge is innocent or guilty."

"I don't believe that."

"Believe what you want. The newspaper has covered a lot of murder cases during the time that I worked there. Brad Mills has told me about a number of cases that had holes in them wide enough to drive a truck through. But the DA still got the conviction because she was able to convince a jury that some poor guy was guilty of the crime he was charged with."

Wes noticed the look of surprise on Natalie's face and realized that he had raised his voice. She crossed her arms and looked down at the floor.

"I'm sorry, Natalie. I'm just really upset by this whole thing."

"Of course you are," Natalie said quietly. "I'll go warm up your dinner."

CHAPTER 16
April 2010

It was still dark when the alarm went off, bringing an abrupt end to Wes's dream. He couldn't remember all of the details, but the dream involved Nicole. They had gone to a store to look at some plasma screen televisions, and Nicole found one she wanted to buy. The price was $3,000. When Wes told her they couldn't afford it, she began to chastise him. She referred to his job as menial and even questioned his manhood. Wes, suddenly aware that everyone in the store was watching, demanded Nicole stop. His demand made her angrier, and she finally punched the television. The screen shattered, and there was blood on her hand. Nicole cried out in pain and then waved her bloody fist at Wes, blaming him for her injury.

Mercifully, the alarm brought the dream to an end. Wes glanced at the clock and did a double-take before remembering why he had set the alarm for 5:30 a.m. Wes looked forward to the luxury of sleeping in on most Saturday mornings, but today was different. He had to be at Nicole's office in an hour to meet members of the Texas State REACT Council, the Heidi Search Center, and others area volunteers who were gathering to spend a day searching for Nicole. It had been two weeks since she had disappeared.

The bright spot in the day for Wes was an opportunity to spend more time with Natalie. He hadn't seen her since Tuesday because he left for work shortly after 3:00 p.m. every day, and she didn't arrive at the house until five. Natalie stayed there until Summer was tucked into bed, and then she left. By the time Wes got home, everyone was in bed. Wes would go into the bedroom of each of his children and check on them. He'd watch them sleeping peacefully in their beds and find some comfort in that.

It wasn't that the family wasn't still feeling the effects of the tumultuous events of the previous week. Nicole's disappearance had hit the family like a phantom storm. In the past week, Wes had thought of his family in likeness to a sailing vessel, diminutive, buffeted about by roaring seas, and hopelessly adrift. Then along had come Natalie, steadfast and sure, and had lashed them safely about her. Wes believed they would be able to navigate the storm with her help.

As he showered, Wes's thoughts turned to Nicole. Would they find the body today? Scores of people would be looking, but there was a lot of ground to cover. It was not uncommon for searches like this one to drag on for a long time, but Wes was confident that searchers would keep looking until they turned up something. He wondered how the children would react. Had the children already begun preparing themselves for the inevitable?

The inevitable was that some day Nicole's body would be found. They would then bury her amid much grieving, and then the healing process would begin. It occurred to Wes that he had never made arrangements for a place to bury his wife, or himself. After all, why would anyone in their early forties even think of such an eventuality? But death came to everyone, and Nicole's death would have to be dealt with.

Wes finished dressing in front of the bathroom mirror before turning off the light and heading into the kitchen. He noticed a green light on the counter and remembered he had programmed the coffeemaker the previous night to come on at 5:30. He poured himself a cup, wrote a note for the children, and left the house quietly.

Natalie was dressed in jeans and a flannel shirt when she came to the door. He handed her a cup of coffee in a travel mug, and she smiled. When they pulled into the parking lot at Nicole's office, Wes saw a truck parked out front. A grizzled, middle-aged cowboy stepped out of the cab when Wes pulled up next to him. "You must be Wes Tanner?" the man said as he extended his hand.

"That's right," Wes said, shaking his hand. He nodded to Natalie. "This is Natalie Guerra, Nicole's sister."

"Nice to meet you. My name's Toby Williams with the Heidi Search Center." The three of them made small talk as other searchers began to arrive. Finally, Wes redirected the conversation back to the subject at hand.

"We should have a hundred people, maybe more, searching the area on foot. We're going to fan out—north, south, east, and west. We're bringing in search dog teams to follow a scented trail. Larry Lindgren, our aircraft pilot, will be flying above us in an ultra-light aircraft equipped with GPS locators and digital cameras to take aerial photos of this area. These aerial photos will be printed out using laptop computers and printers for better planning of the search. We'll search for a few hours this morning and then all meet back here. They'll have box lunches for everyone."

"I can't thank you enough for all your help," Wes said, extending his hand again.

"You bet." Williams shook his hand vigorously. "We're here to help you, Mr. Tanner. You can count on us."

Wes learned against his truck and waved to Williams as he drove off. They had spent more than twelve hours searching the area, starting at the real estate offices and moving out across the streets, fields, and creek beds in the Alamo Heights area. The search had been in vain. Wes was exhausted, but he didn't want to

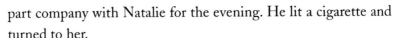

part company with Natalie for the evening. He lit a cigarette and turned to her.

"You really should quit," Natalie said, pointing at the cigarette.

"Again."

"Permanently."

"I'll bet you're glad the fifteenth has come and gone," Wes said, changing the subject.

"Yeah. Now I can start on all of the returns I extended."

"Hey, you deserve a break young lady. Come over and pick out a movie from the Tanner collection," Wes said with a smile. "Plenty of chick flicks to choose from."

"I can't," Natalie said, looking off to the west at the last rays of light fading from the western sky.

"Why not? Do you have a hot date?"

"I have a date."

The smile vanished from Wes's face as he thought about Natalie with another man. For some unexplainable reason, Wes felt betrayed. Natalie never mentioned other men, and Wes just assumed she didn't date. It wasn't as if Natalie wasn't free to see anyone she chose. But the idea of her being with another man made him jealous, in spite of the fact that he had no right to be jealous.

"Have you been out with this guy before?"

"No. This is our first date."

"Where did you meet him?"

"At my office. He's a financial advisor, and we have a common client."

"So, you'll mix a little business with pleasure?" Wes tried to sound lighthearted.

"We'll see."

Natalie continued to stare at the horizon. Wes looked at her face, still visible in the fading light. It was set in a series of curves. High cheekbones, large eyes, and a delicate chin balancing a rounded forehead. Her dark hair hung straight down and ended in one inward curve to her shoulders. The curves continued down through a slim neck to a narrow waist and long legs. She lacked Nicole's stunning physical beauty, but she possessed a more subtle beauty that was accentuated by a purity that seemed to radiate from her at all times. At that moment, Wes wanted to take that face in his hands and kiss those thin lips. But he knew he couldn't do that or even tell Natalie how he still felt about her. Wes wished the feelings would just go away.

"I'd better get you home, then," Wes said. He unlocked the car and held the door open for her as she climbed in.

CHAPTER 17
April 2010

Feeling tired and unmotivated, Natalie stared at the 1040 tax return form, wanting only to go home, curl up in bed, and take a nap. Despite the fact that she didn't take naps, Natalie felt inclined to put her head down on her desk for a moment and close her eyes. She had worked two months' worth of fifteen-hour days, culminating in a marathon eighteen-hour day last Thursday. The day after the tax filing deadline, everyone in her small accounting office cleared out for vacation. Natalie stayed behind and turned her attention to a stack of returns that had been extended until October 15. Better to keep working and avoid thinking about her personal life outside of work.

There wasn't that much of a personal life to think about. She did have a date on Saturday night with the financial advisor. He was a bore. The man spent the entire evening talking about himself. Exhausted from a day of searching for Nicole, she nodded off several times. Her date didn't even notice. It occurred to Natalie at one point that she could have gotten up and left during one of his monologues, and he wouldn't have missed her. Natalie's dating experiences in recent years were similar to this one. These were men with inflated egos that just wanted an audience to tell them how wonderful they were.

With little interest in dating and no close girlfriends, Natalie found the only life she had beyond the four walls of her office had been with Wes and his children. And that was a life borrowed from another, her missing sister, Nicole. Poor Nicole. Natalie's mother was now talking about hiring a psychic to find out what happened to her daughter. Natalie didn't put any stock in that sort of thing, but she had to be realistic. It was just a matter of time before they found Nicole's body. When that happened—in a week, a month, or a year—there would be closure. It would then be time for all of them to move on. It would also mean that Wes would be free to begin a new life with someone else.

Natalie felt certain Wes had feelings for her. She had sensed this even before Nicole disappeared, and it was clearer to her now as he looked to her continually for emotional support. Natalie recalled vividly the crushing blow she had felt twenty years earlier when Wes told her he wanted to start dating Nicole. Her sister had used all her charms to win him away. Her charms and her body. How could any man resist such a combination? As it turned out, Wes couldn't resist Nicole, and he came to Natalie and told her it was over between them. With tears in his eyes, Wes said he would always love her, but it was time for him to start a new chapter in his life.

That chapter was drawing to a close. Natalie wondered if there was a future for her with Wes. Could it be that she would finally be with the man she loved? Perhaps, she thought to herself, if God willed it. But this was not the time to think or dream about that. So, she decided to throw herself into her work. She figured that if she could keep her mind busy, she could get through this. That's why she worked like a dog during the day and read herself to sleep at night.

The ringing telephone ended that thought abruptly. Natalie's first inclination was to let the call go to voice mail. Everyone else in the office did this. They were busy people, so they screened their calls and returned only the ones they wanted to return. Natalie was different. Believing that hiding behind voice mail was dishonest, she always took calls when she was at her desk. Even at those times when she was exhausted and couldn't bear the thought of talking to one more person, she answered her phone.

"Hello?"

"Natalie," the familiar voice said. "I'm in a bind."

"What's wrong, Mom?"

"I need to pick someone up at the airport, and my car won't start."

"Who do you have to pick up at the airport?"

"Mother Love."

"You must be kidding me," Natalie said disgustedly, recalling the name of the psychic her mother had heard on a radio talk show. "She's coming to San Antonio?"

"Yes, dear, and I'm supposed to pick her up in less than an hour. Can you please come and pick me up?"

"I'm working, Mom. Can't Nina pick you up?"

"She doesn't answer." *Smart girl*, Natalie thought to herself. Nina, who didn't work outside the home, screened her calls. When she saw her mother's phone number, she never picked up the phone. Nina had told Natalie this, never feeling guilty about being so narcissistic.

"I'll be there in fifteen minutes," Natalie said.

"Thank you, dear."

Forty minutes later, the two women were standing together outside the baggage claim area of the airport terminal. Nancy was holding a cardboard sign that simply read: "*Mother Love?*"

"Are you sure this was her flight?" Natalie asked as she watched the stream of people coming down the stairs. Expecting to see some wild-eyed woman with a python around her neck, Natalie was surprised when a tall, willowy woman with ash-blond hair stopped in front of them. She was wearing a navy blue business suit.

"I'm Mother Love," the woman said, holding out a languid, manicured hand, accentuated with red fingernail polish. Natalie guessed Love was in her late fifties.

"I'm Nancy Hobbs," Nancy said, grabbing Love's hand with both of her own. "Thank you so much for coming." Love turned her attention to Natalie, seeming to size her up. "This is my daughter, Natalie."

"You don't like me, do you?" Love said with a smile.

"Of course she likes you," Nancy interjected. "Natalie has a heart of gold. She likes everyone."

"I could tell that about you," Love said, nodding. Her eyes were locked on Natalie. "Your heart is too good."

"How could my heart be too good?"

"You're taken advantage of easily, Natalie. People push you around all the time. Am I right?"

"You're right!" Nancy exclaimed. "See, Natalie? I told you Mother Love was the real deal. She already knows you."

"She doesn't believe it." Love shook her head sadly. "Capricorn. Right?"

Natalie stared at her blankly.

Nancy nodded. "Yes, she's a Capricorn."

"Practical, prudent, patient, disciplined, careful, reserved, and skeptical," Love ticked off the traits.

"Yes. That's Natalie through and through," Nancy said.

"We better get your luggage," Natalie said. "I need to get back to the office."

"Natalie's a certified public accountant," Nancy said proudly. "She's the brains of the family."

"A very smart woman," Love agreed as they walked toward the baggage carousel. "Natalie, I hope we can become friends during my stay in San Antonio."

"How long are you going to be here?" Natalie asked.

"Until my job is done."

"Finding my sister?"

"Yes."

"And how much are you charging for your service?"

"Natalie," Nancy scolded. "This is not the time or place for that."

"I don't mind," Love cooed. "Your daughter is a financial person. She always wants the bottom line. It's five thousand dollars if I'm able to complete my work. Of course, I won't charge that much if I can't make contact. To get started, it's seven hundred dollars for the first reading."

"Reading?"

"With the cards."

"Tarot cards," Nancy explained.

"Then what?" Natalie asked.

"Scrying is one hundred dollars per hour," Love said, stepping forward to hoist her suitcase off the conveyor.

"Scrying?"

"Seeing and interpreting images in the crystals."

Natalie looked at her mother incredulously. "Crystal-ball gazing?" "Your Capricorn remains skeptical." Love said, nodding to the door. "Are you parked out there?"

"Yes," Nancy said. "I'm sure my daughter will come around, though. She'll see how it works."

"Yes," Love agreed as they walked through the sliding glass doors. "The proof is always in the pudding."

CHAPTER 18
April 2010

Summer wore an uncustomary smile when she woke up Wes early on a Friday morning. The children were out of school for Fiesta, but Wes knew it was more than a day off that put the smile on his daughter's face. Wes had promised Summer last week they would attend the Battle of Flowers parade if she got out of bed and went to school each morning. Summer appeared to be experiencing separation anxiety in the three weeks since Nicole had disappeared. She didn't want to get up in the morning, and she didn't want to let her father, or Aunt Natalie, out of her sight. Wes chose to combat the problem with bribery. When Summer was reluctant to do something she needed to do, Wes would warn her that she couldn't attend the parade unless she complied. The bribery had worked.

"We're going to the parade," Summer announced to Jordan when she sat down at the table. Jordan looked like a deer in the headlights as she shot a glance at Wes.

"I don't have to go, do I?"

"You used to love the parade. What happened?"

"I grew up," Jordan said as she jumped up from the table and carried her plate to the kitchen. "Don't you have to go to work today?"

"I'm off. What are your plans for the day?"

"Amy and I are going to Starbucks."

"And meet boys," Summer added. Jordan shot her a menacing glance, but her sister ignored it. "That's what she told Amy."

"You'd better stop eavesdropping on my conversations."

"Or what?" Summer said, feeling safe with her father just a few feet away.

"Your sister would never hurt you," Wes said, noticing she was wearing the revealing halter top. "You can go to Starbucks with Amy when you change that top."

"Dad." Jordan rolled her eyes. "It's not that showy."

"Change it."

"Oh, Dad." Jordan looked disgusted as she headed upstairs.

With the halter top battle behind them, Wes and Summer left the house. Monty had also turned down an invitation to join them, opting instead to ride his bike to meet a friend. Wes and Summer drove to Natalie's house and found her in the front yard weeding a flowerbed. Natalie had packed sandwiches and brought a flower arrangement. The threesome was ready to head downtown and find a good spot to watch the parade.

The Battle of Flowers parade was an annual extravaganza commemorating the Battle at San Jacinto in 1836. This was the battle where Texas won its independence from Mexico. The parade, held at the end of Fiesta week, attracted hundreds of thousands of spectators each year. The first parade was held in 1891 to honor those who fought and died at the Battle of the Alamo. Remembering the heroes of the Alamo had remained the focus of the parade, and participants were asked to bring a floral tribute to be placed on the lawn in front of the Alamo. Wes promised Summer they would leave their flower arrangement at the Alamo after the parade.

"Look! A princess!" Summer exclaimed as they stood in the midst of the crowd and watched the colorful floats pass. Summer, perched on Wes's shoulders so she wouldn't miss any of the action, waved frantically. She giggled with delight when the princess waved back. Natalie smiled at Summer and then gave Wes a look of approval. They both knew this was just what Summer needed to take her mind off the tumultuous events of the past month.

When there was a break in the action, Wes put his daughter down to rest his shoulders. Summer spotted a vendor across the street and licked her lips. "Cotton candy!" she cried out. "I want cotton candy."

"I don't see anything," Wes said.

"Right there!" Summer pointed at the vendor.

"I still don't see anything."

"Daddy! Stop it!"

Natalie laughed. "He's mean, isn't he?"

Summer nodded emphatically.

"Don't worry. I'll get you some, sweetheart."

"Thank you."

"Here." Wes reached into his wallet and tried to hand her a five-dollar bill. Natalie waved him off.

"No way, Aunt Natalie's buying," she said before crossing the street. "You're not getting any credit for this after the way you acted."

"Wes." Wes heard the voice behind him and turned to see one of his coworkers from the newspaper approaching. He was accompanied by his wife and two sons. Wes visited with his friend for a moment before Natalie returned with the cotton candy.

"Wes." Natalie was looking around. "Where's Summer?"

"Summer?" Wes glanced around. A wave of fear swept over him when he realized his daughter was no longer standing beside him. He scanned the sunny street in both directions. "Summer?"

"Summer!" Natalie called, looking around anxiously.

Wes squatted down and looked through the crowd at a level that would have been Summer's height. She couldn't have gone far, but where was she? Wes suddenly realized that his fists were tightly clenched. His breathing had become rapid and shallow. "Natalie, I don't see her anywhere."

"Don't panic," Natalie said, looking nervous herself.

"Let's split up," Wes said, breaking into a trot.

"Wes!" He turned. "Shouldn't I stay here? This is where we last saw her."

"Yes. Stay there," Wes said, disappearing into the crowd. Gripped with panic, he stopped to ask a young couple if they had seen a little girl in a pink blouse. They seemed genuinely concerned as they looked toward each other and then back at Wes. But they were shaking their heads. They had not seen her. Wes hurried on, walking and running down the sidewalk as he frantically scanned the landscape for anyone wearing pink.

Wes had traveled a block when he spotted a police officer. He was on a bicycle, following the parade route. Running hard, Wes caught up with him. "My little girl is missing," he said, his eyes begging for help.

"Where did you last see her?"

"A block back," Wes said, pointing in the direction that he had come from.

"Don't worry, Dad. We'll find her," the officer said. He reached for the mike button on his two way radio attached to his jersey epaulet. There was a crackling on the other end, then a clear message of "10-4" from dispatch. The officer keyed off his radio and reached behind him into his waistband for a metal, flip-open report pad. Wearing the typical uniform of a bicycle officer, the young man looked to Wes like a Malibu cop who had just stepped off of the set of *Baywatch*. Just as Wes had begun to size him up as someone not to be taken seriously, his attention was drawn to a black belt holster, with the butt of his gun showing behind the buckle down strap. Directly in front of his sidearm he wore his leather encased S.A.P.D. badge, folded outward on his belt, with the gold shield showing for quick identification as a police officer.

Looking up frequently to maintain eye contact with his complainant, the officer wrote quickly on his form as updates from headquarters came in staccato bursts over his radio. He had radioed fellow officers in the vicinity, who in turn had relayed critical information about the missing girl to dispatch and to other patrolmen in the area. They quickly set up their net.

Wes folded his arms, breathed in deeply, and let his taut muscles relax. They would find Summer, he thought to himself, if she was lost and wandering. Wes quickly corrected himself: lost, wandering, and scared. He continued to scan the horizon for any sign of her. In his mind, he could see Summer walking down the street, crying, and calling for her father. The image of the lost Summer, as painful as it was, paled with another that was trying to seep into his mind. This was the picture of his daughter in the hands of a pedophile, her innocence being stripped away forever.

Wes was following the officer as they weaved their way through the crowd. The officer stopped periodically to question people. Wes saw one mother grip her own daughter's hand tightly as she was being questioned, clearly glad it wasn't her child who had wandered off.

CHAPTER 19
April 2010

More than an hour after he had completed a police report, Wes stood out in front of the San Antonio Police Department smoking a cigarette as he continued a descent into his own private hell. Roger had just arrived and was inside with Natalie praying for Summer's safe return. His grandfather had invited Wes to join them, but he declined the offer. Wes was thinking about the information the social worker had given him. Almost a million children were reported missing each year. About a third of these children were the victims of family abductions. Another large percentage were runaways. Only about four thousand fall into the category of kidnapping victims.

It seemed certain now that Summer was a victim of kidnapping. Police had received a report earlier of a girl fitting Summer's description getting into a truck a few blocks from where Wes and Natalie had last seen her. There was no guarantee that the girl seen getting into the truck was Summer, but Wes feared the worst. He had asked the social worker what the chances were for Summer to be returned safely. She was evasive at first, but when pressed, she finally told him what he already suspected. If Summer was the victim of a non-family abduction, statistics showed that if the child isn't recovered within a few hours "chances are slim of recovering them alive." Time was running out.

Wes recalled his first encounter with police twenty-eight years earlier. He had been living in a small apartment with his mother and two half-brothers in Chicago. The three boys shared a bedroom, with three single beds lined up on the back wall. There was just enough room to move around in the bedroom.

On this particular night, Wes had tried in vain to wait up for his mother to return home from a night on the town. It was her custom to go out drinking with her girlfriends on a Saturday night. Wes could tell when his mother had been at a bar because she would stagger around and he could smell alcohol on her breath. At thirteen, Wes was frequently left to care for his brothers, ten and eight at the time, on the weekends. Wes was dozing on the couch in the living room when he heard a knock at the door. When he opened his eyes, he noticed it was still dark.

"Who is it?" Wes asked fearfully, standing at the door.

"It's the police. Is this the Thompson residence?"

"Yes."

"Open up, son. I need to talk with you."

"Can I see some identification?" Wes asked, peering through the peephole. Wes could see the officer's badge on the other side of the door before he opened it. There were two middle-aged men in uniform in the hallway.

The two police officers stood there looking at him for a moment as if they didn't know what to say. Wes was still rubbing sleep from his eyes.

"What's your name?" one officer finally asked him.

"Wes."

"You're smart to ask for identification before opening up," the other officer said.

"Can we come in and talk with you?" the first officer asked.

"Sure."

Wes said down on the couch, and the first officer put his hand on Wes's shoulder.

"Son, there's no easy way to tell you this. Your mother is dead."

The reality of the police officer's words didn't really sink in until five days later when Wes attended his mother's funeral. Wes's grandfather had flown up to preside at the service. He had also made arrangements to take Wes back to live with him in Texas. Roger had offered to also take custody of Wes's stepbrothers, but their father wanted them. He made it clear that he didn't want Wes, which suited the boy fine. Wes hated his stepfather, who had been mean to him during the years he was married to Wes's mother.

It rained on the day of Rachel Thompson's funeral. Wes recalled standing next to a fat woman with a round face that claimed to be his aunt. It was a cold, rainy day, and the winter wind caused those in the small crowd attending the graveside service to shiver. But Wes didn't feel the wind, or the rain blowing in his face under the umbrella. He felt nothing except a dull sort of numbness as he tried to get his young mind around the reality set before him. Wes knew this large wooden box contained the body of his mother. He had walked past the open casket and saw her face. Her eyes were closed, and she looked peaceful for the first time since he could recall.

Before the funeral started, Wes overhead a conversation at the back of the church. Two women were telling a third about the details surrounding Rachel's death. It seemed that she had gotten drunk and had driven the wrong way on the interstate. She was killed in the accident, along with both of the other women in her compact car. A family of four had the misfortune of being on the interstate, travelling in the right direction, at 2:00 a.m. The father had elected to travel at night while his two small children slept in the backseat. The father and mother were both killed in the collision. The two orphans managed to survive since they were secured in their car seats.

As the last notes of "Amazing Grace" resonated and died away, Wes suddenly stepped out from under the umbrella, walked over, and touched the casket.

"Wes." The lady with the round face reached out from under the umbrella and tried to grab his hand. "You'll get wet."

But it was too late. He was drenched as he slowly turned his face upward toward heaven. The rain felt cold on his face. The sky was gray, and there appeared to be no end to the dark clouds that hung over him.

"**T**his is not your fault, Wes." Natalie made the emphatic statement with her eyes fastened unwaveringly on his eyes. It was almost 5:00 p.m. as he sat on the bench between Roger and Natalie.

"It *is* my fault. I let go of her hand."

"Do you know how many parents let go of their children's hands every day?"

"That makes them equally guilty. The only difference is that most of them don't lose their children. I lost mine," Wes said, unable to contain his tears.

Natalie took his head and pressed it against her chest. Wes wept as she held him.

"I'm going to be praying every hour of every day until she is home safe," Roger said after Wes had regained a measure of composure. "Just like I'm praying for Nicole."

"But that doesn't guarantee either of them will be found safe."

"I believe they will, and I want you to believe it, too."

"I wish I could believe that, Grandpa," Wes said quietly.

"I believe it," Natalie said. "I'm trusting God for a miracle."

Wes was about to make a disparaging comment about blind faith when the loud pop of the electronically controlled door interrupted him. The three of them looked up into the smiling face of Detective Frank Salas. "I've got good news. Great news, in fact."

"What?" All three of them stood up simultaneously.

"Your daughter is safe," Salas said.

Wes jumped up and embraced the detective. "Thank you, Frank. Thank you."

"Don't thank me." Salas pulled away looking somewhat embarrassed. "You might want to thank God for this one because it was a miracle."

A miracle was not a bad description, even for an agnostic, of the events that had transpired an hour earlier. A San Antonio police officer had spotted a truck on the west side of town with a little girl in the passenger seat. Although he had only a glimpse, the police officer thought the girl was crying. Aware that a six-year-old girl was missing, the officer followed the truck. The truck sped up, and the officer called it in as he gave chase. Two police officers several blocks away alertly put spike strips across the road in front of the oncoming truck. The truck ran over the spike strips, and the kidnapper was soon in custody. Summer was unharmed and on her way back to be reunited with her family.

"We don't have very many happy endings to these kind of situations," Salas said as Wes took turns hugging Natalie and Roger. "Your daughter's guardian angel must have been working overtime."

"Her Heavenly Father was at work," Roger said. "That's for sure."

It's bedtime for Sunshine." Wes smiled, hugging his daughter as they sat on the couch at home. Wes hadn't been able to take his eyes off Summer since they had arrived home two hours earlier, and he couldn't stop hugging her. Natalie had been doing her share of hugging and kissing, too.

"Sunshine doesn't have a bedtime," Summer said playfully.

"Oh, really?"

"Yeah. Sunshine is up all of the time, just like the sun."

"The sun sets every night," Natalie reminded her. "I guess that means your bedtime should be at sundown."

"No!" Summer said emphatically.

"Then you'd better get in bed now," Wes said.

"You need to tuck me in."

"I need to go," Natalie said, rising to her feet.

"Aunt Natalie, I want you to tuck me in, too. Please?"

Natalie scooped up the little girl in her arms. "How can I resist you?"

"You can't." Summer smiled, kissing her on the cheek.

In Summer's bedroom, Wes found the book they had been reading. It was *The Hobbit*, the J.R.R. Tolkien fantasy, which chronicled the adventures of the hobbit Bilbo Baggins as he traveled across the lands of Middle-earth with a band of dwarves and a wizard named Gandalf. When they had finished the chapter, Summer was begging for more.

"No," Wes said.

"Please."

"No. Bedtime."

"Prayer time," Summer said, kneeling by her bed. Wes and Natalie knelt on each side of her. "Lord, thank you for this day," Summer prayed, with her eyes tightly shut.

"And thank you for keeping Summer safe," Natalie added.

"And thank you for keeping me safe when I got into the truck with that man. And thank you for my daddy, and for my sister and brother. And thank you for my aunt Natalie. And thank you for my mommy. And please bring Mommy home safely. Amen."

"Amen," Wes and Natalie echoed.

After sliding under the covers, Summer hugged Wes and then Natalie. "Daddy?"

"Yes?"

"Do you think Mommy's coming home, or is she in heaven?"

"I don't know, Sunshine."

"What do you think, Aunt Natalie?"

"I'm praying hard that she's coming home."

"Me, too," Summer said.

Wes turned off the light, and he was standing at the door when Summer spoke up again. "Can I ask you a question?"

"Sure."

"If Mommy's in heaven, will you marry Aunt Natalie?"

Wes glanced at Natalie before Summer added: "If I need a new mommy, I'd like it to be Aunt Natalie."

CHAPTER 20
May 2010

Life had returned to something resembling normal for the Tanner family in the month since Nicole had disappeared. A strong hint of summer was in the air, with temperatures already climbing into the lower nineties by the first week of May. Natalie was continuing to come over every day after school to check on the children. She would help with homework, prepare dinner for the family, and bring stability. Wes wanted to tell Natalie how he felt about her, but he sensed the time was not right. Nicole was still, officially, missing. There was no closure. Wes knew Natalie wouldn't allow the relationship to progress until Nicole's fate was known.

Wes had considered hiring Ezra Goldstein to track down Raul Gonzalez in Mexico, but he had put the idea on hold. If the bounty hunter agreed to take the case, he would surely want a substantial amount of money. Wes had already been forced to dip into his savings, and he didn't want to spend a fortune on what might amount to a wild goose chase.

Wes was relieved that the children seemed to be doing better as each day passed. Summer was adjusting, and her separation anxiety was easing. Wes knew that Natalie was the reason for that since her aunt would frequently lie in bed with her until she was asleep. Monty occupied himself with baseball, skateboarding, and music when he wasn't in school. Natalie had to stay after him about studying, but that was par for the course with his son. Even Jordan seemed to have settled into a certain, predictable rhythm.

At the suggestion of his grandfather, Wes did take all three children to several counseling sessions with a psychologist. They talked about their mother and about the feelings they had experienced since her disappearance. Summer did more talking than the older children. The psychologist told Wes privately that he felt like they needed more time. Wes wondered how long it would take. At a hundred dollars an hour, he couldn't afford much more time.

"I'm hungry, Dad. Can you offer the blessing so we can eat?" Monty asked. The five of them were sitting at the dinner table on a Wednesday night. Natalie had cooked a delicious meal, and everyone looked happy. Wes thought what a nice family this would make.

Natalie nodded to him, signaling that it was time to bless the food. Wes knew the right words to say, although the words would not be heartfelt.

"God, thank you for the food. We ask that you bless it and use it to nourish our bodies. We pray in Christ's name. Amen."

"Amen," Summer said happily. "I like it when we pray together. I like it when we're all together," Summer said, looking in turn at her aunt and father.

"Dad, Coach Sanchez said I'm starting the game tomorrow night," Monty said.

"I'll be there," Wes assured him. "Wouldn't miss it for the world."

"Can we throw the ball around after dinner?" Monty asked, revealing a mouth full of food. Wes nodded at him, choosing to ignore his bad manners.

"Gross," Jordan said.

"What's your problem?" Monty demanded, still talking with food in his mouth.

"You. You're a pig."

"Shut your face."

"Shut your face. It's full of food," Jordan shot back. Monty immediately opened his mouth so his sister got a view of the partially chewed food. "Dad, make him stop!"

"Monty, would you be so kind as to chew with your mouth closed?" Wes said.

"Yes, sir."

"Thank you," Jordan said, feigning sweetness. "Dad, you remember that prom is Saturday night, don't you?"

"My daughter's first prom. How could I forget?"

"It's a special night."

"It certainly is," Wes said, smiling at Natalie.

"Can I have a later curfew?"

"How late are you asking for?"

"Two."

"Dream on."

"One?"

"Midnight."

"Twelve thirty?"

"Done. Tell Doug he'd better not be late getting you home."

"Not Doug. John," Jordan corrected him.

"John? Who's John?"

"John Thompson."

"The football player?"

"And basketball and baseball. And student president. He's the hottest guy in the entire school," Jordan said wistfully.

"I thought you were going with Doug," Natalie said, looking perplexed.

"I was until John asked me."

"But you told Doug you'd go with him."

"Then I got a better offer."

"But Doug asked you first," Natalie persisted.

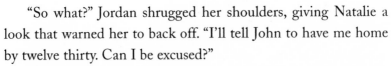

"So what?" Jordan shrugged her shoulders, giving Natalie a look that warned her to back off. "I'll tell John to have me home by twelve thirty. Can I be excused?"

"Okay," Wes said, knowing this was not the right place to argue the issue. Jordan quickly got up from the table and left the room. Wes turned his attention to Summer, asking her for a summation of her day. By the time she was finished, Monty had also excused himself from the table. When Summer left, Wes and Natalie were finally alone. Natalie was staring at him, and Wes knew what was coming.

"It's nice to know she's going to the prom with the hottest guy in her school."

"Yeah." Wes rolled his eyes. "What am I supposed to do?"

"What do you think you should do?"

"I should make her go with Doug."

"I agree that's the right thing to do."

"She won't speak to me for a month."

Wes retreated to the back porch for a cigarette, dreading what was ahead. After he put out the cigarette, Wes went back inside and prepared to confront Jordan. Buoyed by a look of encouragement from Natalie, he proceeded to climb the stairs and knocked on Jordan's bedroom door.

"Come in," said the voice from the other side of the door. Wes entered the room and found Jordan in the bathroom touching up her makeup. He paused to look at the young woman standing in front of the mirror. Wes thought she looked more like her mother every day.

"Hey, princess."

"Hi, Daddy."

"You're a beautiful young lady. Did you know that?"

"Thanks," she said, turning to him curiously after a silent moment. "Is there something else you wanted to say?"

"Yes, there is," Wes said, taking a deep breath. "You need to call John and tell him you can't go to the prom with him."

"What!" Jordan looked like she had been shot. "Why not?"

"Because you told Doug first."

"You can't be serious. Every girl at my school wants to go to the prom with John. He asked me, Dad. He asked *me*."

"I know."

"You can't do this to me, Dad."

"There will be other occasions. Your sixteenth birthday is two weeks away. I agreed to let you start dating, so you can go out with John then."

"But that's not the prom!"

"I'm sorry, Jordan."

"Why are you doing this to me, Dad?"

"Because you told Doug you'd go with him."

"It's funny, Dad." Jordan turned on him, clearly furious.

"What's funny?"

"I can see your lips moving, but I hear Aunt Natalie's voice."

"Your aunt Natalie is right."

"She's not my mother."

"Your mother would have agreed with her."

"No, she wouldn't. She didn't."

"What do you mean?

"Mom said it was okay."

"Mom said what was okay?"

"She said it was okay to go with John if he asked me."

"When did she tell you that?"

"A long time ago. Before she…" Jordan struggled for the right word.

"Disappeared?"

"She knew John was the hottest guy in the school. I told her he was interested in me and that I was hoping he would ask me to prom. Then Doug asked me. I didn't want to miss going, but

I really wanted to go with John. She said if I got a better offer, I should take it. She said it was okay for me to go with John, if he asked. And he asked."

"I'm telling you it's not okay," Wes said firmly, surprised at his own resolve.

"The only reason you're saying that is because of what Aunt Natalie said. Aunt Natalie's a prude, Dad. Even Mom said that. She's a loser. That's why she's alone."

"Jordan, stop it!"

"I hate her!" Jordan said with venom. "I hate you."

Wes stared at her, unable to say anything.

"I'd like for you to leave now."

"We'll talk about this when you're a little calmer."

"Please get out of my room."

CHAPTER 21
May 2010

Natalie was getting worried as the clock struck 1 a.m. Jordan should have been home from the prom by 12:30, but she wasn't. Wes was attending the Spurs playoff game with coworkers, and they had stopped for a drink after the game. He had just texted Natalie to let her know he was on his way home. Natalie said a silent prayer that she would not be alone when Jordan arrived. This time, though, her prayer was not answered as the front door opened and Jordan staggered in. Natalie could smell the alcohol on her breath.

"Jordan, are you drunk?"

"Am I drunk?" Jordan started giggling, trying to focus on her aunt. "What kind of a question is that to ask me? Am I drunk?"

Jordan lost her balance and fell into the wall in the foyer. Natalie reached out to catch her, fearing she would fall to the floor. Jordan sagged into Natalie's arms for a moment and then backed up a step, raised her finger, and pointed at her aunt.

"Am I drunk?" Jordan repeated the question. "Yes, Aunt Natalie, I *am* drunk. But tomorrow, I will be sober. And *you* will still be a prude." The surprised expression on Natalie's face caused Jordan to convulse with laughter. When she sat down on the floor, Duncan came over and started licking her face. This only made Jordan laugh harder.

Natalie found herself at a loss, not knowing what to do with Jordan, who continued to sit on the floor and let the dog lick her face.

"Your father will be home in a few minutes, Jordan. You would be well advised to be in bed before he walks in that door."

Jordan didn't look up. Instead she turned her attention to Duncan. She took his head in her hands and looked into his eyes. "Your father will be home in a few minutes," she told the dog. "You would be well advised to be in bed before he walks in that door."

"Come on, Jordan," Natalie helped her to her feet. Jordan was unsteady and had to be supported to keep from falling back on the floor. Still trying to focus, the teenager tried to speak but let out a loud burp instead. This caused her to start laughing again. After regaining her composure, she pointed her finger at her aunt for a second time.

"As for you, Natalie. *You* would be well advised to stand back as I may heave."

"What?"

"You know, heave. Vomit. Spit up. Regurgitate. Upchuck. Belch forth. Toss my cookies. Have you ever tossed your cookies, Natalie?" Before her aunt could answer, Jordan continued her tirade. "I thought not. You're far too prim and proper for such vile and disgusting behavior."

"Getting drunk doesn't accomplish anything."

"Oh, you're wrong. So wrong. Getting drunk was just what this girl needed. Getting drunk helped me forget how miserable my life is. But just temporarily."

"Come on, Jordan." Natalie put her arm around Jordan's shoulder for support and attempted to lead her to the stairway. Jordan managed to pull away.

"Unhand me, foul beast."

Natalie recoiled as though she had been punched hard in the gut. She realized the alcohol was talking, but the words still stung like a wasp. Natalie had stood in Jordan's way one time too many, and Jordan was letting her real feelings pour out now. This was an eerie reminder of a time when her own sister had done the same thing.

Just weeks after Wes had broken up with Natalie, Nicole came home drunk. When Natalie made the mistake of gently criticizing her, any pretense of civility vanished. Nicole went on the offensive, unleashing a string of profanities and calling Natalie every dirty name that came to mind. She saved the worst for last.

"Wes is such a good lover. Too bad you'll never know."

Looking at Jordan as she went up the stairs, Natalie saw Nicole twenty years ago. They were so much alike, and Natalie feared that her niece would grow up to be just like her mother. *Oh, Lord, please help her,* Natalie uttered a silent prayer just as Wes walked in the door.

Would you mind putting that out?"

Wes had rolled down the window of the truck and lit a cigarette on a quiet car ride to school. Jordan rarely protested when he smoked, so he immediately put the cigarette out in the ash tray. His daughter had barely spoken to him since the confrontation on Friday night, and he was eager to clear the air.

"How long are you going to hold a grudge against me?"

"A long time."

"That's your privilege. You need to understand—"

"Understand what?" Jordan snapped, with her eyes blazing and fixed on him. "That not going to the prom with John was good for me? That it will develop character?"

"Yes."

She rolled her eyes disgustedly. "Please."

"Jordan, this wasn't about a prom date. It was about doing the right thing. You gave your word to Doug. You kept your word. That's a good thing."

"A good thing? You ruined my life!"

"So, you go out and get drunk?"

Jordan just glared at him.

"Well, you'll have some time to think about it. You're grounded for the next week."

Wes was turning into the school parking lot. When the vehicle came to a full stop, Jordan threw open the door and left the car without a word. He shook his head, feeling sad and helpless. Wes had expected Jordan to be upset with him, but he wasn't prepared for her icy silence. At times like this, Wes could see her mother in Jordan.

Wes couldn't count the times that Nicole had treated him with the same attitude. In fact, it seemed to happen every time she didn't get her way. Wes had been in the habit of giving Nicole her way most of the time, choosing to pick his battles carefully.

At least Jordan hadn't resorted to the degrading comments yet. But she wasn't quite sixteen. Wes feared that the time would come when she would respond to him just like her mother did. Then their relationship would slowly deteriorate—just like his relationship with Nicole had soured. Wes turned out of the school parking lot and headed for the office. He had a column to write and then he could go home and escape for a few hours into his make-believe world of fiction where no one could hurt him.

CHAPTER 22
May 2010

Wes arrived at the *Express-News* shortly before 9:30 a.m. and found out the editor wanted to meet with him. He had no idea why he was being summoned by his boss. Wes had known Rob Reynolds since he had joined the editorial staff at the paper almost twenty years ago. Since being promoted to columnist several years earlier, Reynolds seldom spoke to Wes, except for small talk, or to compliment him on one of his columns. He had been in the group that had attended the basketball game Saturday night, and the editor seemed to be avoiding him.

"Wes, how are you doing?" Reynolds asked as Wes settled into a chair across the desk from him. Reynolds tapped the desk nervously with the pen in his hand.

"I'm doing okay."

"The Spurs really stunk up the place the other night."

"They sure did."

"I figured we'd lose to the Suns but not a sweep."

Wes didn't respond, choosing to wait for Reynolds to tell him the reason for the meeting. Judging from the expression on his face, the meeting would not be pleasant.

"Any news on your wife?"

"Nothing new."

"What about that guy in Mexico?"

"Still there, I guess," Wes said, not wanting to talk about the subject.

"Are they going to extradite him?"

"No indication."

"How are your kids doing?"

"They're okay."

"Wes, I've got some bad news," Reynolds said, looking down at his desk.

"What is it?"

"It's this damn economy. It's the paper. We're still losing money. I…"

Reynolds' voice trailed off, and Wes thought the editor was close to tears.

"More layoffs?"

Reynolds nodded.

"And I'm one of them?"

"I'm sorry, Wes. Really sorry. You're a great writer. I love your columns and so do our readers."

"There's just not enough of them."

"I guess that's what it boils down to. I know there's no good time to lose your job. But this is really bad timing for you, I know. I'm really sorry."

"It's not your fault, Rob."

"There is a silver lining."

"What's that?"

"There's a severance package. Two weeks for every year of service. How long have you worked for the *Express-News*, Wes?"

"It'll be twenty years next month. Only job I've ever had."

"I'll try and get you credit for the full twenty," Reynolds promised.

After he left the paper, Wes drove around the city for two hours until he had smoked a pack of cigarettes. The news that he was unemployed was gradually sinking in. In addition to losing a job he loved, Wes knew he was facing an escalating financial crisis. With Nicole gone, he couldn't make ends meet on his salary, and now that would soon be gone, too. Wes would tighten his belt as much as possible, but he needed to get another job soon. But what did a forty-one-year-old newspaper man have to offer in a tight job market? He might be unemployed for a long time.

There was the $500,000 life insurance policy on Nicole, and Wes desperately needed that money. But his agent had told him there was no way to collect until her body was found. Even then, the insurance company wouldn't pay if Wes was considered a murder suspect. Where would the money he needed come from? Nicole's Mercedes was worth more than thirty thousand, but he couldn't sell it because they were upside down in the note. If he stopped paying on it, it would be repossessed and his credit would be ruined. Better to have damaged credit than to lose the house, which was also a possibility.

Flashbacks from his adolescent years suddenly overwhelmed him. Wes recalled the fear he had experienced when his mother told him there wasn't enough money to buy groceries for him and his two brothers. How could he forget those nights when he would wait outside a fast-food restaurant for his friend to sneak food to him to dull his hunger? When he moved in with his grandfather, he thought those days were behind him forever. Now, he feared the same fate lay in store for his family.

Wes found himself on the east side of downtown, driving through an African-American neighborhood. On the street corner, a fire hydrant was spewing water. Wes watched two adolescent boys toss their shoes to the gutter, roll up their pants, and start dancing in the gushing water. Why weren't they in school? Wes wondered. He rolled the window down in the truck to let the warm air rush in. He could hear the water gushing from the hydrant.

Across the street from the waterworks, two old men had dragged out a card table and were playing checkers. They were also watching the boys playing in the water. Wes thought about how different the world was over here, away from the yuppie hustle and bustle of the north side. People weren't out chasing the mighty buck here. They took time to enjoy the simpler things in life.

Wes pulled up in front of Reagan High School a few minutes before 4:00 p.m. He hoped to catch Jordan before she boarded the bus. Wes had been thinking about her all day, hoping she had softened her stance. He wasn't going to apologize because he hadn't done anything wrong. He just wanted to reach out to his daughter and let her know how much he loved her. Wes also wanted her to know he understood how she felt. Life was full of disappointments. No one knew that better than him. What they really needed was some time together. Wes would see if he could interest Jordan in dinner at her favorite restaurant. On second thought, maybe a trip to Starbucks would be more economical.

Wes was standing in front of his truck, watching students board the buses when he spotted Jordan. He started to call to her, but he was afraid he might embarrass her in front of her friends. Wes decided to walk toward her, hoping to reach her before she got on the bus. Instead of getting in the line to board the bus, Jordan pushed through the crowd of students, passed the bus, and walked toward the front of the school. Peering into the distance, Wes saw two men standing in the driveway by a black Cadillac. It was Niebring and Mendoza, and Jordan was headed straight for them.

CHAPTER 23
May 2010

Wes was watching from the window when the Cadillac pulled up in front of his house. In an instant, he threw the front door open and burst out of the house. Mendoza had opened the car door for Jordan, and she was getting out as Wes reached them. "Jordan, go inside."

"Hello, Mr. Tanner," Mendoza said with a smile. Jordan turned and obediently walked toward the house. Wes waited until she was inside before he turned his anger on the detectives.

"You have no business talking to my daughter."

"On the contrary, this is my business," Niebring said as he walked around from the other side of the car. "Your wife is missing and may have been murdered. It's my job to follow up on every lead."

"Keep my daughter out of this."

"Your daughter doesn't want to stay out of this."

"What do you mean?"

"Your daughter called me, Mr. Tanner. She had something she wanted to tell us."

"What?" Wes was reeling, realizing he had been betrayed by his own daughter.

"She believes her aunt murdered your wife."

"That's absurd."

"She also told me that you left the house on the night your wife disappeared."

"Of course I did. Jordan and I drove to Nicole's office. I told you that."

"But you didn't tell me you went out earlier in the evening. You failed to mention that to us in your statement."

"I went to the bookstore."

"Did you?" Niebring raised his eyebrows. "Do you have anyone that can corroborate your story?"

Wes stared at the detective with a look of pure disdain. "Why don't you go ahead and charge me."

"Charge you with what?"

"Murder. Charge me right now, or get off of my property."

"Simmer down, Mr. Tanner." Mendoza raised his hand. "We're not charging you with anything. We're just conducting an investigation."

Wes continued to stare at Niebring, ignoring Mendoza.

"You amaze me, Detective." Niebring returned his stare. "A man threatens my wife. A few days later, he vanishes. He runs to Mexico, and you let him go. Then you try to shake my family upside down looking for a suspect to pin it on."

"I'm not trying to pin this on anyone," Niebring said calmly. "I'm investigating a possible homicide. Raul Gonzalez is a suspect. You're a suspect. Why, everybody in this town's a suspect. I'm going to get to the bottom of this, Tanner. I ain't going away."

Wes stood in the foyer, trying to gather himself before he called his daughter downstairs. Ever since she was very young, Jordan had always been headstrong and defiant. But never in almost sixteen years did Wes feel like his daughter had betrayed him until now. He closed his eyes and took a deep breath.

"Jordan!"

"Yes," Jordan called from upstairs. Her voice sounded innocent, almost angelic.

"Come downstairs. Now!"

Wes heard her bounding down the stairs. A moment later, she appeared in the foyer, looking at him as if nothing out of the ordinary had taken place.

"Yes?"

"I just laid into Detective Niebring. Told him he had no business dragging my daughter into the investigation. Do you know what he told me?"

"No."

"He told me you called him." Wes looked into Jordan's eyes, hoping to see remorse. Instead, he saw something that resembled a smirk. "Is that true?"

"Yes."

"What did you tell him, Jordan?"

"I told him I thought Aunt Natalie murdered Mom."

"What?" Wes asked incredulously. "Are you out of your mind? You actually think Natalie is capable of something like that?"

"Yes."

"Why?"

"Because I know she's in love with you."

"You are out of your mind."

"Am I, Dad?"

Wes hung his head, then turned his back on her and walked slowly into the study. Far from remorseful, Jordan had inflicted her venomous sting, and Wes was unable to fight back. He suddenly felt drained. Emboldened, Jordan followed him into the study.

"Am I? Then tell me why she's always hanging around here?" Jordan asked. She had her hands on her hips. Her look had become fiery, probing. "Why don't you tell me why she spends so much time at your side? Does she really think she can replace Mom?"

"Jordan, what on earth has come over you?" Wes said as he wheeled around to face her. "Your aunt Natalie is one of the sweetest women I've ever known. What she has done has been out of love for our family…your mother's family."

"We're not helpless, Dad. Who asked her to take Mom's place?"

"Your aunt Natalie is devoted to all three of you."

"And to you."

When she saw the hurt in her father's eyes, Jordan stepped back, took her hands from her hips, and let them rest by her side. Her shoulders slumped slightly as she began to fully realize the implications of what she had done. Her tone became soft, and her head was cocked slightly to the side, as if beckoning her father to understand. "She's in love with you, Dad." With that said, Jordan turned and walked out of the study. Wes followed her into the foyer and watched her as she headed up the steps.

CHAPTER 24
May 2010

Natalie tapped her foot nervously as she waited in the hallway outside the San Antonio police detectives' offices. A young Hispanic girl, whom Natalie guessed to be about four years old, jumped playfully between her mom and dad, playing as if to scare one, then the other. For what seemed like a long time, Natalie lost track of everything around her as she lapsed into an unfocused gaze on the little girl. She recalled a time when she played that way with her mother and father. Life was so simple then. Everything changed when her father left them and started a new family.

"Natalie?" Natalie was rocked out of her daydream by the sound of the familiar voice. Wes was walking down the hallway toward her. "I'm sorry I'm late."

"It's okay. The detective hasn't come out yet."

"Good. I didn't want you going back there without me."

"Wes, you don't need to protect me from them. I have nothing to hide. I'm going to tell them the truth."

"We've been telling them the truth. They don't seem to be interested in the truth. If they were, they'd have Raul Gonzalez in custody. I—"

A loud pop interrupted Wes, and Natalie looked up to see a door open. Sgt. Niebring came through the door, extending his right hand to shake her hand, while holding a bulging manila file in his other hand. "Ms. Guerra? Nice to meet you."

Natalie took his hand, and Niebring turned to Wes. "Mr. Tanner?" Natalie could see by the expression on Wes's face that he was full of contempt for the detective. Only reluctantly did he shake Niebring's hand. "Would you follow me, please?" Niebring said as he stepped aside and motioned for them to walk ahead of him through an electronically controlled door.

As Natalie slid past him through the doorway to the interrogation room, she could feel the detective's eyes on her. Niebring was watching them carefully.

"Would you two mind waiting in there? I need to find my partner, and then we'll join you for a short visit."

After Niebring left the room, Wes settled into a chair next to Natalie, looking agitated. Natalie could never remember seeing Wes act this way toward anyone.

"Wes, try and relax."

"I can't relax. Can't you see? Niebring has it in for me."

"I'm the one that's being questioned as a suspect."

"You're not a suspect." Wes shook his head. "He can't possibly think you had anything to do with Nicole's disappearance. He's just trying to make a case against me."

"Wes, calm down. Please."

Natalie stared at Wes for a moment, wondering who this man was that was so full of anger and contempt. She had always known Wes to be gentle and kind. She would have described him as longsuffering during the years of marriage to her sister. Now, she was seeing another side of him that she didn't like. A terrible thought entered Natalie's mind that she didn't want to entertain. What if Niebring was right about Wes? What if he did kill Nicole? Could this be possible?

Before Natalie could say anything else, the door opened, and Niebring entered the room. He was followed by a middle-aged man that Natalie assumed was his partner.

"Ms. Guerra? I'm Detective Mendoza," the man said, extending his hand.

"It's nice to meet you," Natalie said. Mendoza sat down in the corner and started filing his nails. He didn't look up again as his partner took the lead.

"Mr. Tanner, would you please step outside? There is a chair in the hallway."

"Why can't I stay here?"

"Please step out into the hallway," Niebring said firmly.

Wes glared at him as he stood up and strolled toward the door. As soon as Wes had left the room, Niebring turned his attention back to Natalie. "Thank you for coming in, Ms. Guerra."

"I'm happy to do what I can to help find my sister," Natalie said.

"Ms. Guerra, did your sister ever confide in you that she was having any marital problems?" Niebring asked.

"Nicole talked to me on occasion about difficulties she was having with Wes."

"So they were having problems in their marriage?"

"They were having some problems, just like any other married couple."

"You had some problems in your own marriage, didn't you, Ms. Guerra?"

Natalie paused for a moment before answering. "Yes."

"How long have you been divorced from your husband?"

"Nine years."

"How many men have you dated since your divorce?"

"Mr. Niebring, why are you asking me this?"

"An attractive woman like you." Niebring hesitated, searching for the right words. "It's just kind of hard for me to understand why you're still single."

"Thank you, Detective. But this isn't about me, is it?"

Natalie shifted nervously in her chair, crossing her right leg over her left, and then lacing her fingers around the front of her right kneecap. She had been prepared to answer questions about Nicole's disappearance, and she had been ready to discuss her sister's relationship with Wes. She was not prepared to be questioned about her personal life.

There was a knock at the door. Mendoza rose to his feet and opened it. Natalie saw a woman quickly enter the room and approach her. She was a medium-set woman wearing a white uniformed shirt, pressed black Wrangler jeans, and black cowboy boots.

"You must be Nancy's daughter, Natalie," the woman said in a loud and cheery voice. "She was talking to me about how pretty you are. I'm Peggy Turnbow, chief of detectives. I'm so happy to meet you."

"Thank you," Natalie said, surprised.

"And someone else we know also spoke highly of you," Turnbow said.

"Who was that?"

"Mother Love, the psychic. She just raved about you."

"You met Mother Love?"

"Yes. We visited with her about your sister's disappearance. We did so at your mother's request. Mother Love did say that you were skeptical about her *powers*," Turnbow added.

The way the policewoman sarcastically put the emphasis on the word "powers" made Natalie laugh. She felt more comfortable with Turnbow than with the male detectives. Turnbow sat down in the chair that had been vacated by Mendoza. The paunchy detective mumbled something under his breath before excusing himself from the room.

Niebring acknowledged his captain with a cordial nod, and then turned back to Natalie. "How many men have you dated since your divorce?"

"If you must know, I'd say about six or seven."

"And did any of them become serious about you?"

Natalie looked over at Turnbow as she considered whether she would continue to answer these type of questions. Turnbow blinked her eyes slowly and nodded her head to assure her it was okay. Natalie decided to continue, wanting to cooperate with the police.

"A couple of the relationships were serious," Natalie said, after a brief pause.

"Why didn't you marry any of them?"

"Some of them I wasn't interested in marrying."

"They weren't marriage material?"

"Not for me."

"And the others?"

"They all wanted to have children."

"And you can't have children?"

"That's right."

"You wanted children?"

Natalie didn't answer, trying to maintain her composure.

"You wanted children," he repeated. This time, Niebring said it as more of a statement of fact than as a question. She nodded, unable to stop a tear from rolling down her cheek.

"That must have been really hard on you," Turnbow said, sounding sympathetic. She reached across Niebring's desk, grabbed a tissue, and handed it to Natalie. "I bet you love children." Natalie didn't answer as she wiped her eye.

"At least you have your sister's children in your life. Right?" Niebring interjected.

Natalie stared at the desk.

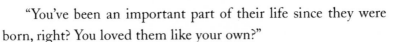

"You've been an important part of their life since they were born, right? You loved them like your own?"

"I never had any of my own, so how would I know?" Natalie said quietly, looking Niebring in the eye.

"Ever wish your sister's kids were your own?"

"No."

"I know you're close to your sister's husband. How long have you known Wes?"

"Almost twenty-three years."

"Since he married your sister?"

"I knew him before that."

"Where did you meet?"

"In college."

"Did you ever date?"

"Yes."

"How long?"

"Almost two years."

"Why did you stop dating him?"

"He started dating my sister."

"How did you feel about that?"

"It hurt for a while."

"Are you in love with Wes Tanner?"

"No."

"Ms. Guerra, did you kill your sister?"

"No!" Natalie turned to Turnbow, wondering if the chief of detectives was going to come to her aid and stop this assault. Turnbow placed her hand over Natalie's and gave her a reassuring smile. Natalie turned back to Niebring.

"Did you help Wes Tanner kill your sister?"

"No!" she said emphatically.

"Thank you for your time," Niebring said with a nod.

Natalie rose quietly from her chair without so much as a glance at either police officer and walked out of the interrogation room.

CHAPTER 25
May 2010

Natalie was having a difficult time seeing the highway through her tears, so she decided to pull off the road at the next exit. She pulled into the parking lot of an office building and parked in the corner. She was far enough away from others cars to hope for a few moments of solitude. The interrogation had evoked painful memories.

"They all wanted to have children."

"And you can't have children?"

"That's right."

"You wanted children? You wanted children," the detective had repeated. It was as though he was chiding her. Yes, she had wanted to have children. More than anything in life. But God hadn't permitted it. Because of this, her husband had left her. Other single men had also broken off the relationship when they learned she was barren.

If she were honest with herself, Natalie would admit that marrying any of these men would have been settling for something far less than her heart desired. What was missing was a spark to ignite the romance that every woman dreams about. Natalie didn't expect a Hollywood fairytale. But she did long for excitement in the relationship. She wanted to feel excitement and passion for the man she married, and she wanted him to feel it for her. This was the missing piece of the relationship puzzle.

Natalie had felt that excitement when she was with Wes. She had never stopped loving him, and her desire to be with him was her deepest and darkest secret. She knew she could be a good wife to Wes and a good mother to his children. Her relationship with Jordan was rocky, but Natalie was convinced she could be won over. After all, Jordan was still dealing with the trauma of losing her mother. She was nothing more than a confused teenager. A hurting and confused teenager crying out desperately for attention and love. Natalie could provide the love she so desperately needed.

Natalie could provide the love all of the Tanner children needed. Someday, all of them could think of her as a mother figure. Natalie closed her eyes and imagined herself sitting in the place of honor reserved for the mother when each child wed. She would be sitting in the front row, next to Wes. People wouldn't even remember that she wasn't their mother. She would be the one playing with their children. Her grandchildren.

As good as that sounded, there was something even better to dream about. In this scenario, she would be Wes Tanner's wife. He needed her. He had always needed her—even after he married Nicole. He had always confided in her. They had been destined for a happy life together until her own sister stole him away. Nicole had seduced him, offering up her body to him. Natalie was unwilling to do that. Wes had been content to wait until they were married, in spite of his male urges. But Nicole didn't make him wait. Nicole could have had any man she wanted. Why did she have to take her man from her? Natalie could only guess that her sister hated her for some reason. Nicole had relished her victory and loved to flaunt the prize under her sister's nose.

Natalie had to admit that there was a time when she had hated Nicole. But that time passed. The dream had died, but the pain still lingered through the years. She watched the couple become a family. She watched Nicole bearing the children that she wanted so desperately. Natalie could never understand why God had allowed it. Had she done something that God had needed to punish her for by cursing her with barrenness? Was her sin so bad that she had to endure so many years of pain?

The ring of her cell phone interrupted Natalie's gloomy ruminations. She quickly picked up the phone and glanced at the caller ID, certain she would see Wes's number. Instead, she saw her mother's number. This was not a good time to talk, so she let the call go to voice mail. Her mother immediately called back.

"Mother? What do you want?" Natalie snapped, surprised at the anger in her own voice. She felt like she was near her breaking point.

"Natalie." Her mother was crying. "Nicole is dead. Nicole is dead."

"What are you talking about?"

"Mother Love just came to see me. She said Nicole is dead. She's at the bottom of a lake somewhere. That man murdered her and dumped her body into a lake," Nancy said, her words punctuated with sobs. "Oh, Natalie. What am I going to do?"

"I'll tell you what you can do, Mother. You can stop believing some phony fruitcake who cares more about taking your money than helping us find Nicole."

Natalie pushed a button to disconnect the call and put her phone on silent. Feeling more lonely now than she had felt in a long time, Natalie longed for Wes. She had left him at the police station and hurried off. Perhaps, she had been worried about her suspicions at that moment. But the crazy thought that had passed through her mind an hour ago had been dismissed. All she wanted now was to move into Wes's arms and let him comfort her. Not prone to making impulsive decisions, Natalie made one. She picked up her cell phone and dialed Wes's phone number.

"Wes? Can you come over?"

Natalie was sitting on the couch in her living room staring at the blank screen of her television when the doorbell rang. Her Irish setter started barking furiously as he raced to the door. The dog immediately stopped barking, a sure sign that he knew the person standing outside. Natalie saw Wes through the window and opened the door.

"Just hold me," Natalie said after he was inside the house. Wes held her close for a moment before she pulled away and looked up at him. "I feel like I'm cracking up."

"I've felt that way for the past two months," Wes said quietly.

Wes continued to stare at her, and she thought he might kiss her. How would she respond? She knew the right thing would be to pull away immediately and create some physical and emotional distance between them. But she wasn't sure she would do that that tonight. Natalie could see this whole thing going in the wrong direction in just a few seconds. She quickly uttered a prayer, asking God to help her practice self-control. But suddenly, the expression on Wes's face changed.

"It's probably a good thing that you called me."

"Why?" Natalie asked, relieved and sorry for the change in his countenance.

"Otherwise, I would have gone home and wrung Jordan's neck."

"She's just confused."

"Confused? She's vindictive. She was mad at you for spilling the beans on her broken prom date. And Niebring somehow gets off on interrogating a fifteen-year-old kid."

"He's just doing his job."

"You're amazing," Wes said, pulling her back into his arms.

"What do you mean?"

"I've never heard you say a bad word about anyone."

"I have."

"No, you haven't. It's not in your DNA. That's what I love about you."

Love? Did he say love? Natalie pressed her body against his, and it felt good. Suddenly, there was a battle raging inside of her as two natures tore at her soul. The old nature seemed to speak to her flesh at that moment, whispering that it would be okay just this once. This was Wes. *You know him, and you love him. He loves you. It would be okay to take him to bed with you tonight.* There would be comfort—such comfort there with him. God would forgive her for a moment of weakness.

But as the old nature spoke into one ear, the new nature was speaking into the other ear. Natalie's new nature told her that it wasn't okay. He was another woman's husband. Wasn't the Bible full of warnings against adultery? Did Natalie really want to become an adulteress, incurring the displeasure and wrath of God? If Nicole was dead, it would still be fornication, which was just as wrong in the eyes of God. Could the passing pleasure of sin ever be worth grieving the Lord?

As Wes continued to stare at her, he seemed to sense the turmoil within her heart. She could see that the moment was passing now, and she would let it go. Somehow, by faith, she would trust that God would bring them together in his time—if it was His will.

"I'd better get home," Wes finally said.

Wes smoked a cigarette as he rode home in silence. Silence was something Wes was seldom willing to endure except when he found time to write. Silence was uncomfortable to him, which was one of the few things he had in common with Nicole. Why was that? Wes knew the reason was because silence inevitably led to introspection, and introspection led to depression. But this was a moment that compelled him to introspection. Moments ago, Natalie had pressed her body against

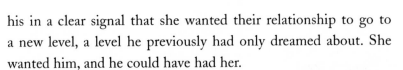

his in a clear signal that she wanted their relationship to go to a new level, a level he previously had only dreamed about. She wanted him, and he could have had her.

If Natalie was ready to make love to him, why had he left her? It certainly wasn't because of any lack of desire on his part. On the surface, the answer was simple. If he had taken advantage of a weak moment, she might have never forgiven him. Wes did not want to risk losing her love again, now that it appeared they might have a second chance. He could certainly wait until the time was right.

But there was more to this than Wes's fear of losing Natalie. It was as though he felt like he was about to violate the moral order of the universe by going to bed with her. Did this mean he was actually opening himself up to the possibility that Natalie and his grandfather might be right about their view of life and a moral order established by a sovereign God?

Wes's primary objection to Christianity and the whole idea of a loving God was how a good God could allow so much suffering to occur in the world. This was an important and personal question for Wes because he had endured more than his share of suffering in his four decades of life. Growing up without a father, Wes endured a difficult childhood with stepbrothers and an unstable mother. Widowed at twenty, Rachel Tanner Thompson married a drunk named Butch Thompson when Wes was five. The marriage lasted six long years, during which time his stepfather beat his mother and Wes repeatedly.

The happiest day of Wes's life came when his stepfather left his mother for another woman. Wes never understood why Rachel cried herself to sleep every night following his departure. They should have had an endless party to celebrate. After enduring years of suffering under the cruel Butch Thompson regime, bad times got worse. Rachel struggled to support her three children on a schoolteacher's salary, and they were frequently short of food, clothing, and even shelter when they were evicted from

their apartment. Wes's stepfather had been mean, but at least he provided the essentials for his family.

Along with the deprivation came degradation. Wes despised hearing the sounds of his mother's lovers through the thin walls of their two-bedroom apartment at night. Wes wanted to run away, but where could an adolescent boy go? It was only after the death of his mother that Wes was able to leave that nightmare behind and move to Texas with his grandfather. But it was too late. The damage had been done to Wes, and the boy knew it.

The damage was to his soul. This was why Wes refused to consider the idea of a God that was all-powerful and good. If there was a God, he might be good, but he wasn't powerful because he couldn't end the suffering of the human race. Even worse, if he was all-powerful, he wasn't good. Either way, the all-good, all-powerful God of the Bible couldn't exist. This was the argument put forth by Ivan Fyodorovich Karamazov, the articulate skeptic in *The Brothers Karamazov* by Fyodor Dostoyevsky, and Wes had been in complete agreement. But Roger argued there was a reason for a good God to allow the existence of evil. The reason was that evil and suffering exposed the depth of man's sinful nature and the need for the forgiveness of that sin. And God gave man the ability to choose to accept that forgiveness or continue with the burden of sin.

Wes didn't have a problem believing in sin. He saw it all around him and even detected it in his own being. But the idea that God wanted to forgive all sins of man and would do so through faith in his Son was difficult to comprehend. Wes recalled a lively discussion with his grandfather on the subject of Jesus Christ's death on the cross. Wes told Roger that Jesus would have convinced everyone that he was God if he had come down off the cross on Good Friday. Roger countered by saying that if Jesus had come down off the cross, he wouldn't have died for the sins of mankind and been able to offer the gift of salvation.

Roger had asked Wes many times to put his faith in Christ. Natalie had also talked to him about this, but Wes wasn't ready. How could he know it was true? How could he know God was real? Something was stirring inside Wes, and now for the first time he felt compelled to find an answer to these questions. Wes uttered a quick, silent prayer to God. If God did exist and really cared about him, Wes asked for a sign.

CHAPTER 26
May 2010

Wes walked in the front door shortly after 7 p.m. and was greeted first by his son. Sounding indignant, Monty informed his father that he was starving to death and he held his father responsible for this atrocity. He had eaten the last box of crackers an hour ago.

"I forgot to take the casserole out of the freezer." Wes looked down at the floor, shaking his head as he retreated into the study, where he had hoped to hide out for the remainder of the evening. "I guess I can make a burger run."

Monty's countenance improved suddenly. "Great."

Wes knew the last thing he needed to do was spend money on fast food, but he doubted his son would tolerate the wait while he tried to cook dinner. Nor did Wes want to spend his time doing that. He was eager to hole up in the study and write for a few hours. He hoped to focus on his characters' problems for the evening, forgetting his own.

"Hi, Daddy."

Wes looked up and smiled at Summer. Jordan was standing right behind her.

"Did I hear someone say something about food?" Jordan asked.

Wes ignored her and embraced Summer, who had run into his arms.

"I'll bet you're hungry," Wes said in his youngest daughter's ear.

"Yes, I am."

"I'm hungry, too," Jordan said quietly, looking for him to acknowledge her.

Wes couldn't bear to look at Jordan without becoming angry again. He had barely spoken to her since the previous day when she had gone to the detectives with her accusations about Natalie. Finding it difficult to forgive her, he was gaining a measure of satisfaction from hurting her now with his indifference.

"Dad?" Wes was moving toward the car when he heard Jordan's voice behind. He didn't turn around but kept walking away. "Can I ride with you?"

"I'd rather be by myself right now."

"Dad?"

"What do you want?" Wes turned around and glared at her.

"Why are you so mad at me?"

"What do you think?"

"Because I talked to the detectives?"

"It's not that you talked to the detectives," Wes said tersely. "If you really had something to tell them, we could have talked to them together. But you went behind my back and told them something that did absolutely nothing to help their investigation. And it harmed someone I care deeply about."

"Aunt Natalie?"

"Those detectives tore her apart."

"They did?" Jordan said, looking down at her feet.

"Did you really think your aunt Natalie could have killed your mother?"

"No."

"What if they charge her with murder?"

"You really think they're going to charge her with Mom's murder?"

"I don't know what they're going to do."

"I'm sorry," Jordan said softly, close to tears.

"Sorry doesn't fix it."

"Dad?" Jordan was still looking at him. Her lower lip had begun to tremble. "Do you think they might charge *you* with murder?"

Wes shrugged, opening the car door. "Who knows?"

"What about that man that came on to Mom at the house? He threatened her. Why don't they charge him with murder?"

"Because he's in Mexico."

"Why don't they bring him back?" Jordan started crying. "Why are they letting him get away with it?

"I don't know. You'll have to ask your friend, Detective Niebring."

"He's not my friend," Jordan said through her tears.

Wes left Jordan standing in the driveway, and he glanced at her in his rearview mirror as he drove down the street. She was still crying, and Wes almost turned around and went back to try and comfort her. But he decided she needed some time to think about what she had done to Natalie.

When Wes got back with the food, Monty and Summer were waiting by the door. They eagerly dug into their dinner, but Jordan remained upstairs. After the three of them had eaten, Wes went into the study and booted up his computer. He thought about checking on Jordan, but he dismissed the idea.

It was almost 2:00 a.m., and Wes sat on his back porch smoking the last cigarette in his last pack. He was too upset by the events of the evening to contemplate going to bed. Maybe he'd make a quick run to the convenience store to buy another carton. Out of work and needing to cut expenses, Wes knew it made sense to quit smoking. After all, wasn't he courting cancer with every puff? But he couldn't consider putting up the cigarettes right now.

Life was way too stressful. On his way to the convenience store, Wes decided to get back in touch with Ezra Goldstein and see if he would be willing to track down Raul Gonzalez in Mexico and return him to police custody in the United States. If the bounty hunter did the police's work for them, perhaps Gonzalez would be charged, and the police would stop harassing Wes and Natalie. He would call Goldstein tomorrow.

When Wes came through the front door, Duncan raised his head off the carpet. After a few flops of his tail, he closed his eyes again. The dog waited dutifully by the door every time his master went outside. Wes patted the dog's head and then went into the study to boot up his computer. He'd spend some time writing, and then he'd be ready to fall asleep.

Wes had just called up his manuscript when a loud thud above him seemed to shake the house. The last time Wes had heard this kind of a sound was when Monty and some friends decided to have a wrestling match upstairs. But Monty didn't have any friends over tonight, and Wes knew his son had gone to bed hours ago.

Hurrying out of the study, Wes turned on a light in the foyer and ran upstairs. He glanced in the direction of Monty's room, but he could see no light coming from under the door. Jordan's room also appeared to be dark. Wes was standing in the hallway, uncertain what to do, when Monty's door opened and his son came out into the hallway.

"Dad! It's Jordan. Come quick."

Wes followed Monty into his bedroom and then into the bathroom he shared with his sister. Jordan was lying on the floor next to the toilet where she had apparently collapsed.

"Jordan!"

She was lying on her side and appeared to be unconscious.

"Jordan!"

Wes knelt down next to her, his heart racing. He shook her by the shoulder, but she lay motionless.

"Jordan! Jordan! Jordan!"

"Dad? What's wrong with her?" Monty asked.

"I don't know. Jordan!" Wes shook her hard, trying desperately to arouse her.

"Dad!" Wes looked up at his son, who was holding a medicine bottle.

"Let me see it!" Wes screamed. He grabbed it away from Monty and read the label of the empty bottle. *Xanax.* It was the anti-anxiety drug that Nicole had been taking for several months before she disappeared. Wes didn't know much about Xanax, but the overdose appeared to have put Jordan in a coma. He ran to the phone on Jordan's dresser bureau and dialed 911, telling the dispatcher he needed an ambulance. Wes was trying to describe what happened to his daughter when Monty rushed into the bedroom.

"Dad, I don't think she's breathing."

"Oh, my God."

Wes raced back into the bathroom and dropped to his knees beside her. When his children were younger, he had thought at times about learning cardiopulmonary resuscitation. He had heard the stories about how CPR saved a child's life by restoring breathing and circulation until emergency help arrived. Wes had missed his chance. *God, I'll do anything,* Wes prayed silently as he gathered Jordan into his arms. *What kind of a bargain can we strike? Please spare my daughter! Please don't let her die,* he prayed.

What happened next was difficult for Wes to understand. Suddenly, feeling calm again, he found himself lifting up Jordan's head, tilting it back, and gently pinching her nose shut with his thumb and index finger. He then placed his mouth over Jordan's mouth, making a seal. Wes started breathing slowly, in and out, pausing in between each breath to let the air flow out. After several moments, Jordan's chest began to rise, and Wes could see she was breathing again.

Wes decided to carry Jordan downstairs where there would be more light, and where they would be closer to the ambulance personnel when they arrived. As he walked out of the bedroom, he passed Summer in the hallway.

"Daddy? What are you doing with Jordan?"

"She won't wake up," Wes said evenly. "Don't worry, Sunshine. Help is on its way."

"Why won't she wake up?" Summer asked as she followed her father downstairs. Wes lay Jordan's limp body on the couch. "Daddy? Why won't she wake up?"

"She took a bunch of pills," Monty said as he followed them downstairs.

"Why did she take a bunch of pills?"

"Shut up, Summer!" Monty snapped. The tone of his voice startled Wes.

"It's okay, Summer," Wes said, trying to sound calm. How long would it take for the ambulance to arrive? *Oh, God. Oh, God. Oh, God*, Wes kept repeating to himself. *Please, don't let her die.*

"Jordan!" Wes shook her arm. *Please! Just open your eyes.*

"Daddy, is Jordan going to be okay?" Summer asked anxiously.

"Just pray, Summer," Wes said in a quiet voice. "That's all we can do right now."

"Lord, please let Jordan be okay," Summer prayed out loud, and Wes closed his eyes.

Several minutes seemed like an eternity before Wes heard the sound of the approaching ambulance. A moment later, he heard the knock on the door. Before he could say a word, someone was trying to force the door open. Realizing he had locked up hours ago, Wes ran to the door. He found two paramedics on the other side staring at him curiously. "Sir? Did you call—"

"She's in here," Wes said, running back into the living room with the two men running close behind. "I think she took an overdose of Xanax."

"How many?"

"I don't know. The bottle was empty," Wes said as a paramedic knelt down beside her and checked her vitals and breath sounds.

"How long ago did you find her like this?"

"Just a few minutes ago. I heard a thud upstairs."

"What's her age?"

"Fifteen. She'll be sixteen next week."

"Does she have any allergies?"

"No."

"Does she take any medications?"

"No."

"Does she have any health history?"

"No. She's always been very healthy."

"How much does your daughter weigh?" he asked Wes.

"A hundred and ten pounds. Is she still breathing?" Wes asked anxiously.

"She's breathing but we need to get her to the hospital."

"Let's rock and roll," his partner said. The two men gently moved Jordan onto the mobile cot and headed for the door. Wes followed behind them, noticing his children standing at the bottom of the stairs.

"We're going to the hospital."

"When will you be back?" Monty asked.

"I don't know. Take care of your sister."

"I will."

"Daddy, is Jordan going to be okay?" Summer asked.

"Yes," Wes answered quickly, fearing that Jordan was listening to their conversation. He wanted to sound optimistic. "We need to pray."

"I've been praying," Summer said.

"Me, too," Monty said as Wes followed the paramedics out the door. Outside, the night was cool and still.

"Can I ride with you?" Wes asked.

"No," the first paramedic said firmly.

"Please!"

"Insurance won't let us," his partner explained. "You can follow us in your car. We're going to North Central."

Wes watched them load Jordan into the back of the ambulance. It looked to Wes like she was laboring to breathe, and her eyelids fluttered slightly as if she was trying to open them. The first paramedic was talking on his cell phone in the back of the vehicle as the second paramedic closed the inward-folding rear doors to the ambulance and climbed in on the driver's side door. The ambulance moved away slowly at first but quickly gathered speed as the siren sounded. The red emergency lights cast an eerie pall over the deserted street leading north away from the house.

As Wes had watched the paramedics work, he was assured in his own mind that Jordan was in good hands. She would soon be in the even more professional hands of the doctors at the hospital. But he knew there was no guarantee she would be alive tomorrow. There was nothing he could do now but keep praying to a God that he wasn't sure even existed. He hoped He did because God was all he had to turn to for help.

Just seconds ago he had been in a hurry to jump into his car and chase them to the hospital. But now he simply stood in the driveway and watched until the red tail lights of the ambulance disappeared as the vehicle rounded the corner. Wes's eyes were glazed with tears as he felt his gaze being pulled slowly toward the canopy of stars overhead. A brisk breeze had picked up from the south and bristled the hairs on the back of his neck. There, high in the north sky, stood the center stone in an elegant bracelet of stars. It was unwavering, brilliant, timeless, and strong. Wes fell to his knees in the middle of the driveway, hung his head, and began to cry.

CHAPTER 27

May 2010

Jordan had been drifting in and out of sleep. Sitting in a chair by his daughter's bed, Wes had been watching her for the past hour. There was no night and day in the ICU. Only a clock on the wall reminded Wes that it had been light outside for some time now. There were no windows to let sunlight in the quiet room illuminated only by the soft glow of the dimmed and softly humming fluorescent ceiling light directly above Jordan's bed.

Suddenly, Jordan opened her eyes and rolled her head slowly to the left. She was looking at the chrome intravenous stand laden with bags of IV fluid. Her eyes focused on the slow but steady drip of the liquid crawling along a length of sterile tubing and down into her arm.

"Hi, sweetheart." Wes touched her hand. His daughter turned her head, surprised but clearly pleased to see him. He took her hand and kissed her forehead.

"I'm glad to see you're awake," a cheery nurse said as she appeared from the other side of the curtain and smiled at Jordan. "I know your dad is, too. He's been by your bed ever since they brought you in here. We couldn't make him leave."

The curtain moved again, and a middle-aged man in a white coat walked over to Jordan's bed. Wes assumed this was another doctor. He had met several since Jordan had arrived at the emergency room. "Hi, Jordan. I'm Doctor Simpson," the physician said, checking her chart. "It looks like you took enough Xanax to insure you'll have no more anxious moments for the remainder of your life." Jordan didn't appear to be amused by the good-natured physician.

Simpson stepped up to her bedside, gently picked up her wrist, and began to check her pulse. The doctor had a nice manner, and he seemed to be more relational than the other doctors that had treated Jordan during the night. "Your lab values indicate you like to wash down your Xanax with some alcohol. I'm not sure I'd try to do that again anytime soon."

Jordan had been looking up at the ceiling, but now she rolled her head slowly toward him and nodded before closing her eyes.

"Jordan," Wes said, fearing she was slipping away again.

"It's okay," Simpson said. "She just needs to get some more sleep."

Wes followed Simpson out of the ICU. He wanted to talk with the doctor without Jordan being able to overhear their conversation. Simpson needed to check on a patient and then he would meet him back in the waiting room. Wes hadn't had a cigarette in several hours, so he went outside to feed his nicotine habit before returning to the waiting room to wait on Simpson. When he sagged into a chair, Wes was suddenly aware of how exhausted he felt. He was also emotionally spent.

Thinking back on the events of the day, Wes could only be thankful now that Jordan appeared to be out of danger. For a man that seldom prayed, Wes had amazed himself at his ability to pray fervently for hours while his daughter's life hung in the balance. Never before had life seemed so out of control. Wes would never be able to erase the picture from his mind of Jordan lying on the floor, her lips tinged blue from lack of oxygen. Wes was at a loss to explain how he had been able to administer CPR when he had never been trained in the art. It was as though something, or someone, had taken over at the moment he bent over her.

When they arrived at the emergency room, Jordan's stomach was emptied by gastric lavage, an IV was started, and oxygen was administered. In the next few hours, Jordan's condition stabilized. After Jordan was admitted to the hospital, Wes learned that his daughter could have died, or had brain damage if the rescue breathing hadn't worked. The attending physician in the ER had told Wes that if Jordan hadn't collapsed, and if he hadn't found her immediately, it probably would have been too late to save her. Now, she was on her way to making a complete recovery.

While her physical progress was encouraging, Wes knew Jordan's psychological and emotional state were more difficult to monitor. He had assumed that Simpson was a psychiatrist, and the doctor confirmed this when he returned to the waiting room and sat down in the chair next to him. Simpson noticed the Bible open in Wes's lap.

"Good book?"

"Pun intended?"

"Yeah." Simpson smiled. "Can I ask you a question?"

"Sure."

"I know your wife's disappearance has been on the news. I've seen and heard several stories. How has your daughter reacted to all of this?"

"I would have said she was handling it pretty well."

"Before she tried to kill herself?"

Wes nodded.

"That's a lot for a fifteen-year-old to handle."

"I know it is."

"Has she received any counseling?"

"I've taken all three of my children for counseling."

"Good. Do you know what might have triggered the suicide attempt?"

Wes proceeded to describe the events leading up to the moment when she was discovered on the floor of her bathroom. As Wes told the story, and Simpson peppered him with questions, feelings of guilt began to sink into his soul. He felt responsible for pushing Jordan to the point where she wanted to end her life.

"When did Jordan first mention that she thought her aunt might have murdered her mother?" Simpson asked him.

"The first time I heard about it was when she told the detective yesterday."

"How did you react?"

"I was pretty upset. I accused her of going behind my back and hurting someone who loves her very much."

"Her aunt?" Wes nodded. "But if she really suspected her aunt murdered her mother, she needed to tell someone about that."

"She admitted she didn't really believe that."

"Then why did she approach the detective?"

"She was mad at her aunt. She blamed her for spoiling her prom."

"How did her aunt spoil her prom?"

"Jordan had told a boy she'd go with him to the prom. Then another boy asked her. She planned to go with the second boy, but her aunt got wind of it. Natalie told her that wasn't the right thing to do and convinced me to make her go with the first boy."

"So you think the meeting with the detectives was just a vindictive act by your daughter?" Wes nodded. "Is Natalie your sister?"

"No. She's my wife's sister."

"And she's pretty close to your family?"

"Yes."

"So you were really upset at Jordan?"

"Yes."

"What did you say to her?"

"I told her Natalie might be charged with murder."

"And it was her fault?"

"I didn't say that."

"Did you imply it?"

"I probably did." Wes looked away, suddenly feeling guilty, even more guilty. "She apologized. I told her, 'Sorry doesn't fix it.'"

"Did she say anything else that you can remember?"

"She asked me if I thought police might charge me with the murder."

"What did you say?"

"I said it was possible. I guess that pushed her over the edge."

"Could be," Simpson said, standing up. "Fortunately, young people are quite resilient. I'll see her for the next few months on an outpatient basis. We'll see what we can do to restore you daughter to All-American teendom again."

Wes had a quizzical look on his face. "What's 'All-American teendom' mean?"

"Grouchy, pouty, hormone-imbalanced and obsessed with her make-up and every boy that comes along," Simpson said. He winked at Wes, shook his hand, and was gone.

CHAPTER 28

May 2010

"Do you believe in God?"

Wes was sitting in a chair next to Jordan's bed an hour after she had been moved from ICU to a private room. His daughter didn't have much to say to him on the day after attempting to take her own life. However, she seemed eager to listen to him talk about anything. So Wes had rambled on about news, sports, weather, and even mentioned that one of their neighbors had purchased a new car. Jordan's question came out of the blue.

Wes furrowed his brow. "Do I believe in God?"

"That was my question."

"You know I've never been very religious, but I sure have been praying for you."

"I guess I left you in a foxhole, huh?"

"Yeah. No atheists in here."

"Dad, if you don't believe in God, why were you praying?"

"I had nowhere else to turn. I actually made a deal with God last night."

"What kind of a deal?" Jordan looked interested.

"You know how people pray that if God will come through for them, they'll turn their life over to him? Well, I would have offered to do that, but I didn't want to be a hypocrite. So I told God if you pulled through, I'd check him out with an open mind."

"How are you going to do that?"

"I started reading the Bible."

"I didn't know you owned a Bible."

"I don't," Wes admitted. "Aunt Natalie loaned me one."

"She's got plenty; I'm sure. So what's your conclusion, so far?"

"I'm only in Exodus, but it's pretty interesting stuff. I'm not really sure how Jesus fits into all of this yet, but I'm going to keep reading."

"Pa-Pa told me about a good church in Stone Oak."

"Really? What church?"

"Stone Oak Bible Church. Would you take me?"

"You bet," Wes said. "I'm just very thankful right now that I've still got you around. I was so scared, Jordan. I thought I was going to lose you, too," Wes said the last words in a faltering voice. Jordan took his hand and squeezed it.

"I love you, Dad."

"I love you, too, sweetheart."

A knock on the open door interrupted them. Simpson was smiling at Jordan as he entered the room. "You look a lot better. Would you like to race me around the building?"

Jordan made eye contact with the doctor and smiled. Wes decided to take the cue.

"I'll be back later," he said, bending over to kiss Jordan on the forehead.

"Promise?" she asked.

"Promise," Wes said.

"**Y**ou need to get some sleep."

It was 10:00 p.m., and Wes was having a difficult time keeping his eyes open as he sat in the chair next to Natalie in the waiting room.

"What makes you think I need to get some sleep?"

"Because your eyes keep closing. It's ten." Natalie glanced at her watch. "I'd better go and relieve my mother."

Wes had almost forgotten that he had two other children at home with their grandmother. He had been at the hospital all day and had only spoken to Monty and Summer once on the phone. Natalie had gone by after work and fixed them dinner. Later, Nancy had stopped in to watch them so that Natalie could see Jordan before visiting hours ended.

"You don't have to do that. I'm going home," Wes said.

"I'll be glad to stay with Monty and Summer."

"I appreciate that, but I really need to go home and spend some time with them. Nat, can I ask you a question?" Wes asked her as she got up from the chair.

"Sure."

"Do you believe in miracles?"

"Yes. Why?"

"Because I think I experienced one."

"What do you mean?" Natalie's interest was piqued as she sat back down next to him.

"Jordan stopped breathing last night. I was kneeling beside her, feeling more helpless than I had ever felt. So, I did something crazy. I prayed."

"You prayed?"

"I prayed to a God I doubted even exists. And suddenly I knew exactly what to do. I performed CPR on my daughter."

"I didn't realize you knew CPR?"

"I don't." Wes shook his head. "It was like something came over me, and I knew exactly what to do. I lifted up her head, tilted it back, pinched her nose shut with my fingers, and started breathing into her mouth. In a few minutes, she was breathing again."

"That was God, Wes. *He* came over you."

Before they left, Wes and Natalie paid a visit to Jordan. After visiting with her for a few minutes, Wes was reassured she was in good hands. He promised to return the next morning.

"Bring me real food," Jordan begged. "The stuff they serve here is killing me."

"I have another question," Wes said after he had walked Natalie to her car.

"Shoot."

"Do you really believe what the Bible says?"

"Yes."

"So you believe in heaven and hell?"

"Yes."

"Do you think Nicole's in heaven right now?"

"I don't know." The expression on Natalie's face was somber.

"You don't know?"

"Wes, we're saved when we put our faith in Jesus Christ. I talked to Nicole about that on many occasions. But I don't know if she ever made that decision."

"What did she say about God?"

"She said she'd think about it later."

"I guess she thought she had plenty of time." Wes shook his head. "I was married to Nicole for almost twenty years, and we never talked about dying."

"It's not something most people think about when they're young."

"I wonder if she knew."

"Knew what?"

"She was going to die. Was she scared? Did she fight?"

"I don't know. Death is something we all have to face at some point."

"Are you afraid to die, Natalie?"

"No."

"You know you're going to heaven?"

Natalie nodded.

"How do you know? Heaven isn't a place you can visit on this side of the grave. You can't see it or hear it or touch it or smell it or taste it. How do you know it's a real place?"

"Have you ever been to Australia?" Natalie asked him.

"No."

"How do you know it exists?"

"I've read the accounts of others that have been there."

"Well, I've read the account of a man that's been to heaven and back."

"Who?"

"A man named John. His account is in the book of Revelation."

"I'll have to read about that," Wes said.

"Buckle your seatbelt. Revelation is quite a ride."

CHAPTER 29
May 2010

Wes was able to bring Jordan home three days after her suicide attempt. When they pulled into the driveway, both father and daughter were surprised to see the two live oak trees in the front yard decorated with yellow ribbons. A huge banner adorned the front of the house. It read: *Welcome Home, Jordan!* Before Wes could shut the car engine off, Natalie, Summer, Monty, Roger, and Nancy poured out of the house, cheering and applauding the arrival. Jordan was overwhelmed. "I don't believe this!"

"We love you, Jordan," Natalie said as she hugged her niece. Jordan burst into tears.

Inside, Wes saw more decorations, and he noticed the dining room table was set with the Tanners' best china. The family hardly ever used the formal dining room. It was as though royalty was joining them for the homecoming celebration.

"Wow," Jordan said as she looked at the table set for seven.

"We've killed the fatted calf tonight," Roger said.

"Killed the fatted calf?" Jordan looked puzzled.

"It's the parable of the prodigal son." Roger smiled. "Jesus told the story of a son that left home, vowing to never return. His father thought he was dead, but one day the son showed up, begging for forgiveness. The father ordered the servants to kill the fatted calf to make a feast because his son, once thought dead,

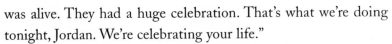

was alive. They had a huge celebration. That's what we're doing tonight, Jordan. We're celebrating your life."

"Daddy, I want to start going to church," Summer said.

"Dad said he'd take us to church," Jordan said. "Pa-pa knows a good church close by."

"That's right," Roger said. "I know the pastor. He's a good man."

Wes smiled at his family. "We're going to visit that church on Sunday morning."

"Oh no," Monty groaned. "Don't they have any church services at night?"

"They have an eleven o'clock service," Roger offered.

"Okay. I guess I can do eleven," Monty conceded.

Wes looked at the faces of his children in amazement. Summer was the only one of the three who had ever expressed an interest in attending church until recently. Now, all three wanted to go. What else could he do but take them? The strangest thing of all was that Wes found himself wanting to go. He hadn't desired to darken the door of any church before, considering it a waste of time. But something was happening to him. Something was changing inside, and he had a desire now to reach out to God.

It was an hour later when they all sat down together for dinner that Wes turned to Roger with a simple request.

"Would you offer the blessing?"

"My pleasure," Roger said.

With six heads bowed, he prayed. "Lord, we thank you for your great love. Thank you for bringing Jordan back home to us. Strengthen us for whatever lies ahead, and please bless this food. In Christ's name, amen."

Around the linen-lined dining table candles, set in sterling silver holders, flickered as the family conversed openly. Then suddenly the conversation died. Each person had succumbed to the innermost harboring of his own thought. Amid the softness of the eerily quiet room, it was almost as if one's thoughts could be heard aloud. Jordan had come home safely, but Nicole was gone. Although the subject had become taboo in recent days in the Tanner home, there remained an ever-present, gnawing realization of the loss.

For several minutes all that could be heard was the soft clinking of crystal and china. It was as if, of one mind, all were sending an inquiry heavenward to which no one expected an audible answer. The youngest member of the dinner party broke the silence.

"Daddy, may I be excused?" Summer asked. "I want to go to my room."

Natalie and Nancy were washing dishes in the kitchen when Wes entered, carrying his plate. He stared at Natalie's figure from behind and felt a desire to wrap his arms around her and kiss her neck. That would certainly shock her and her mother. Wes smiled at the thought.

"That was the best dinner I've had in forever," he said, setting the plates down on the counter. "You went all out."

"We can't take any credit for those steaks," Natalie said with a smile. "Your grandfather grilled those to perfection."

"I suspect you two had a hand in everything else."

"Natalie did most of the work," Nancy said.

"Nancy, I haven't heard you say anything about your psychic friend recently," Wes said. "What's up with Mother Love?"

"She went back to Georgia," Nancy said sadly. "She had a vision that she saw Nicole's face at the bottom of a lake. She was trying to give the detectives information on where to look, but they wouldn't work with her."

"I can't imagine why." Natalie shook her head. "I really thought the detectives would like all that crystal ball stuff."

"I know," Nancy said, oblivious to her daughter's sarcastic tone. "She really tried to help them, but they just wouldn't take her seriously."

"How much of your money did she leave with?" Natalie asked.

"Not that much. It would have been worth every penny if they had found Nicole. I'm sure—" Nancy stopped in mid-sentence as Jordan entered the room. The teenager was looking directly at Natalie.

"Aunt Natalie?"

"Yes, dear?"

"Why don't you hate me?"

"Why would I hate you?"

"Because of what I told the police."

"I could never hate you. You're my niece, and I love you very much," Natalie said as Jordan began to cry and ran into her aunt's arms.

"I'm sorry, Aunt Natalie."

"It's okay," Natalie said as she kissed her forehead.

"I need a cigarette."

Wes was sitting on the couch talking to Roger. Natalie had left, and the children, sated by their huge meal, had gone to bed. Wes had been trying to resist his urge to smoke, but his craving for another nicotine fix was simply too strong.

"You should quit smoking, Wes."

"I know, Grandpa. I want to quit, but I can't."

"You've quit before."

"I've quit a hundred times. And I always start again. Nicole would nag me into stopping, and then she'd beg me to start smoking again."

"Why?"

"Because I wasn't much fun to be around. I was irritable, impatience, restless, and I would always start putting on weight."

172

"I had a hard time quitting, too."

"You smoked?" Wes asked incredulously. "When?"

"I smoked for the better part of twenty years. Started smoking when I was a teenager. Smoked while I was in the army and for many years after I got out."

"When did you quit?"

"I quit fifty years ago."

"How much did you smoke?"

"Two, three, four packs a day. I lost count. Cigarettes were cheap back then. I don't know how you afford them anymore."

"I can't afford them, but I can't live without them. How did you quit?"

"I fasted and prayed," Roger said with those penetrating eyes looking directly at Wes. "This was before the surgeon general's report. People didn't really know how bad smoking was for your health, but I knew it wasn't good for me. I had tried many times, like you. Finally, I told God I really meant it, and he gave me the strength to do it."

"Cold turkey?"

"Cold turkey. It wasn't easy, but I was able to do it with God's help. Every time I got that terrible craving for a cigarette, I just prayed."

"Did you put on weight?"

"I lost weight. I told you, I fasted."

"You're stronger than me, Grandpa."

"No, I'm not. But I have the Holy Spirit living inside me. He did it. Not me."

"What does it mean to have the Holy Spirit living inside you?" Wes asked.

"When you accept Christ as your savior, he sends his spirit to live inside you. His spirit works in conjunction with your spirit to transform you into a new person."

"Just like that?"

"Salvation is instantaneous," Roger said, snapping his fingers. "Just like that. The moment you accept Christ. Romans 10:9 says, 'That if you confess with your mouth Jesus is Lord and believe in your heart that God raised him from the dead, you will be saved.' But the transformation process takes a lifetime."

CHAPTER 30
May 2010

Wes stared at the familiar sign hanging over the door. It read: *Ezra Goldstein. Confidential Investigations.* He read the Bible verse he had first seen what felt like a lifetime ago: "Behold, he shall come up like a lion from the swelling of Jordan against the habitation of the strong" (Jeremiah 49:19). Seven short weeks ago he had been here to interview the bounty hunter. Now, he was here to try and hire him to hunt down Raul Gonzalez in Mexico.

When Wes entered Goldstein's building, the bounty hunter was waiting for him, wearing a pair of Levi jeans, a faded black turtleneck sweater, and a pair of Tony Llama ostrich skin cowboy boots that appeared to be well broken in.

"Wes Tanner." Goldstein extended his hand. "You made me a famous man."

"Did you like the column?"

"Frankly, it was the best article ever written about me. Not that there has been that much written, but the best nevertheless. I've got two new cases because of you."

"Actually, that's why I'm here," Wes said quietly.

"So this is about business, not pleasure? I thought you'd come back around to try a glass of my cognac."

"If that's an offer, I accept."

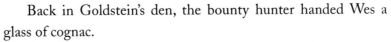

Back in Goldstein's den, the bounty hunter handed Wes a glass of cognac.

"Here's to peace in Jerusalem." Goldstein raised his glass. "So what business did you have to discuss with an old rabbi like me?"

"Nothing with the old rabbi, although I might ask you a few questions about the Old Testament at a later date. What I would like to discuss is a case."

"What kind of a case?"

"There's a man hiding in Mexico. I need a bounty hunter to capture him and bring him back to San Antonio."

"You would be referring to the man that recently left town after the story in the paper about him threatening your wife before her disappearance?"

"I forgot you read the newspaper." Wes laughed.

"And watch some television news, too. The case of Nicole Tanner has gained a great deal of notoriety in the past few weeks. The media have really come down on our local police for the way they've handled the case."

"Don't you agree?"

"I don't think you should blame them. If they had arrested the man, he would have posted bail and probably headed for Mexico."

"And the police probably would have let him go."

"But a bail bondsman would be offering me the job instead of you."

"Would you take the job?"

"Mexico is a treacherous place these days to hunt down fugitives. If I were to take this job—and I say if—I would need a fee commensurate with the degree of difficulty involved with the case."

"How much," Wes interrupted him.

"Twenty thousand. Is this man worth that much to you?"

"Yes and no."

"Yes, you'd pay my fee if you had it. And, no, you don't have it. Correct?"

"I'm sorry to waste your time."

Wes rose to his feet and extended his hand. Goldstein motioned for him to sit back down. "You haven't finished your drink, Wes. That cognac is far too good to waste." Wes eyed him skeptically, wondering what the bounty hunter had up his sleeve. "Something comes to my mind right now from the Torah. Exodus 23:3: 'Nor shall you be partial to a poor man in his dispute.'"

Thirty minutes later, after another glass of cognac, Wes and the bounty hunter had a deal. Goldstein would take the case, meaning that he would pursue Gonzalez and try to capture him. The price they agreed upon was $10,000 flat—all the money Wes had in his savings account. Goldstein offered no guarantees, but Wes felt confident in this man's abilities.

After Wes left, Goldstein sat in his chair and wondered if he had made a mistake in accepting the case that would take him into Mexico to pursue and try to capture the man named Raul Gonzalez. It was a hasty decision, but Goldstein had a habit of making decisions quickly. He trusted his gut feelings, and his gut told him that he needed to try and help this man. Whether the law had erred by allowing Gonzalez to escape south of the border or not was a moot point. Goldstein knew that no one in the San Antonio Police Department was going to expend much effort to bring him back, either. Justice had not been served, and it might not be served if Goldstein didn't take action.

On the other hand, to act would put Goldstein at risk. He knew that it would be no easy manner to travel to Mexico and apprehend Gonzalez. Then there was the matter of getting him back across the border. Goldstein wondered if he had bitten off more than he could chew. He could still back out of this case.

What he needed was some time to think and pray about his decision.

Letting his head fall back into the plush foam-padded headrest, he knew it was time for some quiet reflection. Often times, he had the inclination to quickly add two and two and come up with an answer other than four. Goldstein couldn't count all the times he had been wrong in this business. And it was always the same. To get something wrong was not so much something that you did, but someone whom you misread. For that reason, it was vital that he try to get a proper gauge on the intentions of the people with whom he would be dealing.

First, Goldstein must consider everything he knew about Wes Tanner. Tanner had openly admitted that he was now considered a suspect in his wife's disappearance. Goldstein was certain the police had their reasons for this, but the private investigator had to come to his own conclusion. Plenty of innocent men had been suspected—even convicted—of murder. On the other hand, a man like Wes Tanner might be smart enough to fool many people, including Goldstein. This was the matter that now occupied his mind.

More than twenty years of experience in the field of private investigations had convinced Goldstein that the party most often to be mistrusted was the hiring party, the client himself. Frequently, the client would be a woman, seeking some resolution to a romantic tryst of some sort.

"I think my husband is having an affair. I need to know for sure," the woman might say. "Can you find out for sure, and can you get pictures?" Goldstein would look knowingly at the woman and assure her that, yes, he could probably find out, and he could probably even produce for her some pictures. But, all the while, he would know that it was generally money that the woman was concerned about. In most cases, women already knew about the infidelity.

Truth was often an elusive commodity. No matter how hard Goldstein tried to reassure his clients that all information would be held in strict confidence, he could not get them to be completely truthful with him. They would withhold information, which would cause him to spend more time digging, and which in turn would cost his client thousands of extra dollars in fees at best. At worst, it put Goldstein in danger.

Goldstein thought of his conversation with Tanner. Had Mr. Wes Tanner told him everything? Likely, he had not. But what, if anything, had he left out? Tanner had admitted that the detectives assigned to the case suspected him of murdering his wife. Did they have it right? Was Tanner the killer? Goldstein's impression, based upon the interview of his client, was that Tanner probably didn't have it in him to kill another person. Another possibility was someone Tanner was involved with—a mistress—had killed Mrs. Tanner and that he was trying to cover it up to protect her. This was also a possibility, but Goldstein also doubted this was the case.

Goldstein's conclusion was that Tanner believed Gonzalez either killed his wife or had information that would be helpful in solving the crime. Tanner had specifically instructed Goldstein to bring the man back alive. If Tanner were guilty, what could possibly be gained by paying Goldstein to bring an innocent man back to the United States? If Gonzalez knew something that might implicate Tanner in his wife's murder, then it seemed logical that Tanner would simply have tried to hire someone to go and kill the man. But he hadn't. Tanner had said he wanted Gonzalez brought back alive. The logical conclusion was that Tanner was either very crafty, or he was innocent.

Goldstein picked up the telephone and dialed a number. Moments later, he had gleaned a few more facts from Rudy Mendoza, his contact within the detectives' division at SAPD. Goldstein had helped Mendoza and his partner, Tommy Niebring, break a tough murder case a couple of years ago, and the detective felt like he owed him one. Mendoza had reminded Goldstein that, of course, there was very little he could pass along to him. With that said, he did confirm that Nicole Tanner had disappeared and that the missing woman's sister, husband, and Mr. Gonzalez had all been questioned by detectives. Beyond that, Goldstein was told, the detective could tell him nothing. Goldstein had thanked Mendoza and assured him that was all the information he needed. He was simply checking his client's veracity. The facts, as presented to him by his client, were basically in line with the facts presented by the detective.

It would not be up to the private investigator to solve this case. He had simply been hired to capture this man without incident and bring him back to Texas alive. *Much easier said than done*, he thought to himself. If Goldstein decided to help Tanner by taking this case, he must formulate a plan that he would follow to the letter in his attempt to bring back Raul Gonzalez. This would a great challenge calling for great ingenuity. Goldstein would first need to find out where Gonzalez was most likely headed when he crossed the border. Armed with that information, he would leave San Antonio in pursuit. Once he was in Mexico, the P.I. would purchase an inexpensive car with Mexican plates and begin the long trek into the heart of Mexico.

There was other business to take care of first, and Goldstein had told Tanner that he would not be able to leave the country for several weeks. He had also warned Tanner that he could still change his mind about taking the case. He would do some preliminary investigating. Only when he had made a final decision and was ready to leave, would Tanner pay him the ten thousand dollars. Then the manhunt would begin in earnest.

CHAPTER 31
July 2010

"**D**ad, don't forget that we need to go and buy fireworks."

It was noon, and Monty was finally up and ready to eat some breakfast. Wes was frying some eggs on the stove and feeling rested and strong. It was July 4, and he had been out of work for several weeks. He had been looking for a job, but most of the searching had been done on the internet. The majority of his hours were spent writing and working around the house. It was amazing what several weeks of sleeping in could do for a forty-one-year-old man's body. It had been a relaxing summer for Wes, affording him the first opportunity to spend a significant amount of time with his children since Nicole's disappearance.

Media coverage had died down in the three months since Nicole had vanished from her office, but Wes felt certain that would change when her body was finally found. If it was ever found. Niebring had told Wes that it was just a matter of time before the body showed up. Bodies always "floated to the surface, sooner or later," the detective told him. Then they would ramp up the investigation again, and someone would be charged with murder, Wes had been told.

With possible murder charges hanging over his head, Wes had experienced more than a few anxious thoughts. What if he was convicted? Wes had heard stories about what life was like in a maximum-security prison. Based on those stories, he thought the death penalty might be a better option. In the meantime, all he could do was go on with his life. He would work on his novel for several hours each day, do chores, and read his Bible. Taking Natalie's suggestion, Wes had read the book of Revelation and then the Gospel of John. Before he finished John, he gave his life to Jesus Christ. It was much simpler than Wes had imagined. One day, he just bowed his head and invited Jesus to come into his heart.

Wes had told Natalie he would examine Christianity with the eye of a skeptic. After all, he was a journalist, and a true journalist went looking for the facts. He would take nothing by faith. Natalie said it was an excellent idea and even gave him a book to read by another skeptical journalist named Lee Strobel, a former investigative reporter for the *Chicago Tribune*. When Wes started reading the book, he couldn't put it down. That book, along with the Gospel of John, convinced Wes the claims of Christ were true. He was the Son of God, and he rose from the dead to pay the price for mankind's sins.

Wes's conversion and newfound faith was the only bright spot he could point to since Nicole disappeared. His children were not doing well. By the end of the school year, Jordan had again attracted the attention of John Thompson, the boy she had hoped would take her to the prom. Wes had agreed to allow his daughter to start dating when she turned sixteen, and she was soon seeing Thompson on a steady basis. Wes had been led to believe that Thompson was okay. He was polite and said he attended church. Then Wes caught them under the covers in Jordan's bed one afternoon.

After the incident in the bedroom, Wes forbid Jordan to see Thompson. She was furious. Two weeks later, Wes became suspicious and followed her one night after she told her father she was going to meet a girlfriend. Jordan drove straight to

Thompson's house. When Wes knocked on the door, he found out they were alone. Wes grounded Jordan for a month and took her cell phone away. Two weeks into the grounding, Wes was certain his relationship with his daughter was irreparably damaged.

Jordan hardly spoke to Wes until Natalie sat down and had a heartfelt talk with her niece. After that, things got better, and Wes ended her grounding a week early to coincide with a planned family vacation. Wes had taken her out to dinner the night before they left for the coast, and they had had a wonderful time and talked openly about everything. But Wes knew there would be other obstacles ahead for them. Jordan was too much like her mother for Wes to expect anything less than a challenging next few years.

Jordan wasn't the only Tanner child having problems. Less than a week after school ended, Monty was caught smoking pot with his friends. Always a jock, Monty had lost interest in sports that summer and spent much of his free time skateboarding. Wes didn't like the new crowd his son was hanging out with, and he told him this but to no avail. Wes had always liked Monty's friends before the skateboarding crowd entered the picture. These kids seemed to be enamored with the punk scene, and the marijuana incident was more evidence that Monty was headed in the wrong direction. Wes felt helpless. His son barely listened to him anymore.

While the problems with Jordan and Monty were more obvious, Wes also had Summer to worry about. His youngest daughter had always done well in school until Nicole vanished. Her grades began slipping before the school year ended. The teacher said she wouldn't pay attention in class, and Wes found it difficult to motivate her to do better. A counselor recommended having her tested for attention deficit disorder, but the test results were not conclusive. In the end, Wes knew that losing her mother had a profound effect on his younger daughter.

But the worst news of all came a week earlier. Roger had summoned Wes to his home in Kerrville. Wes knew something was wrong, but his grandfather wouldn't tell him the news over the phone. Roger asked Wes to bring the children. When they arrived, Roger had a big meal prepared. His grandfather was a wonderful cook, and everyone was in a good mood until Roger broke the news.

"I've been diagnosed with lung cancer."

There was stunned silence, followed by a barrage of questions from the children. Wes, for his part, had little to say. He broke down and wept uncontrollably for several minutes. Roger was eighty-six years old, and Wes knew he wasn't going to live forever. But he never expected anything like this. He was certain his grandfather would live to be a hundred and that he had many more years to enjoy with him. But God had other plans.

In the midst of all of these challenges, Wes found himself turning to God for strength on a continual basis. Wes read his Bible and prayed every day. He began to experience a peace that he had never known before. Natalie was his biggest cheerleader, encouraging him to dig deeply into God's Word. They attended church every Sunday at Stone Oak Bible Church. Ernesto Garcia, the senior pastor, invited Wes to meet privately with him and began to disciple him.

Reverend Garcia was the kind of man Wes wanted to become. A year older than Wes, he had been widowed when his two children were in preschool. He had raised them himself while also caring for a growing congregation. The minister had a deep love for Jesus Christ and a deep love for people.

It took every ounce of Wes's newly discovered strength to show restraint in his relationship with Natalie. He was still in love with her, and he believed she felt the same way. This was in spite of the fact that neither of them had ever said a word about their feelings. There seemed to be an unspoken understanding between them that their relationship could not progress until there was closure on Nicole's fate.

In the meantime, Wes had turned his focus to his faith and his children. The four of them had just returned the previous day from a four-day trip to Port Aransas. They had played on the beach for hours and stayed up late playing cards and other games. Tonight, they were going to Kerrville to shoot off fireworks with Roger. Tomorrow, he was taking them to play miniature golf. Wes knew he had to watch his pennies since he was still unemployed, but he also wasn't going to stop living. He did have eight months of severance. But in the end, he trusted that God would provide for them.

When Wes had returned from the beach, he had a message on his answering machine from Ezra Goldstein. Goldstein said he wanted to come by and discuss the case. This was an answer to prayer. Wes called him back, and they were scheduled to meet that afternoon.

As was his custom, Ezra Goldstein arrived for his meeting with Wes a few minutes early. He sat in his car until it was time and rang the doorbell at 1:00 p.m. sharp. Goldstein heard a dog barking inside the house, and then Wes opened the door. He looked tanned, fit, and more relaxed than the last time they had seen each other.

"So when are you leaving for Mexico?"

"If I go to Mexico, I'll be leaving on Monday morning," Goldstein told him as he sat at the breakfast table and sipped a glass of iced tea.

"You haven't decided if you're going?"

"Not yet."

"I don't understand. You told me six weeks ago you would take my case."

"I told you I was inclined to take the case, but I had to give it some serious thought and prayer. Mexico is becoming a more dangerous place each day. This is not something I'm prepared to rush into."

"I can understand that," Wes said with a somber nod.

"I've spent the past few weeks conducting my own investigation into the case. I wanted to be sure I wasn't missing any important facts. I've questioned all of the people at your wife's real estate office, friends, and family members."

"What's your conclusion?"

"I feel like I'm missing a piece of the puzzle."

"I think that piece of the puzzle is Raul Gonzalez."

"May I ask you a question, Mr. Tanner?"

"Go ahead."

"Why do you think Raul Gonzalez murdered your wife?"

"The threat he made. You know about the voice mail?"

"Yes, but I'm asking you what his motive might have been?"

"I don't know. I hope to find out when he's finally brought to justice."

"Does it seem like a bit of a stretch that he would murder your wife just for turning him in to the police? He wasn't even charged with a crime."

"I don't know the answer to that, either." Wes shook his head. "Maybe, he went to see her that night to talk with her, and things got out of hand. Maybe, he's crazy. Believe me, Mr. Goldstein, I want to know the truth about what happened that night. That's why I hope you can find Raul Gonzalez and bring him back."

"Are you prepared to pay me up front?"

"Ten thousand dollars. I can write you a check right now."

"Then I'll leave Monday. Mr. Tanner, you understand this will be no easy task."

"I understand that, but I will be praying for your success."

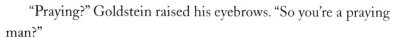

"Praying?" Goldstein raised his eyebrows. "So you're a praying man?"

"I have been for the past month."

"You weren't before?"

"No."

"What changed?"

"I accepted Jesus Christ as my personal Savior."

"So you're a new Christian?"

"That's right."

"Well, we share one thing in common."

"We do?" Wes looked at him curiously.

"We read our Bible and we pray. We pray to the same God, Mr. Tanner."

"There's only one."

CHAPTER 32

September 2010

Death had been on Ezra Goldstein's mind all day.

The private investigator's mind had been banging back and forth like a pendulum, swinging between the dualities of darkness and light, evil and good, death and renewal, as he drove his truck slowly down the dirt street in Mexico City. Nearing his destination, Goldstein was cognizant that fear was stalking him now just as he stalked another. Goldstein knew about fear. Some people were excited by fear and liked to play with it. They savored the taste and smell as it teased their senses and finally intoxicated them with its power. Others were destroyed by its poison—eaten away like a senseless, insidious acid seeping into their brains.

Goldstein had experienced both sides of fear, savoring and abhorring it. As he grew older, though, it was mostly the latter. Goldstein didn't always understand what made him afraid. His commanding officer in the Israeli army had once told him that fear conditioning could result from a single episode, because that was the way the human brain operated. It was a mechanism to prevent you from returning to a dangerous situation. A sound, a smell, or a movement could trigger a memory that stimulated fear. Goldstein knew that something had stimulated fear inside him, but he wasn't sure exactly what had done it.

Feeling this fear and a heavy spirit, Goldstein spent much of the day in the Museum of Anthropology. He found peace in the solitude of those hours, wandering through the rooms of the famous museum. Built in the early 1960s, it housed extensive collections of pre-Columbian artifacts collected from sites throughout Mexico. Goldstein was fascinated by the history of the pre-Columbian period and the cultures in that era before Christopher Columbus and the European influence. These great indigenous civilizations, such as the Aztecs, Mayas, and Incas, had left giant footprints on the New World before they were conquered and then absorbed by the Europeans. It reminded him of the impermanence of life. "Generations come and generations go," King Solomon wrote. "Meaningless! Meaningless! Utterly meaningless!"

Goldstein spent a considerable amount of time in prayer, asking for relief from the heavy spirit inside him. He couldn't help but wonder if God was trying to tell him something. Was coming to Mexico a huge mistake? The private investigator wrestled with this question in his prayers for a few hours but found no answer.

By late afternoon, Goldstein was ready to go after Raul Gonzalez. Locating Gonzalez had been a long and tedious process. After much work on the other side of the border, Goldstein had finally crossed into Mexico. He had been in Mexico City for more than two weeks, and he had located the home of the man he sought. It was a fortress. Goldstein had visited under the cover of darkness for a close look one night. He realized there was no way that he could get past the guard gate or scale the fence. Even if he was able to get on the grounds, there were too many armed people milling around for him to nab this man. Goldstein would have to apprehend him away from his home.

He had decided to try to capture Gonzalez near his office. The private investigator rented a "perch" across the street from the beer distribution company where Gonzalez worked. A "perch," in P.I. jargon, was simply a rented house, apartment, or a motel room, from which the P.I. could comfortably keep an eye on his quarry from the relative obscurity of his rented quarters. Goldstein would rent such a place for a week or more, giving him time to observe his prey's daily movements.

In this case, Goldstein's perch was a room on the third floor of a boarding house. The location was perfect. He had feared that he might not be able to find a room on one of the upper floors. Years ago, he had learned from army intelligence people that a man at ground level was much more likely to be spotted than one who conducted surveillance from a high perch. "A badger sees a badger much more quickly than he sees an elephant," an old, gray-haired colonel had once told him.

From his boarding house perch, Goldstein was able to watch Gonzalez and familiarize himself with the man's routine for a solid week. Above all, Goldstein was meticulous. On a table beside his chair, he kept a notepad and pen. Each time Gonzalez was seen coming or going, Goldstein was careful to make a note of the exact time of each movement. He also noted the type of vehicle that Gonzalez was in each time he left or returned to his office.

Before setting up his surveillance, Goldstein had pulled the blinds almost closed over the big picture window that looked out over the street. He left enough of an opening to give him good scanning range with his binoculars. Goldstein had also brought with him his 35-mm Nikon camera with motorized advance for rapid shooting. In the lens receptacle was the pride and joy of his photo equipment—a slow F-stop 400-800 mm telescoping lens. If Goldstein spotted anything out of the ordinary he would snap a few shots of it. He had already snapped photos of the license plates of all incoming vehicles in which Gonzalez had been a passenger, including a couple of the delivery trucks. Later, he took the film to a photo developing shop far removed from the area in order to lower the risk of someone in the shop knowing this man and tipping him off.

Goldstein had vowed to quit smoking a thousand times, but he was resigned to the fact that while on this job and during the ultra-boring hours of daylong surveillance, he would smoke. Besides, it was in the tax-free zones of Mexico that Goldstein had been able to find the pungent French Galoises cigarettes, for which he had developed a taste during his time in the army. He reached over to the table, lit one, and inhaled deeply.

While Goldstein did indulge himself with cigarettes, there was one thing he would not do—at least not until after his working day had ended. He would not drink anything alcoholic. Earlier, he had ordered a large decanter of fresh papaya juice and a bucket of ice from the front desk. He took a long sip of the juice, set his cigarette in the ashtray and reached for his binoculars.

There was no sign of Gonzalez. Goldstein found his mind wandering back to his favorite western. *Winchester 73* was an old Jimmy Stewart movie made before the P.I. was even born. The story was about a man who won a "one-in-a-thousand" Winchester rifle in a shooting contest, only to have it stolen. While Stewart's character pursued the rifle, it kept changing hands, touching a number of lives.

Goldstein thought about how many years he had spent pursuing men like the Stewart character had done. The climax of "Winchester 73" had been a shootout on a rocky mountain precipice. The P.I. had been forced to shoot it out a few times with his quarry. The day might come when the man he hunted was faster, or shot straighter. That would be Goldstein's last day.

Goldstein saw someone leaving the building across the street. He reached again for his binoculars for a closer look. It was Gonzalez leaving for lunch. The P.I. picked up his pen and notebook and made an entry. He had observed that Gonzalez's daily routine was to arrive at the office about 9:00 a.m., take a two-hour lunch break, beginning about 1:00 p.m., and then leave the office about 6:00 p.m. each day.

When Gonzalez left the office, he typically accompanied his brother and several other coworkers to the cantina across the street. The cantina, a staple of Mexican culture, was the place where men often joined together in a daily ritual of drinking several tequilas and singing rancheras, the traditional music of their land. After getting their quota of spirits, the men were ready to head home to their families. Gonzalez's departure from the cantina typically occurred sometime after eight. Frequently, he lingered in front of the bar to visit for a few minutes before crossing the street. Then he would pass through an alley, lined with white stucco walls, and enter the company parking lot, located behind the office building.

Unfortunately, Gonzalez was almost always with his brother. This posed a problem since Goldstein knew he needed to have his target isolated in order to effect the capture. The Gonzalez brothers rode to work in the same car and also rode home together at night. Goldstein determined that Raul Gonzalez's brother must, somehow, be detained, or distracted. This became an essential part of the plan that began to take shape in Goldstein's mind.

Goldstein had worked in Mexico City on other occasions and had a small network of people he knew and trusted. One was a taxi driver who was always eager to earn extra money. Goldstein also knew a young couple willing to take a risk for a relatively small price. The young woman, named Maria, was the daughter of a friend Goldstein had known for more than twenty years. Maria and her husband, Carlos, both in their twenties, had three children and always struggled to make ends meet. When Goldstein met Maria and Carlos for dinner, he was introduced to Carlos' sister, Anita. After a short discussion, Anita also expressed a willingness to play a role in Goldstein's plan. Sizing her up, the private investigator felt like she would perform more than adequately. With preparations complete, Goldstein was ready to attempt the capture of Raul Gonzalez.

CHAPTER 33
September 2010

Wes quickly typed the e-mail and then hit the send button on his computer an instant before he realized he had forgotten to attach the document. "Shoot!"

"What's wrong, Dad?" Jordan asked from the doorway. Dressed in her cheerleading outfit, she was on her way out the door. Tonight was the home opener for Ronald Reagan High School's football team, and Wes was eager to e-mail his completed screenplay to his agent and get to the stadium early and find a good seat for the game.

Wes had finished his novel two months earlier. He had been surprised at how easy it was to write with so much free time. The novel was still being shopped around with several publishers. Wes's new agent had been optimistic when they started marketing it, but he wasn't as optimistic now after three rejections. Two publishers had liked the story but didn't want to take a chance on a new writer. The other one had just passed on it. Wes had been down this road before with other novels he had written, and it always led to discouragement. He had been dealing with this kind of rejection for twenty years.

The feedback that Wes had received through the years led him to believe that he had the ability to create a compelling story. He had been told that his storylines and plot twists were excellent. Many of his characters were memorable. But something was

193

missing. Wes had to conclude that the problem was the writing itself. He had always marveled at great writers like Stephen King and their ability to communicate excitement and stir emotions. Wes was no Stephen King. He knew he was a better writer today than he was in the 1990s, but the market was tougher. He often doubted he would ever get his break. But he kept on trying, hoping, and now even praying.

Wes had signed with his seventh agent in July. Most of the previous agents that had represented him were based in New York. Wes had always heard that a New York agent had the best chance of selling a novel because New York was still the capital city of publishing. The agents could meet with the big-time editors at cocktail parties and build those important relationships. However, no one had ever sold a thing for him from New York, so Wes decided to try an agent from Los Angeles this time. The agent loved the story, based on Wes's own life, and he pitched it to a movie producer. Wes was more than a little surprised when the agent called him a month ago with the news that the producer wanted to see a screenplay adaptation of the novel.

"I don't know anything about writing a screenplay," Wes told him.

"Learn."

Wes bought a couple of "how to" books and a software program. Without wasting much time, he started working on the screenplay. To his amazement, it seemed much easier to write a script than a novel. The long, descriptive passages needed for a novel were absent from a screenplay. Seven days after he wrote the words fade in on the first page, he was writing the words fade out on the last page. It took Wes months to write a novel, but it only took him a week to adapt it. He e-mailed the screenplay to his agent. One day later, he received a curt, two-line e-mail: "It's too long. Cut it down."

"Too long?" Wes wrote back. "It's only 150 pages." Wes's novel was 400 pages. He had cut out all of the subplots and focused on the main storyline, deleting everything except what he felt was essential to the story.

"It can't be more than 120 pages," the agent e-mailed back. "Cut thirty pages. No one will look at anything over 120." Wes went through the screenplay, line-by-line, and he cut more scenes. Many were scenes he loved. He felt a pang each time he was forced to delete something that was close to his heart. But he now had a 120-page screenplay to send to his agent. Wes was sending it without much hope, but what did he have to lose?

Security floodlights shone above the garages of a few houses on the block, but most of the homes were darkened in quiet slumber as Natalie sat quietly on the front porch. Iron-green, Boston-style street lights dotted the avenue, casting soft halos of gold into the darkness. Natalie breathed in the cool night air and held it in her lungs for a moment before exhaling.

Natalie was aware of the sadness in her heart. The busy activities of the day could crowd the sadness out for a time, but it always managed to seep back in at night. It seemed the sadness had taken up a permanent residence there since Natalie had stopped spending time alone with Wes three months ago. She had been painfully honest with him. If they continued to spend time alone, they would eventually give in to sexual temptation. Natalie knew that once it started, it would be difficult to ever stop. She saw him now only when she stopped by to see the children and never alone.

Wes was a new Christian now, and she would do anything to encourage his spiritual growth. She attended church with him every week. The last thing in the world she wanted was to be a stumbling block for him. If God wanted to bring them together, it would happen. If not, she needed to be able to go on with her own life. Matters of the heart had always been difficult for Natalie to understand. Comfortable with mathematics, where there was always one right answer, Natalie was perplexed by an equation like this one that simply could not be solved.

There was a Bible sitting on the table next to her, and Natalie picked it up. She was searching for answers tonight, trying to understand why the sadness wouldn't depart after such a long time. How long would her own heart be held hostage by a man with whom she could not share life? Why couldn't she just forget about Wes Tanner? Perhaps it was because he was now the epitome of what she was looking for in a husband. Wes was a Christian and growing in his faith every day. He was devoted to his children, and he had even managed to quit smoking after more than twenty years.

Natalie began turning the pages in her Bible. She stopped in the fourth chapter of Ecclesiastes. "Two are better than one, because they have a good return for their work: If one falls down, his friend can help him up. Also, if two lie down together, they will keep warm. But how can one keep warm alone? Though one may be overpowered, two can defend themselves. A cord of three strands is not quickly broken."

Bowing her head, Natalie offered up a silent prayer to God. She asked the Lord to make it possible for her to be with Wes or to free her of the pain. She thought about all of the times in the past month that she had wanted to pick up the phone and call him. Natalie wanted to be alone with him again, to touch him and be held by him. Sighing deeply, she went back into the house and started getting ready for bed.

CHAPTER 34
September 2010

Shortly before 5:30 p.m., Ezra Goldstein was on the street in front of the cantina. Wearing sandals, a white shirt, a leather vest, dark trousers, a brightly striped serape and a sombrero, the private investigator looked like a laborer. His eyes roamed the street idly in the working-class neighborhood, where he blended into the crowd. Goldstein liked Mexico City because he had always found it easy to sink into the background in the bustling city of thirty million. People minded their own business in this city where drug dealings, kidnappings, and other crimes were all too common. The war against poverty resulted in the greatest battles fought but never won.

At 5:45 p.m., a taxi pulled up and Anita exited. She passed Goldstein without speaking and entered the cantina. Goldstein climbed into the cab and departed. Ten minutes later, he received a call on his cell phone from Anita. Gonzalez and his brother, with six other men, had entered the cantina and ordered drinks.

As the cab sped on eastward through the city, Goldstein lit a cigarette and then called Maria. She was told to take up her position on the park bench across from the cantina. Carlos was nearby. They would stay in their places until Gonzalez left the facility and headed for his car. At that time, Goldstein would be notified.

The phone call came at 8:15 p.m. Carlos was calling to say that Gonzalez had left the cantina alone. Anita, the decoy, had done her job in detaining the brother. She had probably enticed him to buy her a drink with a payoff promised later. Maria, the pigeon, crossed the street and stood near the entrance to the alley. She wore a stylish black evening dress, with a modest neckline and a hemline resting just a couple of inches above the knee. Maria also wore a string of brilliant white pearls around her neck. Her hair was dark, long, and wavy. Her shoes were of fine black Italian leather, and a black Gucci leather handbag hung loosely from her left shoulder.

Gonzalez, who had stopped in front of the cantina to light a cigarette, saw Maria. He watched her as she lingered at the entrance to the alley. Walking briskly from across the street and out of view from Maria, Carlos began his approach. Suddenly, he was yelling at her. The angry words caused Maria to recoil from him, and she began to retreat into the alley. Carlos gave chase, but not before cutting directly in front of Gonzalez. The latter didn't move from his spot, but he was watching the couple intently. Carlos caught up to Maria a few feet from the end of the alley. Now, it was time to see if Gonzalez would take the bait. If Gonzalez didn't choose to intervene in the altercation, the plan would fail, and it would be time to go back to the drawing board.

Goldstein could hear two sets of footsteps approaching him as he stood just out of view at the far end of the alley. Carlos was yelling and threatening Maria in Spanish. Goldstein heard Carlos slap her, and he heard Maria cry out. They were playing their roles to the hilt. Now, they were just a few feet away. Then Goldstein heard Gonzalez's voice. He was yelling: "*Sálgala solo*," or "leave her alone."

Carlos tore past Goldstein and jumped into the back of the taxi, which was parked ten feet away. If Gonzalez followed, Goldstein would stop him. But he wasn't counting on that. Maria would do everything in her power to keep Gonzalez occupied in the alley.

"*¿Está bien usted?*" It was Gonzalez's voice, asking Maria if she was okay. The woman had been instructed to position her body in such a way that Gonzalez would have his back to Goldstein when the P.I. made his move. With gun drawn, Goldstein came around the corner of the building and found things just as had hoped to find them.

Gonzalez was gripping Maria's arms, with his back to Goldstein, as the P.I. approached him without being detected.

"Both hands in the open," Goldstein said firmly as he jammed his Walther automatic pistol into the man's back.

"*Ambas manos en el abierto*," Goldstein repeated the command in Spanish, and Gonzalez complied.

"Don't shoot. I will give you my wallet," Gonzalez said in broken English, after taking a moment to measure the odds. "May I reach for it?"

"Move your hand and you die."

"Don't shoot! My wallet is in my back pocket. Just take it and go."

Goldstein had his left arm around the man's neck. "Back up. Slowly." The P.I. could tell Gonzalez was frightened, and this worked to Goldstein's advantage. "Back up slowly, and you won't get hurt." The taxi had moved forward, with the back door open, and Goldstein shoved Gonzalez in the vehicle next to Carlos, who also had a gun leveled at the man's chest. An instant later, Goldstein was in the back, and the cab sped off.

Goldstein had spent many hours planning the capture of Raul Gonzalez and returning him to San Antonio. After he had accepted the job months ago, he had his regrets. There was no logical reason to take such a difficult case for a mere ten thousand dollars. From a business perspective, Goldstein should have turned down the job or at least tripled his price. But he believed God had told him to take the assignment. He had no idea why, but he wasn't going to second-guess it now. And he had given Wes Tanner his word. Now, he must do his best to complete the job.

The first part of the job had gone well. Gonzalez had been captured. Sitting next to his captive, Goldstein glanced at him and then at Carlos, who still had his gun pointed at Gonzalez. They would soon be in his car, the Impala sedan he had purchased in Nuevo Laredo. They would head north toward the border. But there were many pitfalls in the second part of the job that had to be avoided. A mistake could result in Goldstein's arrest or even his death. Bounty hunting was not only illegal in Mexico, but the practice was despised by Mexican police, who saw it as an affront to their authority. If Goldstein were caught, he was certain the Mexican judicial system would go to no small lengths to see to it that he spent many years behind bars.

Goldstein had enough cash to buy himself out of a jam under most circumstances. But there was no guarantee. It was better to avoid the problem, which meant not arousing suspicions. But avoiding suspicion was difficult while essentially kidnapping a man out of his own country. Goldstein looked at Gonzalez again. He noticed him stealing a glance at Carlos's gun.

"Sir, I will tell you one more time so that you will know what you have done wrong just before you die," Goldstein said. "If you move in the direction of that gun, my friend will immediately shoot you dead. There will be no warning."

On cue, Carlos pushed the nose of his pistol into Gonzalez's ribs. Gonzalez looked first at Carlos, then at Goldstein. The taxicab was turning off of the main road now, and it proceeded a short distance before stopping under some trees in a secluded area where Goldstein had pre-positioned his Chevy sedan. "*Estamos aquí*," the taxi driver said.

Goldstein handed the driver his payment as he looked around cautiously. No one was visible in this remote section of town. "Thank you, my friend."

"Mucho gracias, señor."

Goldstein propped himself over the seat by his left elbow and leaned very close to Gonzalez's face as he spoke quietly.

"My colleague, Carlos, has a .45 caliber pistol trained on your back, and I have a pistol trained on your head. Do I need to say more?" If Goldstein's words failed to convey his intentions, his cold, slate-gray eyes left no room for doubt. Gonzalez slowly nodded his head to show that he fully understood.

"Why are you kidnapping me? My family will pay you no ransom."

"I'm not seeking a ransom," Goldstein said.

"What are you doing?"

"I am simply returning you to San Antonio."

"Why?" Gonzalez looked bewildered.

"You are a suspect in connection with a woman's disappearance."

Goldstein and Carlos kept their pistols trained on Gonzalez as he walked a couple of paces ahead of them to the Chevy.

"I did not do anything to that woman."

"Mr. Gonzalez, if you are innocent of this crime, why did you flee to Mexico?"

"The husband told the paper I killed his wife. I was afraid I would be arrested."

"But you told me you're innocent. Why were you afraid?"

"I have much fear about this. I read in your papers about men who have been convicted and executed. Only later, do they find that these men were innocent."

When they reached the vehicle, Goldstein threw the car keys to Carlos, ordering him to drive the car. Goldstein had decided that he, and not his operative, would hold a pistol on Gonzalez during their trip to the border.

Gonzalez was told to get into the back seat and lay face down, with his hands placed behind him in the small of his back. Golstein put his knee in the small of Gonzalez's back and bound his captive's hands with a length of nylon cord. Then Goldstein wrapped Gonzalez's ankles with another length of cord. Carlos climbed in behind the wheel and started the engine as Goldstein bound the captive's hands. Then the P.I. slid into the passenger seat. Golstein glanced back at Gonzalez as the pale light of the night filtered through the rear window and illuminated his face. The man looked more bewildered than frightened.

Goldstein reached into his front shirt pocket for the last of his Galoise cigarettes, lit it, and inhaled deeply. He allowed his gaze to focus for a moment on the moonlit strip of highway ahead as they rode in silence. Carlos steered the car expertly along the road, dodging the occasional potholes that had resulted from the incessant pounding of heavy truck traffic. Goldstein reached up to turn the inside rearview mirror to focus on the man in the back seat. Gonzalez appeared to be asleep, as the liquor took its effect.

As they rode in silence, Goldstein took a moment to reflect on his predicament. He was deep within the tiger's lair, and he knew it. Another three hundred miles lay ahead of them before they reached the border. They would need to stop once for gasoline. There, they would also get food. Anyone who needed to use the toilet would have to relieve himself on the side of the road.

Barring any unforeseen difficulty, that would leave only one very large hurdle to clear. The three of them still would have to pass through the U.S. Customs checkpoint north of Laredo. When this was accomplished, they would have a three-hour car ride to San Antonio.

Goldstein took another long pull on his cigarette and then pitched it out the window. He turned his head toward the side window and briefly saw his reflection in it. Had he aged so much in so short a time? The shadows of the night landscape had suddenly begun to take on grotesque shapes. The lonely howl of a coyote cut through the night air from somewhere off to his right. He closed his eyes and softly uttered a prayer, as the car sped on through the still night.

CHAPTER 35
September 2010

I t was a beautiful morning, and Wes took a break from his writing to sit on the back porch and enjoy the morning air. The children were in school, and the house was too quiet. Staring into the backyard, Wes's eyes fell on a chaise lounge where Nicole had sunbathed during the seemingly endless summer days when temperatures hovered near the century mark in San Antonio. On those days, Wes usually stayed inside until the sun set and the evening breeze brought some relief. But Nicole loved to bake in the sun, and in recent years, her skin was starting to show some wear and tear from nature's own tanning salon.

Staring at the chaise lounge, Wes could see the flowered cushions that her slender body had concealed during those many hours in the sun. He even thought he caught a whiff of coconut oil in the air. Wes recalled a summer day the previous year when he had found Nicole out there sunbathing in the heat of the day. One glance at her long, tanned legs sent amorous thoughts flooding into his mind. Wes had been turned down enough times to be gun-shy about approaching her, but on this occasion she smiled invitingly. Soon, they were necking on the chaise lounge, and it culminated later in lovemaking.

The intimate encounters, which were few and far between, were the only times that Wes felt loved by Nicole in later years. Feeling increasingly lonely in a loveless marriage, he had spent more and more time writing. He found that he could escape into his stories and characters, shutting out the sadness in the real world for a period of time.

Wes started his first novel just days after they had returned from their honeymoon in Cancun to begin life as man and wife. The couple was already fighting, and Wes found himself pulling away from Nicole. Wes was working at the newspaper, while Nicole started a job at a department store in North Star Mall. Money was tight, but his wife kept buying all of the nice things they couldn't afford. After only six months of marriage, they owed three thousand dollars in credit card debt. One night, Wes angrily cut up the cards after Nicole went to bed. When she woke up the next day, another bitter argument ensued. Nicole soon had another credit card, and the cycle started again.

After getting them into debt, Nicole decided they had to buy a house. Wes couldn't understand his wife's obsession with owning a home. He was quite content to keep living in their one-bedroom apartment for $400 per month. But, Nicole just had to have a house. So they saved up enough for a down payment on their first house, and then struggled to keep their heads above water after moving into it. They fought all of the time, but that didn't stop Nicole from wanting to start a family. She told him in one of her softer moments that a family was what they needed to bring them together. Wanting to believe her, Wes agreed and Nicole was soon pregnant with Jordan.

When she found out she was pregnant, Nicole decided to look for a new job with more pay. She started selling health plans for an insurance company. Nicole seemed to be gone all the time, and she was making more money, which were both good things from Wes's perspective. By that point in their marriage, he had decided that the less he saw of her, the better. When they were together, they either fought, or simply endured each other in cold silence. Even when they weren't angry with each other, the young couple found little to talk about. Wes was interested in sports, current events, movies, and books. None of these subjects were of any interest to Nicole. She was interested in fashion and fitness. Wes made a feeble effort to talk to her about those subjects, but he found her interests to be shallow.

Wes recalled things taking a brief turn for the better when Jordan was born. The couple finally had something in common, and they talked endlessly about their baby. From the time Wes first laid eyes on Jordan, he felt a love for her that he had never felt for anyone in his life. That love was exhilarating, yet wrenching and frightening.

Six weeks after Jordan was born, Nicole returned to work. Working nights then, Wes assumed the role of primary caregiver for Jordan during the day. When Nicole returned home in the late afternoon, he went to work. Wes was surprised that she wanted to return to her job so quickly. In contrast to the adoring father, Nicole tired quickly of the demands made upon her. Despite wanting so desperately to have children, she was now anxious to get away from Jordan as soon as possible and as often as possible. Wes filled the void as best he could, as his wife spent more and more time away from home selling health plans.

When Monty was born two years later, Wes realized their two-bedroom home was not big enough. Eventually, Monty would need his own room, so they started looking for another house. There was also a new topic to fight about. Nicole now wanted her husband to return to school, get a master's degree in business, and enter the business world. Wes knew this would mean an end to his dream of being a writer, and he wasn't ready to abandon that dream. So the cold war that had stretched over the years of their marriage became hot again. This time, Wes dug in his heels and resisted with all his strength.

"You'll be glad I kept writing when my first novel sells," Wes promised her.

"I'll be glad when you grow up and begin to assume the responsibility of providing for your family," Nicole said.

Wes knew his dream was mere foolishness to her. Nicole had no faith in her husband's writing ability, and she was always quick to point to any shred of evidence supporting her lack of faith. He was never going to sell a novel, and each passing year made this more clear. Nicole couldn't understand why Wes didn't face that fact. It was clearly time to quit his menial newspaper job and start on a new career path. Nicole resented every moment he spent writing, and she didn't try to hide her resentment.

In the early years of their marriage, Wes was sure that vindication as a writer was just around the corner in the form of some published work. He was going to sell a novel, and another. Wes reasoned that when he was an established writer, making a good income in royalties, things would change. Nicole would finally respect him. Their marriage would be better, and life would be better. But the faith he had in his ability was slowly eroded by all of the rejection he experienced.

So Wes continued to escape from life. Once, when she was pregnant with Summer, Nicole accused him of being insensitive. In tears, she had told him that a wall existed between them that prevented them from ever being close. Wes didn't understand what she was talking about, and his inability to comprehend it only made matters worse. One day during the third trimester of her pregnancy, Nicole totally lost it. Wes couldn't remember exactly what triggered her outburst, but she suddenly started hitting him and throwing things. Wes had to wrestle her to the floor before she broke every dish and glass they owned.

Roger happened to arrive at the house shortly after this episode and found his grandson sweeping up broken glass in the kitchen. When he asked what happened, Wes told him the story. Roger, who had counseled many people at his church, brought the young couple together and started asking them a series of

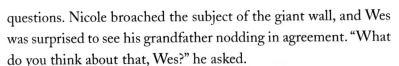

questions. Nicole broached the subject of the giant wall, and Wes was surprised to see his grandfather nodding in agreement. "What do you think about that, Wes?" he asked.

"I don't know," Wes said. "I'm not aware of any wall."

"Do you think you have a tendency to withdraw from difficult circumstances?"

"I don't know," Wes said, wishing he could escape to his typewriter at that minute and resume work on one of his novels or short stories.

"He never shows any emotion except anger," Nicole had said in a quivering voice. "Look at him! He doesn't feel anything."

On this fall morning, Wes had to admit, in retrospect, that she had a point. Wes had learned how to shut off his feelings after his mother's death to avoid pain. But now, the feelings were coming back, and it was frightening for a man devoid of feelings for so long.

CHAPTER 36
September 2010

The early morning sun streaked the sky to their east and shone brightly through the passenger windows of the vehicle. Goldstein winced at the brightness and briefly turned his head away. The lack of sleep from driving through the night and having to keep an eye on Gonzalez had begun to give Goldstein a headache, and the intense sunlight was making matters worse.

"Carlos, turn onto that dirt road and drive until I tell you to stop."

Goldstein had spotted the dirt road ahead that veered off to the right of Highway 85. The road appeared to head off into a vast expanse of open range land to the northeast. Carlos nodded as he slowed down and took the unmarked exit off the main highway.

Carlos drove about three miles and then glanced over at Goldstein for further instructions. The latter simply stared straight ahead, which was a signal that Carlos should keep driving. Ahead in the distance was an earthen dam that rose up off the flat prairie to a height of about twenty feet. Goldstein saw some trees on the top and around the sides of the dam, suggesting a body of water on the other side of the dam.

"Pull around the back side of that dam, and let's check it out," Goldstein said.

Carlos nodded, slowed, and steered the car onto a narrow dirt strip that extended around the top of the dam. Goldstein had been right. Below them was a small reservoir, about fifty yards long by fifty yards across. It was surrounded by native pecan trees that had by nature taken root in the wet and fertile soil provided by the lake. On the far side of the reservoir was a small clearing, which was almost entirely encircled by trees.

Once in the small clearing, Goldstein nodded to him, and Carlos stopped the car under the shade of some trees and cut the engine. Goldstein turned to the back seat. "You were able to sleep some during the night, Mr. Gonzalez. Now, it is our turn to get some rest. We will stay here for several hours. We will then make our final push for the border later in the day."

"May I relieve myself?" Gonzalez asked.

"Of course, but I will be close behind you. I warn you not to try to escape, or I will be forced to shoot you."

"I understand."

Goldstein pointed his gun at Gonzalez, and the captive climbed out of the back seat, stretching his body out after hours of confinement. Goldstein untied the prisoner and then pointed to a grove of pecan trees at the edge of the clearing near the water. The P.I. felt very tired, but he knew that Carlos, too, would be in need of sleep.

"Carlos, I will take first watch, for three hours. Then it will be your turn to guard him for three hours while I sleep," Goldstein said after the two men returned to the car. Carlos' eyes were bloodshot, and his face looked drawn from the stress of the preceding day's events. He was clearly happy to be able to get some sleep. Goldstein decided that the car would serve as his napping place. Goldstein directed Gonzalez back over to the grove of pecans as Carlos pulled off his T-shirt, covered the window facing the rising sun and climbed inside the vehicle to sleep.

"I am very hungry. Is there food for me?" Gonzalez asked.

"Yes," Goldstein said. He returned to the car to find Carlos already asleep in the backseat. He found a box of crackers and walked back over to Gonzalez. "Have as many as you want."

Gonzalez took the crackers and stuffed several into his mouth before Goldstein motioned for him to start walking toward the small cluster of trees. When they reached the trees, Goldstein ordered Gonzalez to sit with his back against a tree while the P.I. tied him up again.

Goldstein leaned down and held a bottle of water to Gonzalez's lips and let him have a long sip. "Enough?"

"Yes. Thank you, sir," Gonzalez said.

Goldstein took the half-finished bottle of water with him and sat down with his back to the trunk of a tree just a few yards from his captive. Determined to stay alert during his watch, Goldstein gave Gonzalez a long look. It was the first time he had been able to look into his eyes since the hectic events of the prior day's capture in Mexico City. Despite what Wes Tanner had told him, Goldstein had been unable to discern any malice in this man. The few words that Gonzalez had spoken to him had either been words of thanks for Goldstein's kindness, or had been words of concern for the safety of his family.

Gonzalez had asked him if he could call his wife, Maria, to let her know that he was alive and unharmed. "She will be very worried," he had told Goldstein. "I just want to tell her that I'm okay and not to worry." Gonzalez had spent some time talking about his wife and how much he missed her. Goldstein wondered why the man's eyes wandered to other women if he loved his wife that much.

Regardless of his own personal doubts about Gonzalez's motives, or his guilt, Goldstein had a contract to perform. His job was to deliver this man safely to his client. Of course, as a licensed private investigator sworn to uphold the law, Goldstein would actually be obligated to deliver the man to the SAPD. He would let Tanner know what he was doing and assure him that the man would be held in the Bexar County jail until authorities decided whether to charge him. In that way, his client would know that Goldstein had successfully completed the transaction without allowing Tanner to be tempted to take the law into his own hands.

Goldstein glanced at his watch. An hour had passed. In two hours, Goldstein would be able to turn the watch over to his operative and then retire to the shade of the Chevy sedan for three hours of desperately needed sleep. The sun had risen to near its noontime zenith. The sky was totally absent of clouds, and the sun was harshly bright on this late summer day. Goldstein's head was aching from the strain of the chase and capture, coupled with the nightlong drive through the badlands of central Mexico.

Taking a long sip of bottled water, Goldstein tried to let his mind settle. This would all be sorted out by evening of the next day, and he could then get back to his normal life in San Antonio. For now, the plan was to spend the day in this isolated place. Then they would proceed to a small town just south of Nuevo Laredo, where the three of them would wait until nightfall. Goldstein had located the tiny village on a map. The town, which lay fives miles south of Nuevo Laredo, was called Charco Largo.

"I'll take the watch now," Carlos's voice jolted Goldstein, who was nodding off under the noonday sun. His companion had strode into the small clearing without detection. Goldstein scolded himself silently, realizing the danger of sleeping on the job. Gonzalez was tied up, but he could have worked himself free and overpowered his unwitting captor under these circumstances.

"You have your pistol with you?" Goldstein asked. Carlos tapped his belt with his hand, indicating that he had his pistol tucked in his waistband. "Keep a close eye on him." Goldstein glanced at his watch. "It is 12:30. I will be back to relieve you at 3:30." Carlos nodded, and Goldstein headed off in the direction of the car.

CHAPTER 37
September 2010

Raul Gonzalez awoke when Goldstein returned to relieve Carlos. Goldstein looked down at Gonzalez as the latter rolled over onto his back in time to see Carlos walking off. He turned his attention to Goldstein and spoke in broken English.

"I do not like this Carlos. He would not allow me to go and relieve myself. He impresses me as being one without compassion or feeling."

"I am sorry for that," Goldstein said. "Will you be trustworthy if I untie your hands and feet?"

"Yes."

Goldstein reached over and untied the cords. He held the man at gunpoint while he urinated and tied him up again. Leaning against a tree, Goldstein placed the gun in his lap. The two men's eyes met, and Gonzalez held his gaze.

"I tell you again, sir, that you have the wrong man. I am not a killer."

"If you're an innocent man, I trust the authorities will conclude that and release you."

"I'm not confident of this," Gonzalez said. "I am a Mexican, and the American laws are not kind to my people."

"I know the law enforcement people in San Antonio. They will be fair."

There was a moment of silence, and Gonzalez shook his head.

"They will not be fair to me. Sir, please. I ask only one thing of you."

"What's that?"

"Dial my wife's number on your phone and let me speak to her for just one moment. Let me tell her that I'm okay and hope to return to her very soon."

Goldstein looked at the man and found himself unable to turn down the request. He dialed the number and placed the cell phone to Gonzalez's ear. "Short and sweet, amigo. And speak only English. Just tell her you're okay."

"Maria," Gonzalez said. "I'm okay…I was captured by an American who is returning me to the United States. He assures me authorities will release me after questioning…" Gonzalez said something in Spanish that Goldstein didn't understand.

"I said English," Goldstein said firmly. "Finish your call quickly."

"Maria, I must go. I love you. *Te amo*, Maria. *Te amo*."

Gonzalez handed the cell phone back to Goldstein. "Thank you."

"Raul, are you hungry?"

"Yes."

"I have part of a sandwich in the car from last night. I'm not really hungry, so I'll get it for you when Carlos returns."

"Thank you, sir."

"Watch him while I double-check the car," Goldstein told Carlos as he nodded toward Gonzalez before lifting the hood of the Chevy and checking the oil and the radiator fluid. Carlos circled around Gonzalez, who stood next to the car, a low growling in his throat and spoke to him in a disparaging tone of voice. The words were in Spanish, so Goldstein couldn't understand him.

"Carlos, stop!" Goldstein ordered. "You are to treat our captive with respect."

Goldstein turned and walked around the car and checked the air pressure in all the tires. It was his habit to be very meticulous in matters like this. The flat, sparsely populated stretch of Highway 85 which lay ahead of them would not be a good place to break down.

When they were ready to leave, Goldstein ordered Carlos to remove Gonzalez's leg bindings but to keep his hands bound. He then ordered Carlos to load Gonzalez into the back seat of the car for the drive to Charco Largo. Goldstein slid in behind the wheel, deciding that for this leg of the trip, Carlos would guard their captive in the backseat. Goldstein did his best thinking while driving.

As night settled across the rugged plains, Goldstein noticed more oncoming headlights. Traffic was picking up considerably. The cars were heading to Queretaro, Monterrey, and beyond—perhaps to Mexico City. The border was near. Once again, Goldstein re-checked his plan in his mind. *So far, so good*, he thought. But there were still major obstacles to avoid before they arrived in San Antonio. Goldstein knew that the closer they got to the border, the more likely they would be to run into federal police prowling for border-bound drug "mules."

The radio was tuned to the only AM station broadcasting in that area. The faint sounds of *norteño* music wafted through the cab as Goldstein steered the car down Highway 85, being careful to mind the speed limit. A road sign loomed on the right, and Goldstein slowed down to get a good look at it. *Charco Largo: 10km.* Goldstein looked out the window to the west, hoping to make out the nature of the landscape by the light of the moon. But he saw no moon. Goldstein glanced to the east, north and south, and still there was no sign of the moon. He spotted a few stars of the southern constellation, but the light from them was dim, casting a faint pall on the surrounding landscape. It was a dark night, with the little town of Charco Largo looming ahead. With a heaviness of spirit, Goldstein wished desperately that he was elsewhere.

"Carlos, Charco Largo is only six miles ahead. Do you recall the plan?"

"Yes, sir," Carlos said as he glanced out the passenger side window for an exit just south of the small town. The plan was to try to find an isolated rural road just south of Charco Largo on which to pull over and make their final preparations to cross the border. As the lights of the town flickered ahead of them, Carlos spotted a road.

"There," Carlos said, pointing.

Goldstein slowed and exited on a dirt service road about two miles south of Charco Largo. He drove for about half of a mile until he ran up on another, smaller dirt road that fed off to the right. Goldstein turned and then proceeded slowly down that road for another half mile. There was no traffic in the area. All was quiet. Goldstein eased the car off the road and onto a grass embankment.

As he opened the driver's side door to exit, Goldstein was startled by a flash of light off to his left. Suddenly, a loud boom shook the ground. Goldstein was still sleep-deprived, and his nerves were raw. He found himself reaching into his waistband for his Walther pistol before he realized that it was just a thunderstorm brewing to the north. More ragged bands of lightning streaked the sky from east to west as peals of thunder rolled like cannon fire through the Rio Grande valley.

"Get him out of the car," Goldstein barked to Carlos. His companion looked stunned by the tone of his voice. Goldstein felt like he was nearing his breaking point as he watched Carlos open the rear passenger side door to let Gonzalez out. Goldstein then ordered Carlos to untie Gonzalez's hands. He was going to allow Gonzalez to drink some water and relieve himself again before they crossed the border. Carlos was standing next to the front passenger door, his pistol trained on Gonzalez, as Goldstein walked around the back of the car in the direction of the two men.

What happened next happened suddenly, as a flurry of lightning strikes shattered the darkness and a spider web of wispy cloud-to-ground lightning lit up the landscape on the outskirts of Charco Largo. Momentarily distracted by the lightning, Carlos turned his head away from Gonzalez and was quickly overpowered. Before Goldstein could raise his gun, Gonzalez stood behind Carlos with his arm around his former captor's neck and a gun in his hand.

"Drop your gun, or I will kill him," Gonzalez said.

Goldstein continued to point his gun at the two men, knowing that he would have to decide quickly what to do. If he dropped his gun, Gonzalez could then easily kill both of them. But if he didn't obey the order, Gonzalez might end Carlos's life.

"You told me you were not a killer," Goldstein said, lowering his gun but not dropping it.

"I am not a killer, but I am not going across the border. Drop your weapon."

Sensing growing agitation in Gonzalez's voice, Goldstein decided to comply. Never taking his eyes off of Gonzalez, he let his pistol drop to the ground. His intuition told him that this man didn't want to kill him. He only wanted to escape.

"Now what?"

"Now, I will need the keys to your car."

"You're taking my car?"

"Borrowing it," Gonzalez said. "It can be retrieved in Mexico City after I return."

"What about Carlos?"

"He is going to drive about a mile with me, and then I will let him off. He can walk back here. You're not far from the border, and I trust you can make it across tonight."

After the car sped off, Goldstein looked east and west down the small dirt road. There was no sign of traffic. Goldstein slowly turned his eyes toward heaven. The lightning and thunder had died down, and the rain began to fall. Drenched and shivering, Goldstein wondered if it was time to retire from this line of work. Suddenly, the private investigator felt a sense of peace. A giant burden had seemingly been lifted when Gonzalez escaped. Goldstein sat down on the ground to await the return of his companion.

CHAPTER 38
September 2010

Wes awoke to the sound of the doorbell, followed by the dog's incessant barking. It was 7:00 a.m., and he groaned at the realization. Wes had had every intention of sleeping late this morning. It was Saturday, and he had been up until three the previous night revising his screenplay. Wes had received a call from his LA agent a few days ago, informing him that the movie producer "loved your screenplay." The agent had "just a few notes" and he wanted a revision done ASAP. The "few notes" turned out to be twenty pages of notes typed into the script and e-mailed to him. The painstaking rewrite process took three solid days. Wes went line-by-line, trying to incorporate each point into his story, before e-mailing the script back to his agent early that morning.

Duncan was still barking as Wes tried to will himself into full consciousness, realizing that the children would be awake soon if he didn't make it to the door quickly. Still wondering who would disturb his family so early, Wes finally pulled himself out of bed, grabbed a robe, and headed for the living room.

When he threw the door open, Wes was surprised to see Ezra Goldstein standing on his front porch. Goldstein looked like he had aged ten years since Wes had last seen him just weeks earlier. When he had left for Mexico, the bounty hunter looked spry and confident, wearing a cheerful countenance. On this morning,

Goldstein looked like he had just stepped off a battlefield on the losing side.

"Shalom," Goldstein said wearily. "May I come in?"

Goldstein entered as Summer appeared in her pajamas. "Who is it, Dad?"

"It's someone to see me," Wes said as he directed Goldstein into his study, where the man sat down wearily on the couch. "Go back to bed, Sunshine."

"Raul Gonzalez escaped," Goldstein said as soon as Wes entered the study.

"What?"

"He got away last night outside of a town called Charco Largo."

Wes collapsed into a chair, and he listened somberly as Goldstein recounted the events leading up to the escape. At the end of the story, the P.I. looked at Wes, waiting for some kind of a response. Wes appeared to be in shock.

"Mr. Goldstein, I really don't know what to say," Wes finally spoke. "I gave you all the money I had to go and find this man. You captured him and brought him back to within a few miles of the border. Then you let him get away."

"I can understand your disappointment. First, let me make it clear, sir, that I will return your ten thousand. Second, I believe that Raul Gonzalez is innocent."

"Innocent?" Wes said indignantly. "He killed my wife."

"Mr. Tanner, I don't think he killed your wife."

"Why do you say that?"

"Call it a hunch, intuition. I spent some time with Raul Gonzalez. I talked to him about the crime you accused him of. I just don't think he did it. If he were a killer, he certainly would have killed Carlos and myself in Charco Largo."

"We'll never know for sure."

"Don't give up," Goldstein said wearily. "The psalmist writes that justice and judgment are the habitation of God's throne. Mercy and truth shall go before His face."

"There are plenty of injustices in the world."

"Yes, sir. But God sets all things right in the end. I wish you well," Goldstein said, extending his hand. "I hope the authorities are able to determine what happened to your wife."

Wes escorted Goldstein to the door and watched him as he walked toward his car.

"Mr. Goldstein?"

Goldstein turned around on the sidewalk as Wes walked toward him.

"Can I ask you a question?"

"Of course."

"If you think Gonzalez is innocent, who do you think killed my wife?"

"I've been puzzling over that one for the past day."

"What's your conclusion?"

"Frankly, I don't know, sir."

"Would you be willing to continue your investigation?"

"Yes." Goldstein nodded. "I would very much like to solve this case."

The next day, Goldstein visited the Alamo Heights real estate office where Nicole had been employed before she disappeared almost six months ago. He spoke to three Realtors that had known her, but none indicated they were close to her. Goldstein learned that the co-worker closest to Nicole no longer worked in residential real estate. Marty Chavez, Nicole's closest friend, had moved on to a new job as a real estate manager. Goldstein obtained the address and drove there.

Chavez greeted Goldstein with a big smile and cheerful "hello." She remembered him from their brief meeting four months ago. Goldstein recalled that Chavez had little to offer him at that time, but now the P.I. was prepared to ask her additional questions. He hoped to spark a memory or ascertain some piece of information that might help him piece together the puzzle of Nicole's mysterious disappearance. At the time, the questions had been of a cursory nature, but these questions would be more pointed.

"How do you like your new job?" Goldstein asked Chavez as she sat behind her desk, sipping a cup of coffee.

"I love it. Don't get me wrong, Mr. Goldstein. I enjoyed being a Realtor, but I just couldn't make a living doing it. Especially in this economy. This job provides a steady paycheck, and hours are better. No more nights and weekends."

"I can imagine it's been tough in residential real estate for some time. How was Nicole doing at the time of her disappearance? Was she enjoying much success?"

"She was struggling like the rest of us," Chavez said. "She was working with some high-end buyers, but her closes were few and far between."

"So she was under financial pressure?"

"Yes. She talked about that a lot. She was frustrated that her husband didn't have a better job. Other Realtors in our office just dabbled in this business, not needing the money because their spouses were the primary breadwinners. But that wasn't the case for Nicole or me."

"Did Nicole ever talk about divorcing her husband?"

"Not in so many words."

Goldstein perked up, sensing he might be on to something. "What do you mean?"

"I knew she was unhappy in her marriage. She never said she was going to divorce her husband, but—"

"But what?"

Chavez hesitated, and Goldstein sensed she was holding back for some reason. He had learned through years of experience that sometimes a moment of silence will compel the reluctant party to speak frankly. He waited patiently until Chavez became uncomfortable with the silence.

"Mr. Goldstein, I was told that Nicole's husband had hired you to track down the man that tried to take advantage of her and threatened her. Is that true?"

"Yes."

"Are you still searching for him?"

"No."

"So you don't think he killed Nicole?"

"No, I don't."

"Do you think Wes killed her?"

"No."

"Who then? Me?"

"No." Goldstein laughed out loud. "I certainly don't think you killed her."

"What's your theory, Mr. Goldstein?"

"I don't have a theory yet, Mrs. Chavez."

"Ms."

"Ms. Chavez, I don't know much of anything at this point. That's why I continue to investigate. Now, if you'll indulge me with a few more questions, perhaps I can help solve the mystery. Will you help me?"

"If I can."

"Nicole never said she was going to divorce her husband, but…?"

"One night, we were having a few drinks after work. We were blowing off steam after a rough day. Nicole had missed out on a big sale that afternoon, and she might have had one too many margaritas. I don't know."

"What did she say?" Goldstein asked after Chavez hesitated again. Goldstein had become adept at reading body language, and he could tell she was holding back.

"She said she often fantasized about meeting Mr. Right."

"And who would Mr. Right be for Nicole?"

"Mr. Right would be Mr. Money Bags."

"Did Nicole know a Mr. Money Bags?"

"Nicole worked with a number of affluent clients," Chavez explained. "Some very affluent. And some were men. She told me about this one buyer she had met from California. She said he was a billionaire. Can you believe that? Not a millionaire. A billionaire. And he was only in his forties."

"He must have had the Midas touch. Why was he in San Antonio?"

"His daughter was going to graduate school, and he wanted to buy her a house. He wound up buying a house for her in The Dominion. Can you imagine? He spent almost a million dollars on a house that his daughter might live in for a year or two."

"That's hard to imagine," Goldstein agreed.

"Do you think that one of her buyers might have killed her?"

"I don't know."

"Maybe she was blackmailing one of those rich dudes and they decided to get rid of her by hiring a professional killer. One of those guys would have plenty of money to hire only the best. I'll bet they thought they'd never get caught."

Goldstein just stared at her with a poker face.

"What do you think about my theory?" Chavez finally asked.

"Anything's possible." Goldstein shrugged, not wanting to tell her that the theory sounded more like a script for an episode of CSI. "Is there anything else that you can think of that might help me, Ms. Chavez? Was Nicole acting strangely around the time of her disappearance? Anything out of the ordinary?"

Chavez thought for a moment, and her face brightened. "There was one thing."

"What's that?"

"I remember a few occasions when I came into her office and saw her clearing her computer screen quickly. Like she didn't want me to see what she was doing."

"Facebook?"

"Sure, Nicole did Facebook. But that wasn't something she would hide from me."

"Wasn't there a company policy against Facebook?"

"No." Chavez shrugged. "They didn't care how much time we spent on Facebook. We worked on commission. You could spend your time any way you wanted as long as you sold enough houses. If you didn't it was your funeral."

CHAPTER 39
September 2010

Wes sat in the front pew at San Fernando Cathedral and watched Natalie light a candle for Nicole. She had performed this ritual once a week for the past twenty-four weeks. She stood over the candle for a moment, her hand cupped around it until the yellow flame grew bigger. Then she knelt, bowed her head, and prayed.

Looking up at the majestic stained glass windows, Wes thought about Natalie's faith and how it differed from his own. Since his conversion, Wes could say they both believed in the Bible, but Natalie also adhered to the catechisms of the Catholic Church. But she had not tried to proselytize him into becoming Catholic.

In the weeks after he had accepted Christ as his Savior, Natalie had attended Sunday services with him at Stone Oak Bible Church, but she also attended Mass. Wes watched as she stood up, blessed herself, and walked down off the carpeted altar to the pew. She nodded to him, indicating a willingness to leave the church.

Outside on the street in front of San Fernando Cathedral, Wes glanced at his cell phone and noticed there was a missed call. He recognized the phone number. Ezra Goldstein had tried to call him while he was inside the church, but his phone had been silenced. Wes had not spoken with Goldstein since the previous

Saturday morning when he had arrived at the house with the disappointing news about Gonzalez.

Wes had felt a large measure of irritation after learning how close Gonzalez was to being returned to San Antonio. When Wes had told his grandfather about his frustration, Roger told him to "take it to the Lord." In addition to encouraging Wes to pray about his feelings, his grandfather had also advised that there was a reason why all of the events were unfolding. God had a plan, and it would be revealed in His timing, Roger said.

Wes listened to Ezra's message and was pleased to learn that the P.I. wanted to meet with him that afternoon. Wes immediately called him back and set the meeting for 4 p.m. at his house. He arrived home shortly before Summer got off the bus. The three of them were playing a game together before Goldstein arrived.

Goldstein was walking toward the house as Natalie got into her car to leave. Wes waved to her and then greeted Goldstein at the door and led him into the study. He closed the door behind him and motioned for him to sit on the sofa. Not a man prone to make small talk, his guest went straight to the point of the visit.

"Since my return, I have talked to everyone that I can think of that might give us some insight into what happened to your wife. I've talked to every family member, including your children, your wife's friends and coworkers. I even spoke with a few of her clients that she saw in the days before her disappearance."

"Have you found out anything useful?"

"I'm not sure," Goldstein admitted. "I do have a question."

"What is it?"

"Did your wife have a personal e-mail account?"

"Yes. She had a Yahoo account, as do I."

"Do you know how to get into her account?"

"Yes." Wes looked at him curiously. "Why do you ask?"

"Would you mind going into her account?"

Wes sat down at his desk in front of the computer and used his web browser to call up the home page and then clicked on the mail button. That took him to the page where a user could sign into their account. Wes typed in her e-mail address in the Yahoo ID box and then entered the password he remembered as hobbs. The message said: "Invalid ID or password. Please try again using your full Yahoo! ID."

"That's funny." Wes scratched his head. "She used her mother's maiden name as her password. But now, it doesn't work."

"Are you sure that was the password?"

"It worked the last time I used it."

"When was that?"

"A long time ago."

"When?" Goldstein persisted.

"A year ago. Maybe more."

"She could have changed it."

"She could have."

Wes heard the front door open and close, and Jordan entered the study. She was surprised to see Goldstein sitting on the couch. "I'm sorry," she said. "Am I interrupting?"

"You remember Mr. Goldstein." Wes nodded as the P.I. rose to his feet and took her hand in both of his graciously.

"Hello, young lady. It's nice to see you again."

"Have you found out something about Mom?" Jordan asked hopefully.

"No." Goldstein shook his head. "Not yet."

"Jordan?" Wes asked. "Do you know the password to get into your mom's e-mail?"

"Why do you want that?"

"Mr. Goldstein wanted to look in there."

"I think the account would have been deleted after this long."

"What do you mean?

"Amy's mother had a Yahoo account that she hadn't used in months," Jordan explained. "One time, I was over at Amy's house, and her mother was complaining about having to get it reinstated again because there was an old e-mail she needed to see."

"It's not telling me it's been deleted," Wes said. "Got any ideas on what your mother might have chosen for a new password?"

"How about your wedding anniversary?" Jordan asked.

Wes typed in the representative numbers and clicked on "sign in." The message on the screen still said: "Invalid ID or password."

"Did she have an old nickname?" Jordan asked.

"Not that I'm aware of."

"Try Wes."

Wes entered it and got the same message indicating an invalid password. "Try Jordan." Wes typed it in. Invalid. "Try Monty." Still invalid. "Try Summer." Invalid.

Wes called Yahoo customer service for some assistance with the password. He explained the situation to a representative. The representative told Wes that without proof of death, they would not provide the password or even verify if the account was active. Wes finally hung up the phone in frustration.

"Any ideas on how to hack into her account?" Wes asked Goldstein.

"I'm very much of a novice when it comes to the computer," Goldstein replied.

"Dad, you might be able to get the password reset. I think all you have to do is answer a couple of security questions and they'll let you reset your password."

"Jordan, would you come over here and do this for me?"

Jordan sat down at the computer, and with a few key strokes arrived at a screen with the first security question. "What is your favorite movie?" Jordan asked.

"*When Harry Met Sally*," Wes said. "She watched it over and over again."

Jordan answered the question, and the next question appeared on the screen. "What was your pet's first name?"

Wes peered over her shoulder, scratching his head. "I think it was Goldie," Wes said.

Jordan looked at him. "Goldie?"

"Yeah, she had a puppy. His name was Goldie, I think."

"If you're wrong, you'll probably be locked out," Jordan told him.

"I'm sorry, but I have more important things to remember," Wes said disgustedly.

Jordan shrugged. "Whatever."

"Who would know?" Goldstein asked.

"Her mother," Wes said. "Jordan, call your grandmother and ask her the name of your mother's first pet."

"Why can't you do it?" Jordan asked.

"Because I told you to do it," Wes replied, "and I think you'll probably want to use my car again sometime in the near future."

"Dialing," Jordan said, picking up the phone. "Grandma? What was the name of Mom's first pet?" She paused and made a face. "Summer has a fish and she wants to name it that."

"Liar, liar. Pants on fire," Wes said under his breath.

"Yes, Grandmother. A fish. A goldfish. Goldie? That's perfect. Goldie, the goldfish. Thanks, Grandma…Yes, yes." Jordan rolled her eyes. "I'd love to have lunch with you real soon. Let me check my schedule and get back with you. Bye." Jordan hung up the phone.

"Goldie?" Wes said. Jordan nodded. "I'm pretty good, aren't I?"

Jordan answered the second security question. "Okay, I'm in. Now, all I have to do is reset the password. What do you want the password to be?" Wes walked around to the other side of the desk.

"Jordan, in your honor," Wes said.

Jordan entered the new password twice and clicked Next. "Thanks, Nicole, your account is up to date," Jordan read. "Now I click on mail and…Hello, Nicole! You have 104 unread messages. It's still a valid account. Let me see when the last e-mail message was sent."

Under Folders, Jordan clicked on "Sent."

"Dad, this message was sent to a Tim Stein on June 25, 2010."

"What?" Wes stared at the screen. "Open it." Jordan clicked on it, and the e-mail opened. They read the e-mail together, and Jordan let out a gasp.

> Dear Tim, I don't know why you won't answer your phone, or return my call. Actually, I do know. You are a coward. If you want to ditch me, you're going to have to face me like a man. How would you like it if I drop in on you and the wife tonight? Call me back, or that is exactly what I will do. Nicole.

Wes and Jordan continued to stare at the computer screen. From the other side of the desk, Goldstein was looking at them, awaiting an explanation. "Nicole is alive," Wes said as Jordan burst into tears and ran out of the house.

CHAPTER 40
September 2010

After Wes had escorted Goldstein to the door, he sat down in his chair and tried to wrap his mind around what had just happened. Wes had known from the beginning that his wife was a selfish person. But never would he have believed she was capable of something like this. Staging her own death and then just disappearing. Clearly, she had no love left in her heart for him, but how could she do this to her own children? How could she put them all through this hell?

Wes wanted to go out and look for Jordan, but he couldn't leave Summer alone. She was upstairs playing in her room, oblivious to what had just happened to their family. He would have to tell her soon. He'd see the joy in her eyes. Mom was alive. It would be a single moment of fleeting euphoria before he would tell her Nicole wasn't coming home. *The fact is, your mother wanted no part in your life.* The news would devastate Summer more than the other two children. Of this, Wes was certain.

Was it worse to live six months under the illusion that your mother had been murdered, or learn that she chose to desert you? If she had been murdered, she would have left them unwillingly. It would have been a tragedy they could have overcome. But how could they overcome this kind of rejection? Nicole didn't just leave Wes for another man. She left her family to start a new life.

If she wanted a new life, she could have one for all that Wes cared. Ironically, her new life hadn't turned out the way that she had hoped. Apparently, this Tim Stein didn't want any part of her. *Smart guy*, Wes thought to himself. Moving the mouse next to his computer, Wes stared at the Sent Items list on the screen. There was a series of e-mails sent to Tim Stein over a period of months. They chronicled the deteriorating relationship. Wes finally worked his way back to one that was sent on the night she disappeared.

Dear Tim, I will be on a bus for LA at 6 a.m. I'm a little nervous about sitting in the bus station all night, but I'm sure it will be okay. I arrive at 8:55 a.m. the next day (Monday). I can't wait to see you and for you to hold me in your arms! Love, Nicole.

The words became fuzzy on the screen in front of him, and Wes realized his vision was blurred by his own tears. "Why couldn't you just be dead?" he asked softly.

"Daddy? What's wrong?"

Wes turned to see Summer standing in the doorway.

"Nothing."

"Yes, there is," Summer said, walking toward him. "You're crying."

Before Wes could answer, Monty walked in the study and saw Summer hugging Wes. "What's wrong, Dad? Did something happen?"

"Have a seat." Wes pointed to the couch. "I have some news for both of you."

Wes picked up Summer in his arms and carried her over, placing her next to Monty. The pair was looking at him curiously. Wes felt sick to his stomach as he prepared to break the news. He knew each one of them was about to ride the same emotional rollercoaster that he had been forced to ride. There would be the initial joy at the news Nicole was alive, followed by disbelief that she would leave without an explanation.

"Your mother is alive."

"Mommy's alive?" Summer said happily. She was the first to speak. Monty looked at him in stunned silence.

"At least she was alive as late as June of this year," Wes added.

"Where is she?" Monty finally asked.

"From what I've read, it appears that she is in Los Angeles."

Monty made a face. "Los Angeles?"

"Why is she in Los Angeles?" Summer looked puzzled.

"Did the kidnapper take her there?" Monty asked.

"She wasn't kidnapped, Son."

Monty and Summer looked at each other and then back at Wes. Their growing sense of bewilderment was evident in their expressions. A moment later, Jordan came through the front door and joined them in the study.

"I guess you told them," Jordan said quietly.

"You know?" Monty asked her. Jordan nodded, and his son turned back to Wes. "How did she get to Los Angeles?"

Jordan looked at him. "Los Angeles?"

"That's what the e-mail indicated," Wes said before proceeding to recount the events of the past hour to them.

"Dad, did she go out there to be with that other man?"

"Yes."

"What?" Monty was indignant.

"She let us believe she was dead," Jordan said bitterly.

The smile had never left Summer's face during the exchange. She didn't seemed to be concerned about the issues being raised by her brother and sister. The facts surrounding Nicole's disappearance were not important to her. Summer's mother was alive, and she was delighted.

"Can I talk to her?" Summer finally asked.

"I don't have her phone number."

"Why didn't she call us?" Summer wondered as the smile slowly evaporated from her face.

"I don't know."

"Why did she leave us, Dad?" Monty asked in a quiet voice.

"I think something happened to her," Wes tried to explain. "Something must have been bothering her deeply."

"She's sick in the head," Jordan said.

"Can we go see her?" Summer asked desperately.

"We don't know where she is, Sunshine."

"You said she was in Los Angeles," Summer said.

"Los Angeles is a big place," Wes replied.

"Can't you do some kind of an internet search and find her?" Monty asked.

"I don't want to find her," Jordan said.

"I do. I want to go see Mommy," Summer said, starting to cry.

"She doesn't want to see us," Jordan said coldly.

"You don't know that, Jordan," Wes said as he put his arm around his younger daughter to comfort her.

"It's not hard to figure out," Jordan said, her eyes now also full of tears. She jumped up from the couch and ran upstairs. Summer was crying even louder, now.

"Tell Mommy we want her to come back. Tell her I'll be good. I'll do everything she says. Please, Daddy. Tell her. Please!" Wes gathered Summer into his arms as she continued to weep, rocking her and trying to comfort her.

Monty was on his feet now. He was quickly becoming sullen and angry. "She doesn't want to see us? I don't want to see her, either." He turned and walked out of the room as Summer continued to cry uncontrollably.

Wes had forgotten that Natalie was coming over to cook dinner for them that evening. He was upstairs reading a story to Summer when he heard her voice downstairs calling to them. Jordan and Monty were in their own rooms, and Jordan almost ran into him in the hallway as he headed for the stairs.

"Jordan, I want to tell her," Wes said firmly. He hurried downstairs and found her in the kitchen. "Natalie?"

"How does Chicken Cordon Bleu sound?" Natalie said, standing in front of the open refrigerator with her back to Wes.

"It sounds great."

At his tone, she shut the fridge door and turned to him. "What's wrong?" Natalie asked, immediately seeing something in his face.

"Come into the study," Wes responded. Natalie followed him through the French doors, and Wes closed them and turned to face her. "You might want to sit down for this one."

"What is it?" Natalie was studying his face with growing concern as he sat down on the couch and motioned for her to sit next to him.

Wes's heart was beating rapidly. "I don't know an easy way to say this."

"What?"

"She's alive, Natalie."

It took a moment for the words to sink in. When they did, all of the color left Natalie's face. "Nicole?" Wes nodded. "Oh, my God. She's alive?" The color came back into Natalie's face, and she smiled radiantly as Wes nodded. Then she closed her eyes.

"Thank you, Jesus." When Natalie opened her eyes again, she was looking for an explanation. Wes quickly related what little he knew, watching Natalie carefully. He had expected—even hoped for—a hint of disappointment. Natalie would know full well that this doomed any chance of them being together.

"She's living in Los Angeles. She apparently left me, or I should say all of us, for another man. According to the e-mails, it didn't appear to work out for her. That's all I know. It's interesting that the romance appears to have been over for three months, but she never made an effort to contact us."

"She was probably too ashamed to call you."

The initial joy of knowing her sister was alive had passed, and Natalie's smile had long since vanished. Was she now struggling with the same dilemma Wes had been struggling with since he had learned the truth? Nicole was alive. Legally, she was still Wes's wife, and that meant his dreams of a life with Natalie were probably dead. He knew his sister-in-law well enough to know that she wouldn't marry Wes now—even if he divorced Nicole. Wes knew Natalie didn't believe in divorce, and she would have no part in it if Wes chose to end his marriage to his wife.

"I'd better go and work on dinner," Natalie said quietly and left the room.

CHAPTER 41
September 2010

The sun was a majestic ball of orange fire as it sat on the horizon briefly and then sank slowly out of sight behind the foothills of the Texas Hill Country. Wes rolled down the windows of the truck as he drove, letting the fall air rush in. It was a beautiful evening in South Texas. With the sun gone, a cool breeze had wafted in from the north and now filled his lungs. Wes started to relax for the first time since he had learned the news that Nicole wasn't dead. He needed time alone to think this through.

The pain that Wes had seen in the children's faces at dinner fueled the anger he was already feeling toward Nicole. He felt like he was going to explode and excused himself before he did. Natalie, her servant's heart always evident, volunteered to stay with the children while he took a drive alone. There were no more words of comfort that Wes could offer his children. Each of them needed to sort through their own thoughts and emotions. Perhaps, later they could all regroup and pray together.

God was all Wes had to lean on right now. He had tried to call his grandfather on his way out of town, but there was no answer. There was no one else to talk with except God, so his thoughts turned to prayer. *Lord, please help me.* Suddenly, anger crowded out the words of prayer. Wes wanted revenge. He wanted to hurt Nicole as much as she had hurt him and the children. But then a still small voice whispered something in his ear. "What would Jesus do?"

"I'm not Jesus," Wes said the words out loud.

"Do you want to be like Him? Or do you want to be like you have always been?"

The two natures of one man battled inside him for the next hour. The old nature told him to head to the courthouse the next day and file for divorce. Who would blame him? But the new nature was telling him something very different. *"I have been crucified with Christ and I no longer live, but Christ lives in me. The life I now live in the body, I live by faith in the Son of God, who loved me and gave himself for me."*

Wes had memorized Galatians 2:20 a few weeks ago, and something made it pop into his head at that moment. Was this the Holy Spirit? Another Bible verse immediately came into his mind. *"And we know that God causes all things to work together for good to those who love God, to those who are called according to His purpose."*

Wes prayed that he might have faith to believe it.

When Wes walked back into the house shortly after 9 p.m., he was surprised to hear a familiar voice coming from the kitchen. It was Roger, and Wes swallowed hard when he emerged from the kitchen with Natalie and all three children. "Grandfather? What are you doing here?" Wes asked, trying to steady his voice as he gazed into the familiar face now ravaged by a deadly disease.

"I got your message and decided to drive down," Roger said.

"And I already scolded him about doing that," Natalie chimed in. "So you don't need to say anything about that. I already told him one of us could drive him home."

"I'll drive him back," Wes said.

"What about my car?" Roger protested.

"Jordan can follow us in your car."

"It's a school night," Natalie pointed out. "I'll follow you up there."

"Let me, let me," Jordan begged, turning her eyes to Summer for help. "If you go, Aunt Natalie, then I'll have to put Summer to bed instead of you."

"I want Aunt Natalie to put me to bed," Summer agreed.

"We'll be back by eleven," Wes said over his shoulder as he headed back out to the car. "She never goes to bed before that."

"So Nicole is alive, " Roger said, as Wes was pulling out of the driveway. The older man was leaning back in the seat. He was having a hard time keeping his eyes open.

"Apparently."

"Praise the Lord, Wes. She's alive."

"I'm not quite there yet, Grandpa," Wes replied, unable to hide the bitterness in his voice.

"I can understand that. If your grandmother had done what Nicole did, I don't think I'd be too excited about having her back, either."

"Who said anything about her coming back?"

"You don't think she wants to come home?"

"Well let's see. She faked her own death and disappeared. She's made no effort to contact me, the children, or anyone else in San Antonio that I know of. She's started a new life without us. No, I don't think she's coming home."

"But what if she did want to come home? Would you take her back?"

"No," Wes said angrily.

"What about the children?"

"They're better off without her."

Wes looked at his grandfather's face. He saw in his eyes a thousand-yard stare— the distant look of a man nearing the brink of eternity and ready to cross to the other side. Wes couldn't bear the thought of losing the man he loved so much, but he knew that the loss would come in the next few months.

A long silence followed before Roger finally spoke again. "Reminds me of a story. Are you familiar with the story of Hosea?"

"No."

"You might want to read the book of Hosea. He was an Old Testament prophet, and he found himself in a similar situation to the one you're in right now. Hosea married a woman named Gomer who was unfaithful to him. She even had children by other men. God told Hosea before the marriage that this would happen. After it happened, God told him to go after her, forgive her, and bring her home again. Do you know why?"

"I have no idea."

"The Lord said, 'Go, show your love to your wife again, though she is loved by another and is an adulteress. Love her as the Lord loves the Israelites, though they turn to other gods.' You see, Gomer's unfaithfulness to Hosea was an object lesson to God's people. We're unfaithful to Him, just like the Israelites were. God asks us to forgive others, just as we ask Him to forgive us."

"So that's what you would advise me to do?" Wes asked.

"Oh, heavens no, Son. I'm not in the advice business. Besides, I believe our Father would know better than I would."

Wes managed a smile as he pondered the older man's wisdom.

"So when do you think I'll hear from Him?"

"As soon as you open your Bible and start reading it again."

CHAPTER 42

October 2010

Wes sat on the wood bench and stared straight ahead at the sign on the wall that read: "HOMICIDE, ROBBERY, SEX CRIMES, NIGHT CID." Then he looked down at the floor and wondered what Sgt. Niebring was about to tell him. Wes had informed police a week ago that Nicole appeared to be alive and living in southern California. Niebring had called him that morning and invited him to come downtown for a meeting. Wes could only assume that they had located Nicole. He wondered if she had been arrested and if she was being brought back to San Antonio to face charges.

Wes heard the loud pop and saw the electronically controlled door open to the left of him. Niebring, dressed in his usual white short-sleeve shirt and tie, approached with his hand extended. His attitude appeared to have changed since he had ruled out Wes as a murder suspect. "Mr. Tanner. Good to see you again." Wes shook his hand, and they made small talk for a moment before the detective led him back to his office.

"You have something to tell me?" Wes asked as he sat down across the desk from the detective. Wes suddenly felt like he needed a cigarette in the worst possible way. This feeling was still familiar even six weeks after he smoked his last cigarette. Every time he felt the old craving, he prayed for strength. So far, he hadn't given into the temptation.

"Mr. Tanner, we found your wife. She's alive and well, as you thought. Of course, we had to confirm your story for ourselves before we could drop our investigation."

"Is she in jail?"

"She wasn't arrested."

"Why not?"

"She didn't break any law that we know of, except possible identity theft."

"She stole someone's identity?"

"I doubt it. She probably just bought the new identity."

"You can do that?"

"Sure. You can purchase a new identity for a few hundred dollars. She's got a new driver's license and Social Security card. We might not have ever found her except for the work of your private investigator. Be sure to thank him for us."

There was a moment of silence as Wes stared out the window. He was in a daze. All kinds of thoughts were going through his mind. He was realizing just how badly his wife wanted a new life. What was so terrible about her old life? This was a question that Wes might ask her someday if he ever saw her again.

"Sergeant Niebring?" Wes broke the silence.

"Yes?"

"Where did you find her?"

"At her office. She works for a real estate company in the Los Angeles area."

"What did she tell police when she was questioned?"

"Not much. She said she was okay."

"Do you have her phone number?"

"Yes."

"Good."

"But I can't give it to you."

"Why not?"

"Because she doesn't want anyone to contact her."

"You've got to be kidding me," Wes said with disgust. "That's okay. I don't want to contact her. She can go to hell as far as I'm concerned."

"I can understand how you feel."

"I doubt that."

"You're right, Mr. Tanner. I probably don't have any idea how you're feeling. I lost my wife a number of years ago, but it wasn't through divorce. She died after a long illness."

"She left you. But not of her own choosing. God took her."

"Cancer took her," Niebring said. "I don't know what God had to do with it."

"I'm sorry for your loss."

"And I'm sorry for your ordeal."

"I appreciate that." Wes nodded, feeling a connection for the first time with the gruff detective. After all, he was a man not unlike Wes, with his own pain and human frailties. "Can you give me the name she's using?"

"I can't do that."

"Can you give me an address?" Wes said desperately. "Can you give me the name of the real estate company out in California?"

"I can't tell you that, either."

"Can you tell me anything?"

"I can tell you only that your wife is alive and living in Los Angeles. She got there on her own, and she has no interest at this time in talking to family members."

"What about her children? Are they going to be allowed to talk to their mother?"

"I'm sorry, Mr. Tanner. She'll have to initiate that."

Wes sat and stared at the floor and then looked up at Niebring.

"You really thought I killed her, didn't you?"

"At one point."

"At one point?"

"It began to dawn on me that she might not be dead."

"Why?"

"All these months. No body. I just had a hunch. People disappear all of the time. Most of them haven't been murdered. They just wanted to disappear."

Wes stared straight ahead as he walked out the door of the police building, but he didn't see a thing. He crossed the street, climbed into his truck, and just sat in the seat for a few minutes, trying to sort things out in his mind. Perhaps there was finally a silver lining in this dark cloud that had hung over his life for so many months. Wes had been studying the Bible recently on the issue of marriage, divorce, and remarriage. He had looked up several verses, including those in Matthew 19 and 1 Corinthians 7. According to the Bible, there were two reasons where divorce was permissible. First, you could divorce and remarry if your spouse was unfaithful. Check. Second, you could divorce and remarry if you were deserted by an unbelieving spouse. Check again.

If God's Word said Wes could move on without committing a sin, then why shouldn't he? If Natalie was willing to be his wife, they could finally have the life they both wanted. However, Wes couldn't stop thinking about the story his grandfather had told him in the truck a week ago. God had told Hosea to take his wayward wife back and show her love in spite of her infidelity. Was God contradicting Himself here, or was there something that Wes was missing?

It was late morning, and traffic was light as he guided the truck through downtown San Antonio. As he cruised up Broadway, Wes decided he wouldn't go directly home. He needed some time to think and even pray about the events that had transpired. There was no question about what he wanted to do. Wes wanted to drive straight over to Natalie's office right now and tell her how he felt. But was this the right thing to do? The Bible said that "the heart is deceitful above all else." Was he being deceived by his own heart?

Twenty minutes later, Wes pulled into the parking lot of Stone Oak Bible Church. He walked around to the side of the building and entered the church office. The secretary greeted him with a smile and escorted Wes into Garcia's office. The senior pastor rose to his feet and shook his hand warmly.

"Wes, I apologize. I had you on the calendar for Friday."

"That's right. Our appointment is Friday. I can come back then if you're busy."

"No, no! Sit down," Garcia said, walking around from behind the desk. He led Wes over to a round table, where the two men sat down.

"Ernesto, I wanted to thank you again for all of the time you've spent with me the past few months. It means a lot to me."

"It means a lot to me, too. There's nothing more exciting for a pastor than to see a young Christian growing in his relationship with the Lord."

"I'm not that young anymore," Wes quipped.

"You're young in the Lord, Wes."

"I understand." There was a pause as Garcia waited patiently for Wes to state the purpose of his drop-in visit. "The police found Nicole."

"Praise the Lord."

"That's exactly what my grandfather said."

"But you're not saying an 'Amen' to that?"

"Don't get me wrong. I'm glad Nicole is alive. It's not like I wanted her to meet some terrible fate. But she left me and the children. She was unfaithful to me. From my reading of scripture, I have grounds for a divorce, with God's blessing."

"I would agree that you have biblical grounds for divorce." Garcia nodded. "But I would take exception with that last statement. Just because God permits something doesn't mean He blesses it."

"What do you mean?"

"Malachi 2:16 says that God hates divorce."

"But I read in Matthew 19 that no sin was committed if a man divorced his wife and remarried. If God hates divorce—"

"Wes, what I have I told you about studying the Bible?"

"Always study it in context," Wes said, feeling like the pastor could see right into his heart as Garcia pushed a Bible across the table.

"Read Matthew 19. Start in verse three."

"Some Pharisees came to him to test him. They asked, 'Is it lawful for a man to divorce his wife for any and every reason?' 'Haven't you read,' he replied, 'that at the beginning the Creator made them male and female and said: For this reason a man will leave his father and mother and be united to his wife, and the two will become one flesh? So they are no longer two, but one flesh. Therefore what God has joined together, let no one separate.' 'Why then,' they asked, 'did Moses command that a man give his wife a certificate of divorce and send her away?' Jesus replied, 'Moses permitted you to divorce your wives because your hearts were hard. But it was not this way from the beginning. I tell you that anyone who divorces his wife, except for sexual immorality, and marries another woman commits adultery.'" Wes finished reading and looked at his mentor inquisitively.

"Can you divorce your unfaithful wife and marry another woman without committing adultery? Yes. Is it God's best for you? In my opinion, the answer is no."

"But I have no reason to believe that Nicole wants to be married to me."

"Perhaps you need to find that out before you make a decision."

CHAPTER 43

October 2010

Wes made a decision on the short drive from his church to his home. He would attempt to find Nicole. His first thought was to send an e-mail to her at the old account he had discovered last week. But it had appeared that this account was no longer being used, and she might not see the e-mail. Wes needed to get the phone number that the police had. He called Brad Mills and asked the police reporter to meet him at the house. Wes thought that he might be able to force the police to release information about Nicole under The Freedom of Information Act.

When Wes arrived at the house, he assembled the children for a meeting and told them the news about their mother being found but not wanting to be contacted. Jordan and Monty had little to say, but Summer burst into tears again. She simply couldn't understand why her mother didn't want her anymore. Wes comforted Summer until she stopped crying and then put a Veggie Tales DVD in for her to watch.

With Summer occupied, Wes went to check on Jordan. She was lying on her bed, staring at the ceiling when he knocked on the door.

"Are you okay?"

"I'm fine," Jordan said, refusing to look at him.

"I don't believe you."

"I'm fine, Dad. Really. I'm glad Mom is alive and well. I hope she has a nice life."

"You must feel rejected."

"Don't you?"

"Yes," Wes admitted. "But I also understand why your mother might not want to see me again. I can't understand her not wanting to see you, Monty, or Summer."

"I guess she got tired of us."

"I don't know what's going through her mind. I'd sure like to find out."

The doorbell rang downstairs.

"Are you expecting someone?" Jordan asked.

"Yes. The newspaper reporter wants to talk to me."

"Why are you talking to a reporter?"

"I'm going to make an appeal to your mother to contact us." Wes told a half-truth. He didn't want to go into all of the details of the FOIA request with his daughter.

"How can she read the story in LA?"

"It'll go on the wire. Hopefully, she'll read it, or someone will tell her about it."

Jordan seemed satisfied with the answer and Wes descended the stairs and headed for the front door. Expecting to see the reporter, Wes turned to find himself staring into the eyes of Ezra Goldstein.

"Wes, I hope I'm not disturbing you."

"You're not what's disturbing me." Wes extended his hand and Goldstein took it.

"Can I have just a moment of your time?"

"Certainly. Let's go into the study," Wes said, opting for a more private location.

Wes led the way into the study, but he didn't close the door behind him as he motioned for Goldstein to sit on the sofa.

Goldstein was quick to the point. "I heard the news."

"The news?"

"About your wife being located. It was on the radio."

"It didn't take long."

"The report said that police wouldn't release information on the new identity, or the whereabouts of your wife."

"That's correct."

"Do you have any interest in locating her in Los Angeles?"

"Yes."

"I may be able to do that."

"I'd settle for a phone number at this point. There's no guarantee she would take my call, but she might. I would like to talk with her one more time."

"I was thinking in terms of flying out to southern California and seeing if I could meet with her."

"Mr. Goldstein, a trip to California is expensive. I don't have any more money."

"I'm not expecting any additional compensation."

"Okay." Wes shrugged. "If you don't have anything better to do with your time."

"Wes?" Natalie looked surprised to see him. She was standing in the doorway, and their eyes met for a moment. Unable to wait any longer, Wes had driven over to her house.

"Did you hear the news?"

Natalie nodded. "They broke in with a bulletin on television. I can't believe they're going to let her continue to live under her new identity. It's just not right."

"Can you believe she wants to? Can you believe anyone would refuse to contact her own children? She's the scum of the earth, Natalie."

"You really need to try and forgive her."

"I want you to read this," Wes said, ignoring her last comment.

"What is it?"

"It's a letter to Nicole. I'm going to send it with Ezra Goldstein."

"He's going to find her?"

"He's going to try."

"I hope he can," Natalie said. "What happens if he does find her?"

"He'll give her this letter, and she'll know how I feel."

"Are you going to take her back?"

"She doesn't want to come back."

"But what if she does?"

Wes took Natalie's hand in his own and looked into her eyes. He could feel his heart pounding like it was coming out of his chest.

"I don't want her back, Nat. I want you."

Natalie looked up into his eyes and held his gaze a moment too long. Wes bent down and kissed her gently on the lips. She pulled away from him quickly.

"No, Wes."

"Why?"

"Nicole is your wife."

"She left me. I'm going to divorce her."

"What about the children?"

"They don't want her, either."

"That's not true." Natalie looked away. "They do want her. She's their mother."

"You've been a better mother to them than Nicole ever was."

"*She's* their mother."

"What about us, Nat?"

"There is no us."

"You don't love me?"

Natalie raised her head and looked into his eyes. Wes saw a tear.

"It doesn't matter."

"Why?"

"Because Nicole is your wife, Wes. You chose her."

When Wes returned to the house, Summer ran into the foyer. She looked into his face, noticing his eyes were red. "What's wrong, Daddy?"

"Nothing."

"You're sad like me, aren't you?"

Wes nodded.

When Summer hugged him, Wes noticed she was holding something in her hand.

"What's that, Sunshine?"

"Daddy, is that man going to find Mommy?"

"What man?"

"That man that came to see you today."

"Were you eavesdropping, Summer?" Wes asked gently.

She nodded. "I'm sorry. But is he?"

"He's going to look for her."

"Could you have him give this to Mommy?"

"Sure," Wes said, taking the note that she was holding out to him. "I'll tell him to give it to your mother when he finds her."

CHAPTER 44
October 2010

Ezra Goldstein disembarked his flight and walked into the spacious terminal area at Los Angeles International's American Airlines gate. He was looking for the sign to baggage claim and spotted it above the down escalator just to his right. Goldstein was eager to reclaim his bags, go outside, and stretch his legs after the long flight from Texas.

It had been a full day of travel already. Goldstein had spent more than three hours in the air, en route from Dallas. Even though San Antonio was the seventh largest city in the country, there were no direct flights to LA, so Goldstein had spent two hours in Dallas waiting for his connection.

As he walked down the blue-carpeted tramway, Goldstein took note of the people walking in the opposite direction toward the boarding gates. Like zombies, each seemed transfixed in his or her own little world. Some were carrying chic shopping bags filled with gifts and souvenirs from LA's many exotic boutiques.

After fishing his black leather carry-all and suit bag from the baggage carousel, Goldstein headed out the nearest exit and into the fresh, breezy southern California afternoon. He liked this airport. The curbside pickup lane was much wider than at most airports, giving travelers plenty of space to rent a cab, hop on a shuttle, or a bus. The curbside was lined with lush palms and plants with red flowering tops.

Goldstein had decided to hire a limo service on this trip to Los Angeles. While he was comfortable driving in the nation's second-largest city, he wanted to avoid the hassle of renting a car and the liability that went along with it. Besides, he did not want plates that could be traced back to him.

Goldstein knew Nicole Tanner was out there somewhere. What he didn't know was what kind of shape he would find her in. On one occasion, he recalled being hired to find a runaway teenager. The father of the girl gave him a recent picture of the girl. She looked just as sweet as a peach, dressed in a cheerleading outfit and clutching pom-poms to her chest. When he finally located her, Goldstein found the cheerleader had become an emaciated, street-hardened, drug-addicted wretch. Goldstein could only hope that a similar fate hadn't befallen Wes Tanner's wife.

Standing on the spacious walk outside LAX, Goldstein lit a Galoise cigarette and took a puff. It had been a long, smokeless flight, and the French cigarette never tasted better. His attention was drawn skyward to the departing and incoming commercial jets. As Goldstein waited for his escort car, he watched as a stream of highly polished Mercedes, Jaguars, and Ferraris zipped up to the curb, scooped up their parties, and drove away quickly in the direction of the freeway interchange.

When Goldstein had made arrangements from San Antonio with the limo service, he had been particular about his needs. He wanted the most obscure automobile available, preferably a ten-year-old model of a large, white sedan—either a Ford or Chevrolet. When he spotted a late nineties model white Chevrolet Caprice slowly cruising up to the curb in front of the terminal, he was pleased. The driver, dressed in a black suit, pulled up to the curb and stepped out of the vehicle to greet him.

"Mr. Goldstein?"

"Yes."

"Welcome to Los Angeles, sir," the driver said, as he walked around in front of the car, took Goldstein's bags, and loaded them into the trunk. Goldstein stepped on the butt of his cigarette and slid into the back seat. The driver's manner was courteous and professional. Goldstein had noticed the driver's physique as he loaded his bags before driving away from the airport. This was a man who spent time working out in a gym. Goldstein was confident he could take care of himself if they should run into any trouble.

Goldstein had been insistent about one other thing from the limo service. For his entire trip in Los Angeles, Goldstein wanted only one driver. When on an out-of-town assignment, the P.I. relied above all on constancy, familiarity, and confidentiality. He had checked out this limo service and was confident it would fill the bill.

"You know the destination?" Goldstein asked.

"Yes, sir, the Three Palms on Wilshire."

Goldstein dozed off once during the drive across town. Upon arrival at the hotel, the driver reached into the glove compartment and gave Goldstein a cell phone with a pre-coded direct dial number to the limo driver. "I am assigned to you for the duration of your trip, Mr. Goldstein. Call me, day or night, and I will answer," the driver said.

"Thank you," Goldstein said as a bellhop gathered up his luggage. Goldstein followed him inside to the check-in counter. After checking in, he headed directly to his room. He wanted to call his colleague Jim Hunt. When Goldstein needed help in southern California, he knew he could count on Hunt. More than once, his friend had been there to fill in the blanks—especially when Goldstein had to track down the address of a contact in Chinatown, Compton, or anywhere hostile to outsiders asking questions.

Goldstein had arranged to meet Jim Hunt at the Peking Duck. It was also one of Hunt's favorite watering holes, and this was the part that bothered Goldstein. It seemed that in recent years when Goldstein had met Hunt for dinner in LA, he noticed that his friend was extra generous with the girls who took the drink orders. As a result, the drinks would come quickly and would be mixed extra strong. Goldstein knew that his friend had a drinking problem, but he just couldn't find it within himself to confront him about it.

"A glass of Manischevitz," Goldstein told the waitress. Goldstein would have one with dinner and one after the meal. In spite of its Welch's grape juice flavor, each glass of Manischevitz sparked warm memories for Goldstein. He fondly recalled the nights he had spent dissipating into a soft and bleary haze with friends at Yeshiva University.

The atmosphere in the restaurant was exquisite. They were seated at a small table near a large fountain that stood in the center of the restaurant. The water flowed from the top of the fountain and cascaded down the sides, which were formed of ornate white rock. Mounted among the rocks and visible through the flowing water were miniature lights of blue, red, green, and amber. Atop the fountain was a large dragon made of black marble. In the retaining pool below, large multicolored carp swam lazily among thousands of shining coins that had been thrown in by patrons.

Above each table at the Peking Duck was a spinning crystal globe that picked up the lights from the fountain and cast a faint rainbow-colored strobe throughout the room. On the walls were murals depicting scenes from ancient China, each etched by hand in ivory. The carpet was blood red , and the walls were azure blue. The restaurant was dark, cool, and private, but alive with muted colors.

Goldstein sipped his drink while Hunt drank heartily. Forgetting himself, Goldstein ordered another glass of wine as the two caught up on old times and shared both humorous and somber stories of their lives on the street.

"Jim, I could use you help," Goldstein said as he fished into his pocket for Nicole Tanner's business card. The card, obtained from Wes Tanner, had a photograph of a smiling Nicole standing in front of a real estate sign. Goldstein proceeded to tell Hunt pertinent facts of the case, including his theory on why she faked her own death.

"Are you sure it was another man?" Hunt asked.

"Yes. Her husband found an e-mail she sent to her lover before she left for LA."

"It will be no easy matter to find this woman. Do you know how and when she arrived here in LA?"

"By bus a little more than five months ago," Goldstein said.

"Can I keep this card?"

"Of course. I have others."

Hunt stared at the business card for a moment. "She's very beautiful, isn't she?"

"Yes."

"Having a beautiful wife is a curse."

"Then may God curse me and let me die a happy man." Goldstein winked.

Goldstein spent the next morning in the lobby of the hotel searching websites on the internet for pictures of local Realtors. He found none that resembled Nicole Tanner. At noon, he took a break and returned to his room. He flipped on the TV and tuned it to CNN. They were covering the crash of some small commuter plane, and Goldstein found himself saddened for the families of all those involved.

There was a knock at the door, and a woman from the kitchen brought lunch, which consisted of a Reuben sandwich with extra sauerkraut and a baked potato with sour cream and chives.

Goldstein was about to bite into his sandwich when the phone rang. He answered it on the first ring.

"Ezra, it's Jim. I think I might have your lady. It seems a woman fitting the description of your target was looking for someone to get her a Social Security card and California driver's license last June."

"You don't say?"

"Yeah, deal is, the guy she went to for the license is a guy that works for me. Hey, guess what else?"

"I'm all ears," Goldstein said, feeling the veins on his neck pumping vigorously with excitement at the break in the case.

"Usually when my guy asks the client for existing ID they almost always tell him they don't have one. But this woman actually produced a Texas driver's license."

"Jim, I owe you big time, old friend. Do you have the name she assumed?"

"I thought you might be interested in that piece of information. It's Mary Worth."

"Mary Worth," Goldstein exhaled softly into the phone.

"Let me make your job even easier, Ezra. Apparently, she didn't want to take a chance coming back to the forger's shop to pick up the ID, so guess what she did."

"Tell me."

"She gave him an address in Beverly Hills to mail it to her. You ready?"

Goldstein grabbed a ballpoint pen and a small pad of paper from the top of the bedside nightstand. "I'm ready."

"264 South La Cienega Boulevard, Box 1491, Beverly Hills, California, 90211."

CHAPTER 45
October 2010

Nicole Tanner had dreamed about living in southern California since she was a little girl. In her dreams, experienced mostly during her waking hours, she would be discovered by a talent scout traveling through South Texas.

The talent scout would just happen to be sitting in the back of the high school auditorium when she played Annie Sullivan in *The Miracle Worker*. Blown away by her beauty and acting skills, he would whisk her off to Hollywood, where she would became a famous movie star. Nicole would get her star on the Hollywood Walk of Fame and buy her mansion on a bluff overlooking the Pacific Ocean.

She actually kept the dream alive in the back of her mind for several years after she married Wes. There was a growing movie industry in Austin, just eighty miles from San Antonio, and Nicole believed she could land a part in an independent film. Hadn't people always told her she had movie star looks? She drove to Austin several times to audition for parts, but she was never called back for a second reading. Wes had not been supportive, and he pressured her to give up her dream. As the years passed, the dream died. Even if she divorced Wes, it was too late. Nicole knew her beauty had begun to fade. The best Nicole could hope for was an occasional trip to southern California.

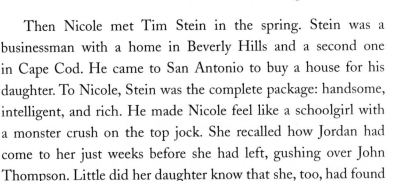

Then Nicole met Tim Stein in the spring. Stein was a businessman with a home in Beverly Hills and a second one in Cape Cod. He came to San Antonio to buy a house for his daughter. To Nicole, Stein was the complete package: handsome, intelligent, and rich. He made Nicole feel like a schoolgirl with a monster crush on the top jock. She recalled how Jordan had come to her just weeks before she had left, gushing over John Thompson. Little did her daughter know that she, too, had found a captivating, new love interest. It wasn't something Nicole could share with Jordan, or anyone else.

On that Saturday evening, Nicole had invited her best friend, Marty Chavez, to Bennigan's for a drink. After downing a few frozen margaritas for courage, she almost told Chavez about her plan to stage her own death, travel by bus to southern California, and take up a new life with Stein. Chavez had known they were having an affair, and she was far from disapproving the idea of Nicole leaving Wes. But Chavez would not have approved of Nicole leaving her children without a word of explanation, or even a good-bye. But that's exactly what Nicole did. She left her old life behind and started a new one. Nicole had expected it to be easy to step into a new life, and it would have been easy if she could have simply become Mrs. Tim Stein. When she arrived in LA on the Greyhound bus, she had every reason to believe it was only a matter of time until she and Stein were married.

As it turned out, Nicole learned a lesson she should have learned a long time ago. Talk is cheap. Stein told her later that he never believed she would leave her family and move to LA. And when he found out about the circumstances surrounding her departure from San Antonio, he used that as an excuse to break off the relationship. She was left with nothing. Broke and without an identity to pursue gainful employment, she had to become resourceful to survive. She heard about the place where the illegal immigrants went to purchase a new identity, and she became

Mary Worth. Nicole took a one-day real estate prep class, studied a few more days, and passed the state exam on her first attempt.

Nicole was soon able to secure employment at one of the top real estate firms in Beverly Hills, and she had been closing bigger sales than she had ever closed in San Antonio. It was hard work selling residential real estate in southern California, but Nicole had never been afraid of hard work. With no husband or children to worry about, she was free to put in the long hours necessary to become successful in the Los Angeles market. With her first big commission check, Nicole was able to move out of the dumpy hotel room she was renting by the week and move into a modest one-story tract house.

It wasn't long before she had turned the little house into a home while she dreamed of buying a nicer place on the ocean. It would happen one day, she promised herself, if she continued to work hard. And she would. The more time she spent working, the less time she had to think about what she had lost. The truth was that she missed Jordan, Monty, and Summer desperately. Sometimes, she even missed Wes.

Nicole refused to dwell on her feelings of loss because she knew there was no turning back. Nicole Tanner no longer existed. She was Mary Worth now, forging a new identity and a new life. Perhaps, some day she would meet a man who would make her happy. She might even have more children, if it wasn't too late. She could be a better mother than she had been to her three children—if she had a second chance.

Everything was starting to come together until the day the police showed up at her office. Nicole called an attorney client for assistance, and he was quick to point out that she hadn't broken any laws. She might be in a little hot water for identity theft, but he could get her out of that. The attorney said she had a right to start a new life in another state if she so desired. After checking with San Antonio police, the local authorities agreed. Nicole's whereabouts would not be disclosed to her husband or anyone else in her old hometown.

Once again, Nicole was free to live her life any way she chose as long as she remained a law-abiding citizen. So Nicole went about her business. She continued to sell houses and make more money. She purchased a nice car. On the surface, life was good. But under the surface beat the heart of a lonely woman. It was much more than just missing a man in her life. In spite of her best efforts, she couldn't push her children out of her mind.

Nicole wondered how Jordan was doing in her junior year in high school. Did Natalie understand the side of Jordan that was so much like her mother? Nicole thought about Monty. He was fourteen now. How was he doing in the awkward period between boyhood and manhood? And then there was Summer. Her youngest daughter, now almost seven, would be getting the love and nurturing she needed from Natalie. However, that didn't quell Nicole's desire to see Summer. She wanted to hold her daughter, kiss her and tell her how she was God's gift to her.

When she was honest with herself, Nicole had to admit that she yearned in the deepest part of her soul for all of her children. When her loneliness reached its apex, she would pick up the phone and start to dial the home number in San Antonio. She wondered who would answer. What would she say? Would she break down and cry? Beg for forgiveness? Ask for permission to come home? At those times, Nicole was prepared to do anything to be reunited with her children.

But one thing kept her from completing the phone call. And that one thing might have kept her from ever calling her children. Fear of rejection. Nicole knew her heart couldn't bear to hear the words of rejection. "We don't want you anymore, Mom. We don't need you. We're just fine without you. We have Dad. And we have Aunt Natalie. She's our mother now."

And what would Natalie think about all of this? Would her Christian morals prevent her from marrying a divorced man upon learning that Wes was not a widower? Natalie could probably find a way to justify marrying Wes after he was divorced. Wes was probably down at the courthouse filing for divorce hours after he learned the news that his wife was alive. Fact was, no one, including Nicole, could blame him. Wes deserved better than what he had received, and he would soon get it with Natalie.

With thoughts of her soon-to-be ex-husband filling her mind, Nicole stepped out of her Cadillac and entered the post office on Wilshire Boulevard. Lost in her own world on a sunny, October day, she didn't even notice the bearded man with the stone-cold eyes that was following her. Inside the building, she turned her key in the post office box and found only junk mail. Disappointed, she turned around and was startled to see someone looking over her shoulder.

"Nicole?"

"Yes?" she said without thinking.

"Nicole Tanner?"

She didn't answer and was only able to stare at the dark eyes that were slowly softening into the weathered skin. The man was reaching into his coat pocket now. Nicole swallowed hard. "I have something for you."

He produced a small, white envelope and handed it to her. She recognized the handwriting on the front. It was simply addressed: *Mommy.*

"Who are you?"

"I'm a private investigator. This young lady wanted me to deliver this to you."

CHAPTER 46
October 2010

Ezra Goldstein was accustomed to catching people off guard in his line of work, but he couldn't recall seeing anyone reeling like Nicole Tanner as she read the letter from her daughter. In a moment, the expression of surprise on the beautiful woman's face had turned into bitter remorse. Teardrops rolled off her face and fell on the handwritten letter, causing some words to smear on the page she held.

"Summer sent you?" Nicole finally managed to ask.

"Yes. Your family misses you, Mrs. Tanner."

"It doesn't matter," she said through sobs. "I can't go back."

Goldstein didn't want to discuss this inside the post office. "Can I buy you a cup of coffee?"

"I wish I had time." Nicole managed a feeble smile. "I have a showing in thirty minutes, and I'm a mess." Nicole's mascara had run, and Goldstein understood the woman needed to get cleaned up if she was going to conceal her recent emotional tumult from her clients.

"Okay. How about tonight? Let's dine together, and we can talk things over."

"I don't know—"

"I saw your family very recently. I can bring you up to date on all of them."

"Okay," Nicole agreed.

"Six o'clock?" Goldstein asked.

"I have a showing at five."

"How about seven?"

"Better make it eight."

"I'll pick you up. Can you give me your address?"

"I'll meet you," Nicole said, and it occurred to Goldstein that her decision could only be viewed as prudent. After all, he was a stranger to her. She had known him all of five minutes. She would certainly be more comfortable meeting him.

"Do you know where the Water Grill is?" Goldstein asked.

"I've heard of it. I can find it."

"I'll see you there."

The sedan from the limo service pulled up in front of the Three Palms Hotel at exactly 7:30 p.m. Goldstein had called the limo driver after the meeting with Nicole in the post office and told him the time he wanted to be picked up. Goldstein was pleased at the punctuality of the driver.

"Good evening, Mr. Goldstein."

"Good evening." Goldstein smiled as he slipped into the backseat. "Please take me to Water Grill. Do you know where it's located?"

"Yes, sir. South Grand Avenue."

The Caprice cruised down the streets that grew darker and more silent, leading away from the crowds. Goldstein peered out of his window and saw a man walking alone on the sidewalk in a rain coat. The temperature had begun to drop, and a storm was on its way. Goldstein noticed all of the stores on the street were locked up behind iron grilles. The driver turned down another street, and in a few minutes they were on Grand and then pulling up in front of the Water Grill. Goldstein wasn't prepared for the wind, which hit him squarely in the face as he stepped out of the car. He hurried across the street, with his light jacket flapping against his body. The skies opened up, and the rain came down hard just as Goldstein reached the entrance to the restaurant. Hopefully, the storm would pass before it was time to be picked up.

Inside the Water Grill, an attractive young lady in a white trouser suit greeted Goldstein with a smile and asked if he had reservations. He did. Goldstein gave her Nicole's description and asked if she had arrived. The hostess told him that she had not, but that she would go ahead and seat him, keeping an eye out for his party. Goldstein agreed and followed the hostess to his table.

The atmosphere inside the restaurant was warm and inviting—fine wood, soft lighting, and an intimate table arrangement. A waiter asked if he was dining alone, and Goldstein told him he expected a female companion to join him shortly. Asked if he would care for a drink, Goldstein mentioned that he had heard good things about their wine cellar. The waiter recommended a bottle of Argyle Nuthouse Willamette Valley Pinot Noir, and Goldstein agreed.

After the waiter left, Goldstein looked around at the people dining at nearby tables. A handsome young man and a beautiful woman held hands across the table and smiled at each other. At another table, a boisterous party of men were toasting one of their own for some sort of business accomplishment. Out of the corner of his eye, Goldstein glimpsed Nicole, wearing a long, black dress, moving toward him. Even though she was holding an umbrella, Goldstein could see that she was drenched.

Goldstein rose to his feet. "Good evening, Mrs. Tanner."

"A lot of good this did." Nicole laughed, holding up the umbrella.

"I thought it never rained in southern California."

"But when it does, it pours."

The waiter was right behind Nicole and held her chair as she sat down. The waiter was also holding the bottle of wine and showed it to Goldstein, awaiting his approval.

"I ordered a bottle wine. Pinot Noir. Do you like wine, Mrs. Tanner?"

"Yes."

"Very well." Goldstein nodded his approval. The waiter opened the bottle and filled the glasses half full. They made small talk for the next twenty minutes, and it was only after they had placed their dinner orders that the conversation turned serious.

"How did you come to know my husband?"

"He hired me."

"To find me?"

"Yes."

"Why? So that he would know it's okay to move on with his life? Well, you found me, and you can tell him he's free to divorce me now and marry his beloved Natalie."

Goldstein took a sip of his wine and studied her face. Her voice didn't betray her emotions, but Goldstein could see the deep sadness in her eyes.

"Mrs. Tanner, I cannot speak directly for the feelings of your family, but I can tell you what I believe based upon my observations of them during this ordeal."

Goldstein leaned forward across the table and spoke in a tone barely above a whisper. "My feeling is that they desire to forgive and that they all want you to come home."

Nicole was looking at his face, but her gaze was blurry and unfocused. She seemed to be looking through him. "If only I could believe that," she finally said softly.

"You can believe it."

"No," Nicole said, and the tears began to roll down her cheeks. "I left my children behind without a word, and I left my husband for another man. I can't believe any of them could ever forgive me for what I've done."

Moved with compassion, Goldstein reached across the table and covered her trembling hand with his. "Mrs. Tanner, I've been in the business of reading people for many years, and I would not tell you this if I did not believe that it was true." Nicole was sobbing gently, and her tears fell freely as she had ceased to even try to wipe them from her face. The scene at their table had caused several other patrons to look curiously in their direction. Goldstein panned the restaurant with a steely glare, and the other patrons quickly looked away.

Nicole's shoulders heaved gently through her sobs as she let her forehead fall onto the back of her wrist on the table. When she looked up from the table, her glistening eyes were still full of sadness. "But Mr. Goldstein, what I have done can't be forgiven."

CHAPTER 47

October 2010

Natalie hadn't seen Wes since they had kissed on her front porch a week earlier. That kiss had stirred up emotions in her heart that had frightened her. There was an inner battle raging. The truth was that Natalie still wanted to be with Wes, and her mind had been working hard since he had called her with the new piece of information.

Nicole had been involved in an affair. Natalie knew her Bible, and she knew he had biblical grounds for divorce. But in her heart, Natalie knew she couldn't do it. At least, not yet. If Nicole wanted to end the marriage, there was nothing they could do about it. If Nicole divorced Wes, he could marry her. But Natalie couldn't encourage any man to divorce his wife. Marriage was a divine institution, a sacred trust. Severing that relationship always had significant consequences.

Fearing her unstable emotions, Natalie had avoided Wes. But on this particular day, she had to visit him because it was his birthday. Jordan had called earlier in the week to invite her over for dinner, but Natalie had refused. She told her niece she had a prior engagement, which was actually true. Natalie had a date that night, and she was glad to have an excuse to get out of an evening at the Tanner house. She would miss spending time with the children, but she didn't trust herself to be alone again with Wes.

Wes was out in the street throwing the football with Monty when Natalie pulled up in front of the house shortly before noon. Natalie took a deep breath, uttered an arrow prayer for strength, and got out of the car.

"Hey, stranger," Wes said as he approached the car.

"Hi, Wes," Natalie said, trying to sound nonchalant. Natalie couldn't recall a time in recent memory when so many days had passed without seeing him. She wondered if he had been thinking about her as much as she had been thinking about him.

"I want to apologize for what I did," Wes said quietly so as to not be overheard.

"It's okay."

"It wasn't okay. It made you uncomfortable. I'm sorry."

"It happened. It's over."

"I don't want it to be over, Nat. Not between us. Not ever."

"Wes, don't start," Natalie begged him. "Please."

Wes started to say something, but Monty was walking up behind him.

"Happy birthday, Wes," Natalie said, handing him a card.

"Thanks." Wes took the card but didn't open it. "Jordan told me that you turned down our dinner invitation. My birthday won't be the same without you."

"I'm sorry."

"Okay, but this is my birthday, so I'm going to insist that you buy me a cup of coffee. Let's drive down to Starbucks."

"Okay," Natalie agreed.

Inside her car, Wes wasted no time in getting right to the point.

"I want you to know that if Goldstein finds Nicole, I'm going to go out there to see her. I need to understand why she did what she did. Then I'm going to tell her good-bye. She made her choice, and now I've made mine. I'm in love with another woman.

A godly woman that I want to spend the rest of my life with, if she'll have me."

"It's not that simple," Natalie said stoically. "She's your wife, Wes."

"She left me for another man."

"You don't know if she's still with him."

"I don't care," Wes said firmly. "I don't want her anymore. I want you."

"You're being impulsive."

"Impulsive? I've been thinking about you and wanting to be with you for ten years. When your divorce was final—"

"Wes! Stop!" She held up her hand, her eyes pleading with him to not say it.

"I'll stop. I'll stop right now, and I'll never bring up the subject again if you'll look into my eyes and tell me that you don't feel the same way."

They were parked in front of Starbucks, and Natalie desperately wanted to become a good liar for just this moment. She could never pull this off, and she knew it. Before she could speak, Wes's cell phone rang. He glanced at it.

"It's Jordan."

"Go ahead and answer it."

"I'll call her back," Wes said, staring into Natalie's eyes.

"Answer it, Wes. It might be important."

Looking disgusted, Wes answered the phone.

"Yes, Jordan?"

Natalie watched his face, and it was clear that something was wrong. Very wrong.

"Okay, I'll be right there." Wes ended the call. "We need to go back home."

"What's wrong?"

"My grandfather is in the hospital."

Roger had grown increasingly ill in recent weeks and had hid it from his family. But there was no hiding it now. On the previous night, he had collapsed on the floor, struggling to breathe. A neighbor had found him that morning, still on the floor and too weak to get up. The neighbor immediately called 911. Roger was admitted to the hospital, and his doctor called Wes. The Tanners drove up that afternoon to visit him.

Sitting next to his grandfather's bed, Wes insisted that the time had come for Roger to move to San Antonio to spend his final days with Wes and the children. If Roger wasn't already weak from the relentless onslaught of the cancer, Wes couldn't have won the battle to get him to move. Roger had lived in the same house for sixty years. He had cared for his wife as she passed her final days there. He had raised his three children there. He had entertained his grandchildren and great-grandchildren there. The idea of leaving his home seemed impossible for Roger to comprehend until now.

Roger's two surviving children lived far away, so Wes made the case that he was the logical choice of caregiver. His grandfather finally agreed to the move with one condition. Wes had to agree to hospice care in the final days of Roger's life. The reason the pastor was insistent on this point was based on his own experience caring for his wife, who also died of cancer more than twenty years earlier. "You don't know how difficult those final days are," Roger had said. Wes didn't argue the point. A day later, Wes rented a small U-Haul trailer and drove to Kerrville to gather Roger's most precious possessions together. Roger had asked that Wes bring the children. It was a sad day for everyone as they faced the impending loss.

Wes was picking up the framed pictures on the mantle in the living room when Roger appeared from his bedroom. He was hooked up to his oxygen to allow him to still breathe through his dying lungs. Jordan and Monty were upstairs, but Summer lingered nearby, studying each of the pictures. "That's Grandfather," she said, pointing to one of a young man in military fatigues. The young man was smiling and had the look of carefree youth.

"That's right," Wes said, taking the picture in his hands and studying the face of the father he never knew.

"How old were you when he died?" Summer asked.

"I wasn't even born yet."

"So you never knew him?"

"No. He died in Vietnam."

"Your grandfather was a war hero," Roger said. He opened a cabinet and brought out a shadow box. It contained a Medal of Honor, and Roger handed it to Summer. She opened the box and examined the medal. She removed a piece of paper.

"Daddy? Can you read this?" She handed Wes the piece of paper.

Roger Tanner, Jr., Corporal, U.S. Marines 2nd Battalion, for conspicuous gallantry and intrepidity in action at the risk of his life and beyond the call of duty during the Battle of Khe Sanh in northwestern Quang Tri Province, Republic of Vietnam on April 3, 1968. Under siege, Corporal Tanner's platoon was in the process of establishing a blocking position when they came under intense automatic weapons fire from close range. As other members maneuvered to assault the enemy position, Corporal Tanner was ordered to provide security for the left flank of the platoon. Suddenly, the left flank received fire from enemy located in a ditch. Realizing the imminent danger to his comrades from this fire, Corporal Tanner fixed his bayonet and moved aggressively into the ditch. His action silenced the sniper fire, enabling the platoon to resume movement toward the main enemy position.

As the platoon continued to advance, the sound of heavy firing emanated from the left flank as a pitched battle ensued in the ditch where Corporal Tanner was fighting. The ditch was actually a well-organized complex of enemy defenses designed to bring devastating flanking fire on the advancing American forces. Corporal Tanner, disregarding the danger to himself, advanced 100 meters along the trench and killed six snipers, who were armed with automatic weapons. Having exhausted his ammunition, Corporal Tanner was mortally wounded when he engaged and killed two more enemy soldiers in fierce hand-to-hand combat.

His unparalleled actions saved the lives of many members of his platoon who otherwise would have fallen to the sniper fire from the ditch, and enabled his platoon to successfully overcome an enemy force of numerical superiority. Corporal Tanner's extraordinary heroism and supreme dedication to his comrades were commensurate with the finest traditions of the military service and remain a tribute to himself, his unit, and the United States Marines.

"Wow, Dad!" Monty said. He had come downstairs with Jordan and was listening while Wes read the account. "You never told me he won the Medal of Honor."

"I'll bet you were very sad growing up without your daddy," Summer said.

Wes lowered his head, surprised to feel the tears welling up inside him. How could he still cry for the loss of a man he never knew? Seeing this, Summer walked over and hugged him. "I'm sorry you lost your daddy."

Tears were rolling down Wes's cheeks as he hugged Summer. Wes looked over at his grandfather and noticed there were also tears in Roger's eyes.

"Do you want to hear something wonderful?" Roger asked Summer.

"What?"

"We're going to see your grandfather again. All of us are."

"In heaven?"

"That's right."

"Me, too?"

"Yes."

"But he's never seen me before," Summer pointed out. "How will he know me?"

Roger smiled. "He'll know you."

CHAPTER 48
October 2010

Nicole met Renée at the health club where she was went each day to work out. A big believer in fitness, Nicole found the club to be a place where she could regenerate her physical and mental energy. Nicole had been a member of a women's health club in San Antonio, and she had missed the workouts since moving out west. Now, finally in a position to afford a membership, she reveled in the time she spent in the Cardio Theater at In-Shape City: Brentwood. Nicole could alternate between the treadmill, elliptical trainer, and stair climber while watching the 46-inch plasma television.

Renée looked like Jordan. She was sixteen with a slim, well-toned figure and silky blonde hair. Their conversation was casual at first, but Nicole's interest in her caused Renée to open up and talk about school, her boyfriend, and her dream of becoming an actress. In a city where lots of pretty girls yearned to be movie stars, Renée had yet to draw any interest in her acting endeavors. But, as Nicole listened with interest, the young girl began to talk with enthusiasm about her hopes for the future. When it was time to go, Nicole gave her a hug and encouraged her to come back soon so they could visit again.

When Nicole hugged Renée, she thought about how long it had been since she had hugged Jordan. Truthfully, she had always found it difficult to hug her older daughter. Unlike Summer, who loved to hug and cuddle, Jordan did not. But on this day, Nicole ached to feel Jordan's arms around her. She thought about how much fun it would be for them to sit on the couch, eat popcorn, and watch a movie. After the movie was over, Jordan could tell Nicole about the boys she liked or the latest fashion trend she had read about. In her mind, Nicole could see Jordan opening up to her just like Renée had.

Nicole thought about all of the missed opportunities. Ever since Jordan was a baby, she had considered her more of a bother than a blessing. She had her children because it seemed to be the thing to do, but Nicole admittedly was more interested in pursuing her own agenda than raising a family. Although she complained to Wes about his paltry salary, she secretly reveled in her own ability to go out and succeed in the business world. After Natalie was divorced and started spending more time at the Tanner home, Nicole seized the opportunity to work and play more apart from her family. Monty and Summer grew up seeing Natalie more than their own mother, who was always on her way out the door to make another appointment, a workout, or meet a friend for a drink.

When Nicole made a decision to start a new life in Los Angeles, she was thinking about no one but herself. A life with Tim Stein brought with it the promise of something fresh and exciting. He had promised her everything while winning her affections in San Antonio, and she was desperate enough to believe him. She was also able to rationalize her decision, telling herself that her family would be better off without her. No one that knew Nicole casually would have ever guessed that she struggled mightily with low self-esteem. She didn't exhibit any characteristics associated with low self-esteem, such as timidity or jealousy. Nor was she prone to make negative comments about herself.

Nicole did not tell many people that her father and mother divorced when she was a baby. They certainly didn't know that her stepfather had fondled her repeatedly when she was an adolescent. Even her mother and sisters didn't know this. Missing the right kind of love from a man in her formative years, she began to search for any kind of love she could find from the boys and later the men in her life. She was promiscuous in high school and even more so in college. After she married Wes, she vowed to be faithful. But it was a vow she couldn't keep. She found herself drawn into several affairs, even before she met Stein. All of them were short-lived.

After each affair, Nicole renewed her commitment to never let it happen again. Then, after a period of months, or years, it would happen again. Each time, she experienced guilt and remorse. Wes never found out about any of her affairs because she was discreet and he was naïve, or preoccupied with his own life. But she knew in her heart that God knew what she had done and did not approve.

Nicole believed in God, and she knew God was displeased with her lifestyle. But she couldn't seem to help herself. Nicole was looking for something to fill that emptiness inside. She tried meditation. She tried sky diving. She even went bungee jumping once, as Marty Chavez cheered her on, but when the thrill was gone, the emptiness returned.

In the days since the end of her relationship with Stein, the emptiness engulfed her. In all of her life, she had never experienced such loneliness. One night, Nicole was so desperate that she drove to a bookstore and purchased a Bible. She read herself to sleep that night and many nights after that, finding a strange comfort inside the pages of the book. Slowly, something started to happen. She began to experience a peace she had never felt before. The peace often evaporated the next day, but it would reappear the next night when she opened her Bible again. After a few weeks, Nicole was reading her Bible at night and in the mornings before work.

As she continued to read her Bible regularly, Nicole found herself praying to God. Initially, she found it strange to pray. It was like talking to herself. But then she started to feel something in her heart as she asked for forgiveness and believed she had received it. Initially, her prayers were for herself. But one day, Nicole even found herself on her knees praying for her children. After that, she offered up prayers for her children on a daily basis. She had no idea what was going on in their lives, but she knew they must be dealing with difficult issues. Perhaps, she was the one responsible for causing most of those issues. This thought broke her heart and caused her to weep more than once.

Several weeks after Nicole started praying for her children, her prayers took on a new sense of urgency. It was the day the police had come to her office, and she knew her family was going to find out she was alive. They would know how she deceived them, and she begged God for her children to find forgiveness in their hearts. She also prayed that they would not be harmed by her actions or feel rejected. Nicole barely slept at all that night. Her heart was full of remorse for what she had done. How could she have been so selfish? She couldn't concentrate on her work at all the next day, so she finally went home. Sitting in her living room, she thought about returning to San Antonio. But what kind of a reception would she get? She finally picked up the phone and dialed her old home phone number. When Wes answered the phone, she hung up.

That day was not the first time she had thought about her husband. As time had passed, Nicole found her heart changing toward Wes. For many years, she had viewed him with disdain. She saw him as meek and mild—something less than a real man. He never had been much of a physical specimen. He didn't like to play sports, except with their children. Wes had been content to earn less money than she did, and he didn't seem to mind her wearing the pants in the family. Once, just a few months before she left, Jordan confronted her mother about this. Her daughter

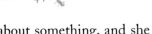

had overheard Nicole lambasting Wes about something, and she angrily accused her mother of emasculating him.

Jordan had been increasingly critical of her mother in those final months before Nicole left. She sided with her father on nearly every occasion. To his credit, Wes would defend her, and this occasion was no exception. He had admonished Jordan to be respectful to her mother. Wes avoided confrontation until Nicole got under his skin, and then he would lash out at her with a barrage of angry words. He would usually apologize later for the outburst. But as she reflected back on his words, she had to admit that Wes was mostly on target. He called her selfish, and she was selfish. He said she wasn't a good mother, and the fact was that she wasn't. He said she was a lousy wife, and she knew she had been just that to him.

Nicole had not wanted to be any kind of wife to Wes during most of the years of their marriage. She would have divorced him except for the children. Now, after months apart, she felt something strange stirring inside her. She knew Wes was a good man. Nicole remembered how he would stay late to listen to someone's problems at work, and he was never too busy to help a friend move, or stop to assist a stranded motorist. He was certainly a good father who was always there when any of the children needed him. She had to admit that he had been a good husband to her. He had tried to make their marriage work, but she wanted no part of him.

Wes deserved a better wife than Nicole, and her children deserved a better mother. That's what she kept telling herself until the day Ezra Goldstein appeared. The man's words that night at dinner had planted the seeds of a new hope in her. Goldstein had told Nicole he believed her husband and children still wanted her—even after what she had done to them. This was hard for her to believe, or accept. How could Wes, or the children, ever forgive her for what she had done? Fearing Goldstein was wrong, she started looking for an affirmation from God.

The affirmation came two nights after the meeting with Goldstein. She opened her Bible to the book of Joel and read: "I will repay you for the years the locusts have eaten…" When she read the words, it was as though Nicole heard God's own voice telling her that He would repay her for the lost years of her own life. That night, Nicole felt as if she had turned a corner. She was ready to change and become someone different. She prayed for Jesus Christ to come into her life and to change her.

After Nicole prayed to receive Christ, she prayed for direction in her life. She wanted to return to her husband and children, but she couldn't bear the thought of being rejected. Before she drifted off to sleep that night, she prayed for a sign from God. The sign she prayed for was that her husband would come for her.

CHAPTER 49
October 2010

"**W**hat the heck is an option?" Wes demanded as he leaned back in his desk chair and scratched the thinning hair on the top of his head. He was talking to his agent on the phone and trying to understand what he meant. The agent had said something about a producer loving his screenplay. That much Wes heard loud and clear. But the producer didn't have the money to buy it, so he wanted to option the script and try to find someone with deeper pockets to fund the movie.

"You need to come out here and pitch this thing," the agent told him.

"Pitch it?"

"Yeah. Tell them the story verbally. Create some heat. Get them excited enough to want to make your movie."

"Will they pay my expenses?"

"Uh, no. You have to pay your own way."

"That's a pretty big gamble for a guy that's unemployed."

"Wes, how bad do you want this thing? You've been trying to make it as a professional writer for how long? Twenty years? You're on the verge of a breakthrough here. Are you really going to let a few hundred dollars stand between you and success?"

Wes was about to share some choice words with the agent when the doorbell rang. "Listen, Stephen. Someone's at the door. I'll think it over and get back to you."

"Don't think too long," the agent said before Wes hung up the phone. He was still shaking his head as he walked to the front door. Suddenly, every thought about his screenplay and future as a writer disappeared from his mind. Ezra Goldstein was standing on the front porch.

"Greetings, Wes," Goldstein said when Wes opened the door.

"Any luck?" Wes whispered, glancing over his shoulder. Goldstein nodded, and Wes stepped out on the front porch. All three children were at home, and he didn't want anyone to overhear their conversation. Wes suggested they get in his car and drive to the nearby coffee shop.

Fifteen minutes later, as Wes sipped his coffee, Goldstein briefed him on how he found Nicole and what she had said. Goldstein concluded the story with the revelation that Nicole wanted to come back.

"I thought I was the bearer of good news."

"This is good news." Wes tried to sound enthusiastic, but he was lying, and his body language must have given him away.

"I dare say you might not be ready to welcome her back with open arms."

"Put yourself in my place. Your wife not only cheats on you, but she fakes her death so that she can leave you and the kids to start a new life with another man. Now she wants to come back. What would you do?"

"I don't know," Goldstein admitted. "In your shoes, I might be inclined to set my feelings aside and consider how my children would feel about her return."

"Summer wants her back—regardless of what she has done. I don't know about her older brother and sister."

"Don't you think all of your children want you two living under the same roof?"

"I can't speak for them."

"I don't want to stick my long, Jewish nose where it doesn't belong, but I do hope you'll consider them before you make your decision. Here's the address," Goldstein said, handing a piece of paper to Wes.

"Did you get her phone number?"

"I'm sorry, sir. I wasn't able to get that. And I need to tell you one more piece of information. You may not be happy about this."

"What is it?"

"I did give your wife the letter your daughter wrote to her, but I lost your letter."

Wes looked at Goldstein, eyes narrowing. "Lost it?"

"I'm so sorry,"—Goldstein appeared to be smirking—"these things happen."

Wes booked his flight to Los Angeles before he spoke to his children about going to see their mother. He had decided their reaction was immaterial in his decision to make the trip. On Saturday morning, Wes sat down at the breakfast table with his three children. Monty had just awakened and was still in a T-shirt and boxers. He had his head over a plate of eggs his father had cooked for him. Summer seemed more interested in a picture she was drawing than what Wes had to say. Only Jordan looked curious.

"What's this all about, Dad?" Jordan asked.

"It's about your mother."

Summer looked up, hopefully. "Did the man find her?"

"Yes."

Jordan and Monty stared at him silently.

"When are you leaving?" Summer asked.

"Tomorrow evening."

The room grew silent. Monty was taking the last bite of his eggs. Summer went back to drawing her picture. Jordan just gazed out the window into the backyard, where a lone bird hopped around looking for something to eat in the grass.

"I miss Mommy." Summer broke the silence.

"Monty, do you have anything to say?" Wes asked.

"I'm still hungry. Can I have some cereal?"

"Sure." Wes nodded. "But I wanted to know if you had anything to say about your mom."

Monty shrugged his shoulders.

"How do you feel about her coming home?"

"Okay, I guess."

Wes turned to his daughter. "Jordan?"

"I don't know," she said, still gazing out the window.

"Do you want your mother to come home?"

"Yes," Summer said emphatically. "I want Mommy to come home." Summer was looking at her older sister with pleading eyes. Jordan still had her eyes on the bird in the backyard and was avoiding eye contact with everyone.

"Jordan? I'd really like to know how you feel about your mother coming home."

"I'd like to know why she left."

"It's a fair question. I think she needs to answer it."

"It was the other man, wasn't it?"

"Yes. But I understand he's not in the picture anymore."

The room fell silent again, and Wes could see the pain in Jordan's eyes. Monty maintained his poker face before he retreated to the pantry for a box of cereal.

"Daddy, if Mommy married another man, would we have two daddies?" Summer asked, her eyes still on her artwork.

"No!" Jordan said angrily. "We have one dad, and he's the best dad in the world." Spontaneously, Jordan was on her feet, leaning in to wrap her arms around Wes's neck.

It was turning out to be a beautiful October day, with the temperature already in the upper seventies, and yet the street was unusually absent of activity as Wes stepped outside. A few weeks ago, at the height of the lawn maintenance season, the street would have been buzzing with the sound of lawnmowers, weed eaters, and electric hedge trimmers. But on this day, all was quiet on his street. There wasn't even one child playing outside. Wes slid behind the wheel of the truck and started the engine. While he was already rehearsing what he would say to Natalie, he was still praying for a miracle. The last thing in the world that Wes wanted to do was what he was about to do.

Fifteen minutes later, Wes turned onto the familiar street and then immediately into the driveway of the small, one-story house. The yard was green, manicured, and perfect as always. Wes noticed the flower beds were still full of color as he passed them. Hours of loving care were clearly evident.

"God, help me," Wes mumbled as he pressed the doorbell. He heard the bark of the yellow lab inside and then he saw the dog named Buddy through the glass as he raced toward the door. A moment later, Natalie appeared. She was wearing a burnt orange University of Texas sweatshirt and jeans.

"Hi, Wes," Natalie said as she opened the door. Her tone was as cool as the autumn breeze. Wes hadn't seen her since his birthday when he had declared his love for her. He had spoken to her on the phone only once, and he had no idea what she had been thinking. Standing in front of him now, her face wasn't giving anything away.

"I have something I need to say to you."

"Wes, I—"

"It's not that." Wes stopped her abruptly. "I just wanted to tell you that I'm leaving tomorrow for LA."

"To see Nicole?"

"That's one of the things on the agenda."

"So you have an address?"

"Yes. Ezra found her."

"Does she know you're coming?"

"No."

"What are you going to say to her?" Natalie asked, looking past him at some imaginary object of interest.

"I'm going to tell her she can come back to us if she wants to. We'll give our marriage another go."

"Good," Natalie said softly, and Wes was surprised to see her eyes moistening. "I'm glad you've decided to give her another chance."

"It's the right thing to do."

"It is the right thing to do," she agreed.

"Thanks," Wes said, trying to smile as he gently wiped away a tear from the corner of her eye. She looked into his eyes and then kissed him gently on the cheek.

"Roger has my number if he needs anything?"

"Yes."

"You said that was one of the things on your agenda. Is there another?"

"Yeah. I'm also going to pitch my screenplay to a movie producer. My agent thinks they're going to go for it."

"What does that mean?"

"I guess they'd make it into a movie."

"Oh, Wes," Natalie said with a smile. "You've waited so long for this."

"It hasn't happened yet. Please keep me in your prayers."

"You're always in my prayers, Wes."

CHAPTER 50
October 2010

Wes glanced at the man occupying the window seat next to him as he unbuckled his seatbelt after the flight from Houston to Los Angeles. The man hadn't said a word during the entire flight, but now he turned to him and smiled. The stranger looked like a movie star, with a handsome face and rugged features. He was wearing white slacks, a white sports coat, and a blue tie dotted with willowy white clouds.

"Is it business or pleasure that brings you to the City of Angels?" the man asked as the roar of the jet engines died down, signaling the end of their trip. He spoke with a strange accent that Wes couldn't identify.

"Business," Wes replied, not wanting to get into a discussion with the odd-sounding stranger at this point.

"Business? What kind of business?"

"I'm a writer, and I'm meeting with my agent and a movie producer to discuss a screenplay I hope to sell."

"What's it about?"

"It's about a man convicted of murdering his wife."

"But he didn't do it?"

"Right. How'd you know?" Wes asked curiously.

"Lucky guess. So what happens to this man?"

"He spends several brutal years on Texas death row before his wife turns up alive and he is finally freed."

"What really happened to his wife during those years?"

"She faked her own death, changed her identity, and ran off with another man. They never got married but lived together until the other man was killed."

"How?"

"It was an accident."

"Sounds realistic. So did the man forgive his wife?"

"Yeah, he did." Wes nodded, feeling a chill running up his spine. It was as though this stranger had read his script. But how was that possible?

"That's a great story. Most people wouldn't forgive someone under those circumstances, but it is the right thing to do. Reminds me of a story I heard about."

"Really?" Wes said, suddenly frightened that his story wasn't as original as he had thought.

"Yeah. I heard about this man from San Antonio whose wife was believed to have been murdered. Several months later, it was reported that she had faked her own death and was alive," he said, staring directly at Wes.

"Are you from San Antonio?" Wes asked him.

"No."

"How'd you hear about the story?"

"Heard about it from someone that had been in San Antonio." The man smiled. "I hope that man can forgive his wife, too. We all need to be forgiven."

"That's true," Wes said with a growing feeling of uneasiness. He was on his feet now and reaching for his carry-on bag above his head.

"Good luck," the man said, extending his hand. "Hope you sell your screenplay."

Wes was still thinking about the stranger on the plane as he walked down the blue-carpeted concourse toward the baggage claim area. He wasn't disturbed by what the man had told him. In fact, he felt encouraged by the stranger and optimistic about what lay ahead for him in the next two days. He claimed his bag and boarded a shuttle to ride to a discount car rental facility in Inglewood.

Wes checked his wallet to see how much cash he had left. He had figured that with plane fare, the hotel, and the car, he was already out seven hundred dollars. And that didn't account for food and other incidentals for the next two days. By the time he put a tank of gas in the car on Tuesday evening he'd be lucky to keep the cost under a thousand dollars. His savings was almost gone, and that left him feeling anxious.

It was almost ten o'clock by the time Wes checked into the hotel with a bag of fast food in his hand. He was exhausted but felt peaceful. After he ate his dinner, he got undressed and readied himself for bed. But when he turned the lights out, he felt anxiety beginning to grip him. What was he afraid of? That the movie producer would reject his screenplay? He'd dealt with almost twenty years of rejection as a writer. That Nicole would reject him? Or somehow find another way to hurt him? There wasn't much else she could do to him. Then he realized that he had no idea what to say to her when he did see her. What words would come out of his mouth?

Wes flipped on the light and opened his suitcase. He quickly realized he had left his Bible at home. Wes opened the top drawer of his dresser and found a Gideon Bible. He opened the book and quickly found his place in the first chapter of the book of James. "If any of you lacks wisdom, he should ask God, who gives generously to all without finding fault, and it will be given to him." Wes knew that was what he needed more than anything else now. Wisdom. He had been relying on his own brain for so long that this idea seemed totally irrational to him. Wes closed the Bible, turned off the light, and said a solemn prayer before falling off to sleep.

"I love it," the producer said, coming out of his chair excitedly. He came around the table and shook Wes's hand. "I think I can speak for the people at the Lifetime Network when I say congratulations. We've got a deal."

"How long will it take?" the agent asked, as the producer released Wes's hand.

"A week. A month. I don't know," the producer said. "The first option period is a year. It should happen before that. "

"I don't want this thing dragging out for a year."

"It's not going to drag out. This is a great story. They're going to want to get this into production ASAP."

Thirty minutes later, Wes walked out of his agent's office, still shaking his head. The pitch had taken less than fifteen minutes, and he was being told they had a deal worth six figures. Even better, the agent told him to start adapting his other unpublished novels into screenplays. Wes was told he could expect phone calls from other producers as soon as news got out in the Hollywood fishbowl that there was a new screenwriter on the scene.

It seemed that after years of futility, Wes had finally gotten his break as a writer. He said a silent prayer of thanksgiving before his thoughts shifted abruptly to Nicole. The magnitude of what lay ahead made him swallow hard. He checked the address and the directions he had pulled off the internet. In just a few short moments, he might be staring into the eyes of his wife for the first time in six months. He tried to remember exactly what she looked like the last time he saw her sitting in their study just hours before she disappeared. She seemed preoccupied with her work, but it wasn't real estate that was on her mind that afternoon. Nicole was about to leave her family with no plan to ever return.

In his mind, Wes could see Nicole sitting at the desk, pretending to study the MLS directory on her computer screen while she pondered a future without them. Wes started to get angry again. Nicole had left him for another man. Worse than that, she had left their children, letting them believe she had been murdered. She didn't deserve to be forgiven. As that thought flashed through Wes's mind, he thought about what the man on the plane had said.

"We all need to be forgiven."

The sun was setting as he neared his destination. It had taken more than an hour to drive across town, and Wes's nerves were on edge after being cut off a dozen times by aggressive drivers on the congested freeways. As Wes did his best to navigate the early evening traffic, he had a chance to mull the implications of the just-completed meeting with the producer. If the movie deal went through, his agent would want him to commit to moving out here. He had told Wes that a working screenwriter had to live in the LA area. You had to be near Hollywood. There were just too many in-person meetings a working screenwriter had to attend. Wes would cross that bridge when he came to it. Right now, he had to prepare himself to meet with Nicole.

Wes felt sick to his stomach as he pulled up in front of the house with the address Goldstein had given him. The house was not large, but Wes guessed it would nonetheless cost a small fortune in the frenzied southern California real estate market. How could Nicole afford to live here? Wes guessed she was just renting the house, but rent payments had to be high, too. Wes knew she had gotten back into selling real estate, and she was probably doing well. Nicole was a natural saleswoman, and her looks and personality attracted people like a magnet. Especially men. Looking around at the simple elegance of the neighborhood, Wes began to wonder if she could even be persuaded to leave here. He got out of the car and approached the front door.

No one came to the door when Wes rang the bell. The thought occurred to him that Nicole might not be home for several hours. Wes began to feel butterflies in his stomach and fought the urge to immediately drive away. But he reminded himself of what

Goldstein had said. The private investigator had told him in no uncertain terms that Nicole wanted to come home. She gave Goldstein the address to give to Wes. She must have wanted him to come for her. But she had no way of knowing if he would come, or when. Wes got back into the car and waited as dusk settled in.

CHAPTER 51

October 2010

Wes reflected on what had happened to him in the past six months as he sat in the car in front of Nicole's house. His wife had disappeared, and she was presumed to have been murdered. Wes became the prime suspect and was dogged by a San Antonio police detective. Summer was kidnapped and miraculously rescued. Jordan had taken an overdose of Xanax and nearly died. Monty and his sisters had all struggled mightily in the months of separation from their mother. It had been the most trying time of their life, but they had made it through. Wes knew in his heart that he hadn't done it alone.

As he waited for Nicole, Wes thought about a sermon that his grandfather had preached a few months ago. He could still recall it in vivid detail. It was a sermon based on the first chapter of James. The writer urged his readers to consider it pure joy whenever they faced trials... Pure joy? Most people believed the trials and tribulations of life were a curse and something to be avoided at all costs. Roger's message that day was a stark contrast to that philosophy.

"We should embrace the trials of life, and the hardships, with grateful hearts," he told his congregation. "Why? James 1:3 answers that question: 'Because you know that the testing of your faith develops perseverance.' Do you really believe that? Paul wrote in Philippians 1:6: 'Being confident of this, that he who began a good work in you will carry it on to completion until the day of Christ Jesus.' To be conformed to the image of Christ, we must go through hardships. The joy is knowing what waits on the other side of life."

At this point in his sermon, Roger quoted an ancient proverb: "Life isn't about waiting for the storm to pass. It's about learning to dance in the rain." As he recalled that sermon, Wes suddenly felt like he had received a word from God. It was as though he now realized what his life on earth was all about. It wasn't a question of *if* but *when* the rain comes. He could try to hide from the storms in life, or enjoy a lifelong series of dances in the rain when it came.

It was almost dark when Wes saw the headlights of a car behind him. He turned his head in time to see a Lexus pull into the driveway. Wes thought his heart was going to beat right through his chest as he climbed out of his rental car. He watched for movement inside the car behind him, but it was too dark to see anything. Wes decided to move toward the car so that Nicole, if it was her, could see him and perhaps recognize him in the streetlight. Slowly, the driver's side door opened, and Nicole stepped out.

Wes could tell that Nicole was looking directly at him. He couldn't see her face, but her body language told him she was surprised.

"Wes?"

"Hi, Nicole," he said, walking slowly toward the car.

He could see her face now. She seemed to have aged some in the last year, but she was still beautiful. Wes was three feet from her when he stopped. They were looking into each other's eyes, each searching for something.

"You came," she managed to gasp. "I didn't think you were going to come."

"I had to come," Wes said flatly.

Nicole's voice was trembling. "I'm glad you did, Wes. I'm so glad..." Her voice trailed off, and her shoulders sagged as she began to sob.

Seeing Nicole crying caused a wave of emotion to sweep over Wes, and he stepped forward and placed his hands on her shoulders. He tried to look into her eyes, but she refused to raise her head. She was overcome as tears of shame and grief streaked her face.

Wes removed his right hand from her shoulder and wiped her tears, first from one side of her face, then from the other. With his fist closed, he reached under her chin, and with the back of his thumb he slowly coaxed her head up until she was looking into his eyes. He saw something in those eyes that he had never seen before.

Their lips were only inches apart. Wes's eyes glazed with tears, but none fell. The sounds of the big city had become distant, as stillness engulfed the scene around them. In the distance, off to the west, the mighty Pacific Ocean heaved and rolled, with the sound of its wondrous, timeless gentle swells providing a soothing refrain.

Wes and Nicole had become players center stage. They stood silent, gazing, searching each other's eyes through the windows to their souls. Wes felt like he had crossed a threshold into some sort of a surreal and sublime place.

"I love you, Nicole," Wes whispered.

Nicole grasped Wes behind his head with both hands and covered his mouth with hers. Wes recoiled slightly, surprised by the urgency and passion of his wife's kiss. He backed away for a moment. He wiped tears from below her eyes with his thumbs and then stepped forward and returned her kiss. The kiss was tender at first, then more passionate as his emotions surged inside him like a raging river. Then his own tears began to flow.

The stars above were like innocent, twinkling eyes, stealing a seat to the act playing out below. Nicole's shoulders trembled as Wes placed his arms behind the small of her back and pulled her hard against his body. After several minutes, they disengaged from their kiss and stood there, cheek-to-cheek, as his tears mixed with hers, forming a sweet, salty stream of soul-cleansing fluid.

Wes pulled his face back from Nicole's and looked into her eyes. "Honey, do you want to come home?"

"Yes. Yes," she said, as if gasping for air. "Wes?"

"Yes?"

"How can you still love me after what I did?"

"How could God still love me after what I've done?"

"God? You've found God?"

Wes nodded. "Jesus Christ died on the cross for my sins. God has forgiven me. How could I not forgive you?"

"I've been reading about forgiveness in the Bible, Wes. It's just that…" She stopped midsentence.

"What?"

"I just couldn't bring myself to believe it could happen for me."

CHAPTER 52
October 2010

Natalie had just finished cleaning the kitchen at the Tanner house and was walking out to her car when she realized she had left her cell phone inside. When she came back inside, she was surprised to see a light on in the kitchen. Roger stood by the cabinet in the kitchen.

"Roger? I thought you were asleep."

"I was just looking for some aspirin," the older man said, unable to hide the pain in his face. Natalie knew the cancer was taking its toll and that his limbs and internal organs were racked with pain. Wes told her that Roger was resistant to the idea of taking the opiates prescribed by his doctor because they were a close derivative of morphine.

"Roger, there's no sin in taking your pain pills."

"I don't like taking them. I feel like some kind of a junkie."

"You're not a junkie." Natalie rubbed his shoulders. "Come on, let's go sit down in the living room and talk for a little while."

"You don't need to stay with me. I'm okay."

"I know I don't need to stay. But I like talking with you."

"Are the children asleep?" Roger asked as they sat on the couch.

"Jordan and Monty are asleep. Summer keeps getting up and coming downstairs to ask me if they're home yet. I don't think she'll go to sleep until she sees Nicole."

"When are they supposed to be here?"

"They were driving Nicole's car back. They left yesterday morning, so I thought they'd be back some time tonight."

"The fact that they're driving back together. It's a good sign."

"It is a good sign," Natalie agreed.

There was silence between them for a moment before Roger spoke again. "It won't be long now, Natalie. I'm ready to go home. I'm just praying that the Lord won't take me for four more days."

"Summer's baptism?"

"Yes." Roger smiled. "I'd really like to see that."

"Are you scared, Roger?"

"After all these years? I'm looking forward to it. Life is a series of passages. You pass into life, you pass through life, and you pass away. I can only imagine what it will be like to see Jesus face-to-face."

"Yes." Natalie closed her eyes. "What will it be like?"

"I had the most amazing dream a little while ago."

"Tell me about it."

"I dreamed I was walking through this beautiful field. It was so green, and there were rolling hills and a stand of trees in the distance. A couple was walking toward me. As they drew closer, I recognized them." Roger's eyes filled with tears. "The woman was Abigail, my late wife. She was even more beautiful than I remembered. The young man was my son, Roger, Wes's dad. He was wearing the same military uniform he wore on the day he left for Vietnam. It was like they were sent to welcome me home."

As Natalie imagined the scene in her mind, she heard the front door open. An instant later, she heard the sound of running feet and then saw Summer coming down the stairs as Nicole came through the front door. Summer rounded the corner and froze in her tracks. The little girl appeared to be fearful that her mother might not be glad to see her.

"Mommy?"

"Summer?"

"Mommy!" Summer said gleefully. Nicole was leaning over to set her purse on the floor as Wes came in the door behind her. Summer propelled herself through the darkness and jumped onto Nicole's chest. The little girl wrapped her legs around her mother's back, and her arms were secure around Nicole's neck. Mother and daughter were crying in unison. After a moment, Nicole tried to let her down so that she could get a closer look at her, but Summer maintained a desperate hold on her mother. She wasn't letting go.

I t was shortly after noon when the congregation began filing out of Stone Oak Bible Church. The weather outside had changed during the church service. A stiff wind blew out of the north as the massive storm clouds had melded into a solid sheet of gray. It was just a matter of time before the heavens opened up.

Wes and Nicole at first had tried to gather up the children and herd them to the car to get out of the weather. Instead, they found themselves caught up in a virtual receiving line of folks outside the church who wanted to congratulate Nicole and Summer on their baptisms. Nicole was too busy shaking hands and trying to keep all of the names straight to pay much attention to the goings-on around her. But Wes managed to break away from the small talk to steal a quick glance at his grandfather. The older man had insisted on attending the service, overcoming Wes's objections.

Wes noticed Roger was pale and short of breath, but looked happy and at ease as he shook hands and accepted all of the congratulations from parishioners. Wes still wanted to get him out of the weather and back home as quickly as possible. Jordan and Monty were standing nearby, but Summer was nowhere in sight. Wes scanned the parking lot until he finally spotted his youngest daughter. She was proudly showing off her gold embossed baptism certificate to some friends near the church van on the far side of the parking lot.

As he watched Summer, Wes noticed Natalie out of the corner of his eye. She was walking across the parking lot with her mother, but Nancy suddenly stopped to talk with someone she knew. Natalie was standing to the side waiting, and he noticed Pastor Garcia walk up to her. He appeared to ask her a question, and they visited for a moment.

After the pastor left Natalie's side, Wes decided to approach her. He hadn't spoken with her since the night he had returned from California, and seeing her again made him sad. His feelings hadn't changed toward Natalie, but God had changed everything. Wes knew they would never be together, and he would be grieving that loss for a long time.

"Hey," Wes said as Natalie caught sight of him and nodded.

"Hey, yourself."

"Thanks for coming."

"It was a beautiful ceremony," Natalie said with a smile tinged with sadness. "Never thought I'd see the day Nicole was baptized. She's a changed woman, Wes."

"Yes, she is."

"Everything turned out for the best."

"I guess it did," Wes said, looking back across the parking lot at Summer. "Summer's sure glad to have her mom back."

"How are Jordan and Monty?"

"They've been more reserved."

"It will take time."

"Yeah," Wes agreed. "I saw you visiting with the pastor. Were y'all having a theological discussion?"

"Not exactly," Natalie said, and Wes noticed she was blushing.

"Oh really? What kind of a discussion were you having?"

"You're kind of nosy, aren't you?" Natalie teased him.

"Yes."

"Ernie just asked me where I wanted to go and eat lunch."

"Ernie? You're dating my pastor?"

"Shhh." Natalie put her finger to her lips. "It's no big deal."

"I think it's great."

Nancy had finished visiting with her friend and was walking toward them as Nicole appeared by Wes's side.

"You looked like an angel up there," Nancy cooed to Nicole.

"Not bad for a woman stuck at the bottom of a lake for who knows how long," Wes said, unable to resist teasing his mother-in-law.

"I want to take everyone to lunch," Nancy said, ignoring the jab.

"I need to get my grandfather home," Wes told her.

"Then I'll take my daughters and my grandchildren."

"I need to go with Wes," Nicole told her.

"And I've got—" Natalie hesitated before Wes interrupted her.

"A date with our pastor."

Nicole and Nancy registered surprise as Natalie shot Wes a dirty look. He took that as a cue to go and retrieve Summer, who was still talking happily with her friends, oblivious to the approaching storm. She looked radiant in her red brushed-suede dress, white knee socks, and black patent leather shoes. Her dark brown hair had been combed straight back wet and had begun to dry and fluff out in the stiff breeze.

"Your grandmother wants you to go to lunch with her," Wes told her.

"I want to show my certificate to Papa first," Summer said, her eyes darting back and forth as she searched for Roger. She spotted him as he stood alone under a tree by the edge of the parking lot. She immediately took off running, and Wes followed her. Roger reached into the inside vest pocket of his suit jacket for his sunglasses and quickly put them on before Summer and Wes could reach his side.

Roger leaned to one knee to give his granddaughter a hug. "Congratulations, honey. Papa is proud of you."

"Thanks, Papa. I love you."

"I love you, too, honey."

Summer turned and spotted Nicole approaching. She ran into her mother's arms and received a hug and a kiss before running off to join her grandmother and siblings. Wes watched them climb in the car as a shivering Nicole hugged him.

"I'm cold," Nicole said as the north wind blew past them.

"Me, too," Roger agreed.

Wes drove, and Nicole and Roger rode in the backseat. Easing the car out of the lot, Wes guided it onto the tree-lined residential street that led from the church. He slowed down and drove very carefully. The street was narrow and there were cars parked on both sides. As the street widened to four lanes, Wes slid over into the slow lane and glanced in the rearview mirror for a quick look at his grandfather. Roger had let his head recline against Nicole's shoulder. The north winds had kicked up dust from a nearby construction site, and the unsettled particles hung in the air like a brown fog.

As Wes turned onto Stone Oak Parkway, less than two miles from their house, the first raindrops began to fall. Wes put the windshield wipers on half speed. He decelerated a little bit and eased over into the right lane for a car to pass. Wes glanced into the rearview mirror, expecting to see Roger still resting his head on Nicole's shoulder. But something was wrong. Roger's glasses hung on his nose and off the side of his face. It was clear he had slumped hard against her. Wes felt his stomach tightening.

The tears on Nicole's face told Wes what he needed to know.

Straight ahead loomed a storm cloud. It towered over the skyline, forming a massive anvil-shaped thunderhead at its top.

With a burst the sky opened and a heavy rain began to fall, showering the parched landscape with a deluge. The traffic had slowed to a crawl as pools of water formed on the road. Nicole gripped his hand.

His sight was fixed on the road, but he felt the pain go through his heart as he was suddenly separated from the grandfather that had been more like a father to him all of these years. Slowly, the blunt pain he felt was replaced by a peace.

EPILOGUE

May 2011

It was a beautiful spring day as Wes Tanner
and his family strolled through Arlington National Cemetery.
The president had given his speech and laid a wreath, in keeping
with the Memorial Day tradition. After his motorcade had left
the military burial ground, things had quieted down. People
were milling about the 612 acres of green grass, quietly paying
their respects at gravesites adorned with white crosses. Arlington
National Cemetery, one of the nation's most important shrines,
contains the remains of more than 260,000 men and women
who made the ultimate sacrifice to preserve America's freedom.
These included Medal of Honor recipients and five-star generals,
along with presidents, and more than 4,700 unidentified soldiers
represented by the Tomb of the Unknown Soldier.

It was Nicole's idea to visit Washington, D.C. over Memorial
Day. Wes had recently received a substantial check from the
Lifetime Movie Network as payment for his original screenplay,
which was now in production. This opened the floodgates for
other offers from television. With the prospects of now having an
income in the mid-six figures, Wes couldn't fall back on the old
excuse that they couldn't afford the trip.

"It's right over there." Nicole had a map that had led them to
the gravesite of Wes's father. It was easy with the number system
utilized at Arlington. The gravestones were graced by American

flags each Memorial Day, and a sea of red, white, and blue colors blended in with the green grass as Wes and Nicole walked hand-in-hand. Wes seemed to be experiencing a greater degree of difficulty maintaining his composure with each step.

Fifty yards ahead, Wes saw a silver-haired man standing with his head bowed. The man seemed to be praying at a gravesite. As they walked up behind him, Nicole nodded silently to Wes. This was where Roger Tanner, Jr. was buried. The man with the silver hair had his eyes closed and didn't notice the family of five. Wes, Nicole, Jordan, and Monty stood back, respectfully, but Summer walked up next to the man.

"Roger Tanner, Jr. Medal of Honor recipient," Summer read the headstone.

The silver-haired man opened his eyes, pleasantly surprised by the appearance of the seven-year-old girl. He looked down at her and smiled.

"This man was my friend. He saved many lives."

"He was my grandpa," Summer explained.

"Grandpa?" The silver-haired man looked stunned. He knelt down on one knee to be at eye level with Summer. "What's your name?"

"Summer."

"That's a beautiful name," the man said. He turned his head and noticed Wes and his family standing a few feet away. "But of course! You're his son!"

Wes froze where he stood. The man jumped to his feet and walked over, unwilling to take his eyes off of Roger Tanner's son.

Wes finally recovered and extended his hand. "I'm Wes Tanner."

"I'm Eric Adams." The silver-haired man gripped Wes's hand firmly. He continued to stare at Wes as though the last piece of a large jigsaw puzzle had just fallen into place.

"I wouldn't be here today if it wasn't for your dad. He saved my life and many others. I'm sure you know that. But he did something even more important for me."

"What?" Summer demanded, looking up at Adams.

"He saved my mortal life but he also led me to eternal life."

"You mean Jesus?"

"Oh, yes. Jesus Christ. Is he your Savior, Summer?"

"Yes. I asked Jesus into my heart," Summer said happily. "So did they."

Summer was pointing her finger at her parents, brother, and sister.

"It's not polite to point," Monty said, looking embarrassed.

Adams took a moment to introduce himself to each family member, staring at them with something akin to wide-eyed wonder.

"Can you tell me a little about my father?" Wes asked.

"I can tell you a lot about him. We went through basic training together and shipped off together to Vietnam. We spent three months together on Hill 881S. Wes, could I have the privilege of taking you and your family to dinner?"

Wes listened like a child to Adams' stories about his father. Some were humorous, some were poignant, and all of them offered insights into the character of Roger Tanner, Jr. Wes didn't want their time together to end, but the children were getting tired. So, with a grateful heart, Wes shook Adams' hand as they stood by his car after leaving the restaurant.

"One more thing," Adams said. He reached into his car and pulled out a worn Bible. "A long time ago, God put it in my heart to keep this with me. I've transferred it to at least a dozen vehicles in the last forty years. I had no way of knowing how to get in touch with you, but I always knew God would bring us together. And I wanted it to be right there, close at hand, when that time came."

Adams handed the Bible to Wes. On the inside page was his father's name, written in his grandfather's handwriting. The inscription said the Bible was a gift for Roger, Jr. on his sixth birthday. As Wes leafed through the pages, he saw countless notes in his father's handwriting. When he reached the book of Second Timothy, a picture fell out. The picture, yellowed by the years, was of his mother. She appeared to be about twenty, and her young face bore none of the stress marks Wes remembered.

Wes's eyes were drawn to some underlined verses on the page the picture had marked for more than forty years. "But you, keep your head in all situations, endure hardship, do the work of an evangelist, discharge all the duties of your ministry. For I am already being poured out like a drink offering, and the time has come for my departure. I have fought the good fight, I have finished the race, I have kept the faith. Now there is in store for me the crown of righteousness, which the Lord, the righteous Judge, will award to me on that day—and not only to me, but also to all who have longed for his appearing."

Wes embraced Adams for a moment, reflecting on how his father and grandfather had managed to also keep that faith and finish strong. With God's help, he would do the same. He knew that he would not be long parted from them. They would have an eternity to spend together, along with the Savior they both loved.

listen|imagine|view|experience

AUDIO BOOK DOWNLOAD INCLUDED WITH THIS BOOK!

In your hands you hold a complete digital entertainment package. In addition to the paper version, you receive a free download of the audio version of this book. Simply use the code listed below when visiting our website. Once downloaded to your computer, you can listen to the book through your computer's speakers, burn it to an audio CD or save the file to your portable music device (such as Apple's popular iPod) and listen on the go!

How to get your free audio book digital download:

1. Visit www.tatepublishing.com and click on the e|LIVE logo on the home page.
2. Enter the following coupon code:
   42a1-a58a-59d3-ccb2-7acb-40fc-cd20-9b38
3. Download the audio book from your e|LIVE digital locker and begin enjoying your new digital entertainment package today!